Stolen Eyes

Book 2 of the Nanobot Wars

Courtney Farrell

Fiction Foundry Press

Stolen Eyes

Fiction Foundry Press
www.courtneyfarrell.com

Editor: Diane Reed
Cover Art: Christa Reed
Photographer: Ivan Warhammer
Formatting: Rik Hall – WildSeasFormatting.com

ISBN: 978-0-9904449-6-1

Dedication

To my muse, who whips me like a rented mule.

Chapter 1

I floated toward the ceiling, hands clutching air. Thrashing in my sleeping bag like a giant worm, I managed to snag the edge of a porthole. Armored glass chilled my bare shoulder as I pulled my legs from the lightweight sleeping sack. The motion sent me into a dizzy midair spin. Everything was harder in zero gravity. I scrunched up the sack and stuck it to a Velcro patch on the wall, cussing out Keenan under my breath. He could have taken two seconds to clip me back in when he got out of our bed. Apparently that was too much to ask.

The year I had on Keenan didn't give me much authority over him. He was already wild when I took him in as an orphaned nine year old. By fifteen, he'd gone completely feral. Not his fault. I did my best, but we all grew up on the streets, fighting for food. That boy was pure savage, and gorgeous too, with golden eyes and long, tawny hair. I'd never been the type to cheat on my boyfriend, but going into quarantine with Keenan, I admit, I was tempted. Three irritating days later, I only hoped I wouldn't punch him in the face before someone came to let us out.

Keenan wasn't the parental type, so it was kind of weird to hear his voice from the other room, talking to three-year-old Tito. "Good job, buddy."

My irritation faded. The sound of their laughter brought a soft smile to my face. Three days locked in with a toddler really made him step up. I was impressed. Until I floated across our quarters, stuck my head in the bathroom, and saw little Tito peeing into midair. In zero gravity, drains don't work. Nasty yellow droplets floated everywhere. Tito had the vacuum thingy in one hand, sucking them up. Him and Keenan were both giggling like crazy.

"He's supposed to pee *down* the tube," I yelled, backpedaling as a few drops flew toward my face. "Eeew! What the hell are you lettin' him do, Keenan?"

"He's still afraid of it," Keenan protested. "He thinks it's gonna vacuum off his--"

I made an aggravated noise, cutting him off. "Clean it up."

Keenan's voice followed me as I retreated. "You're not chief anymore, so quit givin' orders."

That hit me in the gut. It was true. I wasn't chief anymore. Before Bianca's army arrived, I gave the power away. I made my boyfriend chief. It pissed Keenan off, but I had to do it. That forced Dakota to pick the crew over me, and keep the boys safe. The night of the battle, I was pretty sure I wouldn't survive. Not against ten thousand pox-infected animals. Keenan came back for me and Tito. With some inside help, Dakota snuck the other kids on the rocket ship. Old Joe didn't make it. With only one leg, he couldn't run, so he held the door while the boys escaped. He died for us. I hung weightless at the porthole and stared out, my vision hazy through grateful tears. That man was the closest thing I had to a father. The only adult in my life. And he was gone.

Soon our ship would dock at the orbiting space station. We'd get tested for pox, and our quarantine would be over. My crew would be together again. I'd see Dakota! My heart soared.

A gentle hand on my waist turned me. Keenan was there, looking apologetic. He smelled clean, and his long, blond hair was damp from the shower. Tito's happy squeals still echoed from the bathroom.

"He's playin' in the shower. I figured he could use some cleaning up."

"Good," I sighed. "Look, I'm sorry I was such a bitch--"

Keenan stopped me with a soft finger on my lips. "Shh. It's okay." He wrapped his arms around me from behind and pulled me close. He didn't try anything more, so I didn't pull away. The warmth of his body calmed me. We floated in silence, looking through the porthole. Outside, Earth glowed blue against the darkness of space. The sight made me ache. I'd never see the sky again, never run over green grass. I could never go back. Bianca waited for me there.

I know, she wasn't a real person, even though I couldn't help thinking of her that way. Her intelligence was some kind of artificial, computer-generated thing I didn't understand, with a twisted personality that was real as hell. Bianca's submicroscopic nanobots controlled billions of stolen bodies, but she still didn't have the one she wanted. Mine.

"I still can't believe we're in space," Keenan murmured into my ear. "You did good, babe. Real good."

"Uh, thanks," I managed. That touched my heart. Keenan could be such an asshole, and then, out of nowhere, he was incredible.

A rumbling noise came from somewhere deep in the ship, and the view out the window changed. A shining white space station appeared, like a magical floating city in the sky. Me and Keenan pressed our heads together at the window. Delicate spokes connected five rigid rings, all set in the same plane, so bigger loops enclosed smaller ones. A central axle shot through the middle, an arrow dead center on the bull's eye.

The outer ring glided past the porthole, a whole lot huger up close. Yellow lights gleamed from thousands of windows. Only about half the windows in the second and third rings were lit, and the two smallest rings were dark.

"Why'd they abandon the ones in the middle?" Keenan muttered.

I shrugged.

His fingers tightened on my arm. "Doesn't look right to me."

I trusted Keenan's instincts. Always had. So that bugged me. At home, we would have turned around, left that place. I swore under my breath. "It sucks not being in control."

Keenan snickered.

As we passed through the smallest ring, a glimmer of light flickered from one single window. "Did you see that?" I asked. "Who could be in there, all alone?"

"I dunno. Maybe they got some infected locked in there," Keenan said darkly.

I punched his arm, grinning. "Oh, stop it! We're safe. This place is clean, Adam said so."

Jets hissed as our ship bellied up to the central axle, close enough to see the flags of a dozen countries painted on the side. I winced and leaned away, like that would help in a collision.

"Hope that douchebag knows what he's doing," Keenan said. "He's only, what, seventeen? Little young for a pilot."

"Yeah, but Adam trained for this trip his whole life. I woulda studied too, if the alternative was death."

Keenan flashed an insolent grin. "Not me. But here I am. Dodged the rules again."

A bone-deep thud resonated through the walls. "That had to mean the ship just docked," I said. Relief overwhelmed me. There'd be adults on the station. Someone else could take over. I wouldn't have to be responsible anymore. "Keenan, we made it."

He stroked my hair. "Yeah. We're safe now. It's okay, don't cry."

My cheeks heated with shame. I'd never been the teary kind of girl, not as chief of a crew of boys. Maybe I was emotionally exhausted. Maybe it was the big letdown, after we got away. Either way, I wasn't feeling too tough. Keenan turned me to face him, and I leaned against his chest, my face damp with tears.

With a click, our door came unlocked. A second later, the panel slid aside. A strange man's face peered in. He looked like a cartoon thug, with a military crew cut over a cave man's brow ridge. "Thought you two would be happy to get out of here," he leered, waggling his hairy eyebrows suggestively. "Maybe not."

Keenan let go of me fast. I pushed off his chest to get to the door, but that didn't work. We floated away from each other, floundering in midair.

The big man laughed at us. He filled our tiny quarters, floating gracefully despite his bulk. The nametag on the front of his sky blue jumpsuit read *Neilson*. "Stuart. Come with me. Admiral wants to see you."

For a second I just gaped at him. Stuart. That was my new name. The little doctor had signed the adoption papers a few days before he died. An unwelcome memory rose up, almost blinding me. *A tiny, elderly man struggles across a dark, corpse-strewn battlefield, laboring under the weight of the flamethrower on his back. Wet, squelching sounds come from the darkness.* Adrenaline crackled through my body, like the whole, horrible thing was happening all over again.

"Now, Stuart," Neilson growled.

I snapped back to reality. A rough hand caught the front of my jumpsuit. Nielson yanked me through the door, touched a button, and shut the door in Keenan's face. My feet never touched the floor.

"Hey Jackie, wait for me. Hey! What the fuck?" Keenan's muffled shouts came through the closed door, but the astronaut ignored it.

"What about my friends?" I exclaimed, trying to pry off the man's meaty hand.

He hung on easily. "Admiral only wants to talk to you. Not the three-year-old. And not the boy."

I resisted, legs kicking, but in zero gravity I had no traction at all. Without taking a cheap shot, I wouldn't have a chance. I held my temper with an effort. No need to make an enemy on my first day on the station. With his free hand, the man shined a super-bright pen light into my eyes. I blinked against the stabbing pain, eyes watering. Then he swept a handheld UV light over me from head to toe.

"I did that myself, three days ago," I snapped, shielding my eyes with one hand. "And besides, if I was infected, I woulda got you already."

Neilson winced a little at that, but didn't answer. He switched off the glowing violet light. I blinked. The afterimages that splotched my vision slowly faded away.

I looked him over. Not a speck of dirt under those big, square fingernails, and that wasn't the kind of guy who worried about his manicure. I put it all together. "You've been up here a long time, haven't you? What's it been, years?"

The man's grip on my jumpsuit relaxed. He nodded a vague affirmative.

"Bet you've never even seen a pox victim. You let one this close to you, you're done. They're quicker than you think. One scratch is all it takes." I gave his sleeve a sharp tug to make my point.

He nodded grimly, as if memorizing that. My estimation of him went up a notch.

Sounds of heavy breathing came from the end of the hall. My head snapped around. Three white-coated men rounded a corner at the other end of the corridor, flying weightless in single file. They pushed off the walls with hands and feet like they were swimming the breast stroke, and then rocketed along, arms and legs held rigidly behind them. I recoiled, but the door to my quarters had been locked behind me. I was trapped between the fast-moving intruders and Nielson's broad, motionless chest.

The leader tucked his knees up, seized wall-mounted handholds on both sides, and came to a sudden stop, uncomfortably close to me. When he spoke, his hot, moist breath wafted across my face. "What the hell are you doing?"

"Nothing," I stammered. "I was just--"

Nielsen's booming voice drowned me out. "Admiral's orders. She's off to the lab to get tested, then to the bridge."

"We test her *before* she gets the run of the ship, not *after*," the lanky, balding technician spat. "What were you thinking, Nielson?"

I was quickly surrounded. White-jacketed men pinned my arms and legs. Someone jammed a needle into a vein in the crook of my elbow. My punctured vein throbbed. Another guy blasted me with a handheld UV light. I shut my eyes tight and willed my panicked body not to fight. When the violet light went off, I opened my eyes. Two men still held my wrists. The others were riveted to the readout on a boxy piece of equipment. If I was up to no good, that would've been my moment to strike. With an effort, I held still.

A light on the box flashed green. "Negative," the bald man muttered. His partners sighed in relief.

I yanked my arms free. "Nice going, morons. You people better get your shit together, or Bianca's gonna eat you alive."

Nielson's broad face grew red. The bald boss-man narrowed his eyes. He looked mad enough to take a swing at somebody. He pressed his thin lips together, then parted them enough to squeeze out a few words. "She's right."

My eyes widened in surprise. The technicians snapped into formation behind their leader. In seconds they were soaring away, down the white, featureless corridor.

Nielson was lost in thought. "Bianca . . . that's the AI," he repeated, almost to himself. He turned. For the first time, he seemed to really see me. "So it's true what they say about her? She's really female?"

"Yeah," I said. "Only she doesn't have a body of her own. I'm not even sure how she thinks, since she's made of billions of nanobots. I don't get it.

All I know is she jumps from body to body. Possesses people. Stares out their eyes." I shivered. "You can tell, if you look close. If somebody gets taken, you can tell it's not them anymore."

"Like a goddamned demon," Nielson muttered.

I nodded grimly. "She keeps moving. Never stays in one body for long. I think the people she occupies might sicken and die faster than regular infected."

"You wouldn't, though," the big man said in a low, haunted voice. "Would you?"

I wanted to lie. I really did. But everyone already knew about the Class III nanites in my blood. So I made myself admit it. "No, I wouldn't. That's why she wants me."

Neilson squeezed my shoulder, and I knew he saw the fear in my eyes. He gave me a lopsided grin. "Well, we won't let her get you, then."

I let out a shaky breath. "Right. Thanks."

"Okay, off to the bridge with you. Let's go," he said. One big hand shoved me down the corridor.

We left the rocket through the round door of an airlock and took a right turn into the central axle of the space station. The plain white walls of the tube never changed, giving the place a dreamy quality. I felt lost. That bugged me, but I couldn't complain, since I wasn't supposed to be there. Stowing away on the rocket had saved my crew, but I didn't think about what would happen after that. On the station, we were outsiders, unwanted and uninvited. I wasn't shy, but that triggered a huge wave of insecurity. All they had to do to get rid of me was open an airlock.

I figured I'd try and cooperate. So I pushed off wall-mounted handholds as I floated along, trying to swim through the air like the technicians did. I did okay at grabbing for the aluminum bars, but my feet flailed all over the place. One thick-soled boot thumped Nielson in the face. "Sorry," I grunted.

Nielson swore. He hesitated at the door of what looked like an elevator. "Nah," he said. "You ain't ready for that."

"What?"

"The tube system. Those capsules are rocky as hell. Seein' as how it's your first day, I'll take you down one of the spokes instead."

I wouldn't have thought being weightless could tire me out, but after half an hour of pushing off handholds, my arms ached.

Behind me, Nielson was getting impatient. "Move along, we're almost there." He grabbed my boot and shoved me ahead, way faster than I wanted to go.

The far wall was coming up quick, and I had no control. I lunged for a handhold, missed, and braced for impact. A circular airlock at the end of the hall rolled open just in time.

"Whoohoo," I cried, as we floated through, into a small, stainless steel room. Our laughter echoed from the walls of the empty chamber.

I dragged my hands along the shiny ceiling to slow myself down, leaving damp smears. Ahead, an open portal revealed a hallway zipping along sideways, like a high-speed version of an airport walkway. The sign beside it read *Ring 5*. We were on the largest ring of the station, the outer one. Tiny golden lights embedded in the moving floor swept past in a hypnotic river of light.

Nielson guided me lower with a hand on my arm. "Good. Careful, now. Get your feet close to the floor, we're entering the gravity zone."

"Gravity zone?" I shot a questioning look over my shoulder, dragged a toe over the threshold, and stumbled as the artificial gravity caught me. Neilson's grip on my arm kept me from ending up flat on my face.

He chuckled. "The rings spin, so centrifugal force pulls us to the walls. Almost feels normal if you don't look around too much."

He pointed and I set off awkwardly, feeling a little off balance in the false gravity. My head swiveled from side to side, taking in the alien environment. Under our boots, the squishy floor glowed with soft, diffused light. The hallway curved into a loop at least a mile across. We were walking on the inside of a huge donut, with curving walls and a high, arched ceiling. I almost forgot the whole, immense ring was moving until we sailed past another stationary airlock. Open doors offered glimpses into ultra-modern offices that moved with the ring. Every surface was slick, either plastic or steel, and unnaturally clean. It made me miss Joe's diner something fierce, even if the place did smell like dirty socks.

Hundreds of yards away, the corridor slowly arced uphill. I craned my neck to stare at the tiny human figures ahead. "Those people are sticking out sideways," I exclaimed.

Neilson grinned. "Feels right side up once you're there."

"Ug," I muttered, taking a few more heavy steps.

"Muscles don't want to hold you up, do they? Try it after a two month hitch," Nielson grunted. "Guys that don't do their exercises get their asses hauled out on stretchers."

"A two month hitch? Doing what?"

"Construction," Nielson said shortly. "In space suits. Outside."

He stopped at a door on the left. A fake wood placard on the door read *Admiral Bauer*. Nielsen shot me a sidelong wink. "His Lordship Himself," he mouthed, and knocked.

The door slid open sideways, and we stepped into a cylindrical room lined with dozens of glowing computer screens. As I stared, colorful graphs updated themselves in a mesmerizing wave of falling pixels. The single desk in the middle of the floor was unoccupied, so for a second I thought we were alone. Then a silver-haired man strode toward us from halfway up the wall. From my perspective, he was tipped forward, looking down, like any second he'd somersault to the bottom. He finished his eerie descent and came even with us.

"Admiral Bauer." Nielson saluted and left without another word.

The admiral stood still and watched me with solemn blue eyes. I tipped my chin up and held his gaze.

"Jacqueline Stuart." Bauer spoke slowly, his voice a low rumble. "Street fighter. Gang leader. The last free girl. Did you know the press calls you that?"

I shook my head. I didn't even know there was still a press. In my world, newspapers were for starting fires.

"You're something of a folk hero, you know." He raised one mocking silver eyebrow. "The only person ever to go toe to toe with Bianca and walk away unscathed."

I opened my mouth to argue. *I didn't walk away. I bailed. I got chased right off the fucking planet.* But then he said something that pissed me off.

"I saw you on the news, but you're so much smaller in person."

I let out an irritated huff of air through my nose and turned away. In two strides I reached the only chair, a fake leather one in front of a gleaming semicircular desk. Flopping into it, I leaned back to take in the enormous view screen on the narrow end of the room. Past the sleek, curved body of the station, my stolen planet hung like a living jewel.

Weird bumps under the fingers of my right hand made me look down. A panel of multicolored buttons winked from the arm of Bauer's chair. *Shit.* I'd just taken the command chair. *Oh well. Fuck it.* I slid my fingers off the buttons, just in case, but stayed put.

The admiral quirked a lip in amusement, probably because my toes barely touched the floor. "Since you're there, push the amber button on the arm of the chair."

It took me a second to pick out the amber one among the multitude. I pressed it. The view outside was replaced with an image of the North American continent from space.

"These are real-time satellite images," the admiral said. He reached over me to touch a button, and numbers scrolled across the screen. *38.8633° N, 104.7919° W . . . 38.8633° N, 104.7919° W . . . 38.8633° N, 104.7919° W.*

The camera zoomed in, giving me vertigo. My fingers gripped the armrests as if it was me falling through the clouds. The Rocky Mountains appeared, growing larger as we plummeted down. The camera's descent slowed. East of the mountains crouched a bleak Colorado city. Rooftops grew larger, and I recognized a familiar grid of four-story brick buildings. The narrow lane between them was a maze, choked with wrecked cars and rusted old barrels. I knew every last one of them.

"That's our territory," I blurted.

Bauer snorted. "That *was* your territory. Pox owns it now."

I leaned forward, staring intently. At the end of the road stood the familiar, sagging roof of Joe's diner. Nothing moved. No burly, one-legged man limped down the alley. Tightness built in my throat. It was a relief when the camera panned east and stopped over the Tech Center, where humanity made its last stand. The tubes that once connected the buildings had been kicked aside, as if by a giant. *What could do that?*

The admiral's sleeve brushed my arm as he pressed another button. The empty launch pad appeared, growing larger, until the twisted remains of the array filled the screen. My breath caught. Doc Stuart had designed that giant, cone-shaped scaffold with its pox-killing UV lights, knowing he'd bait the trap with me. I agreed to it. There was no other way to lure Bianca in. She showed up, all right. In force. We lost that battle, and I was surprised to escape with my life.

Below the twisted steel scaffold lay the bleached white skeletons of thousands of animals. I peered at the bones. My heart ached for their wasted lives. "The battle only happened three days ago, and they're already picked clean. Nanobots did that."

"Of course. That's not the point," the admiral said impatiently. "Look higher." The camera panned up, following a ladder up the array to a landing where three cracked ultraviolet lights hung crazily from a bent railing.

"I don't get it," I said. "What are we looking for?"

He didn't answer. The camera zoomed closer, past hanging shreds of steel cable, and focused in on the metal mesh catwalk. It took me a minute to make sense of the picture. The steel was slowly liquefying. Rivulets of silver-gray molten metal streamed together, flowed to an upright pylon and spiraled toward the ground. Behind them, the metal gleamed as if it had been polished.

I spoke without taking my eyes from the screen. "The whole thing isn't melting. She's only taking off the surface."

Numbers crowded a blue bar to the right of the image. Most of them didn't make sense. One did--the temperature. 41°F. I was seeing the impossible. Cold metal, melting. My mind connected the dots.

"Oh my God!" I jumped to my feet and leaned forward, hands splayed on his desk. "Nanobots are stripping the array! She's looking for pieces of me. Bits of blood or skin I left behind. I bled up there, I know I did." I collapsed back into the admiral's chair with a groan. "Can she do it? Can she clone me?"

Bauer didn't sugar-coat it. "We think so. Bianca may not be able to generate a functional human body, but she can almost certainly grow enough tissue to appropriate your healing abilities. She'll be entrenched then, virtually unstoppable."

My fingernails dug into the arms of the command chair. When I spoke, my voice came out as a hoarse whisper. "How long?"

Bauer leaned against the other side of his desk, those long-fingered hands gripping the edges harder than they needed to. His gaze flicked back to the flowing metal. "At this point, we think she hasn't found any of your cells yet, or she wouldn't still be searching. We'll know she's been successful when *this* ends." He twitched his chin at the melting array. "After that, maybe two weeks. No more."

Part of me wished he hadn't called me there. So I wouldn't know what was going on, and I could've gone on thinking the adults had it under control. They didn't, though. That much was obvious the second I got out of quarantine.

Bauer stood, hands on hips, and looked me over appraisingly, as if making up his mind about something. Then he opened a cabinet on the wall and pulled out a gleaming silver sphere the size of a soccer ball. Curious, I left the chair and came around to join him on the other side of the crescent moon desk. He settled the heavy metallic ball carefully into my arms. The thing had to weigh twenty pounds.

I spotted a recessed button on one pole and impulsively pressed it. A faint tingling spread into my hands, slowly becoming intolerable. It was all I could do not to drop the ball on his foot. The device warmed until it seemed to pulse with life. Green bars began to creep around the equator.

"Shut it off, shut it off!" The admiral's hand flashed out and pushed the button so the lights went out. "We don't need an EMP going off on the bridge."

"Sorry." I sheepishly handed back the sphere and rubbed my itching palms on my pants. "So this thing is a bomb?"

"No, the device creates an electromagnetic pulse. It'll shut down anything electronic within ten feet. We want to use it on Bianca."

"Sure, that'll help," I sniped. "Maybe we can turn off her lights."

Admiral Bauer tilted his head and stared at me like I was stupid.

Then I got it. "Oh. *Nanobots* are electronic." A second later, the full force of what he was trying to say hit me. "Wait a minute. Ten feet?" I cried. "We have to get this thing within ten feet of Bianca? How are we gonna do that? We don't even know which body she's in."

"We will," the admiral said. "When she comes after you."

"What?" I yelped.

Bauer set the device on his desk. Its flattened poles kept it from rolling away. When he spoke, his voice was gentle. "You heard me, Jacqueline. We want to send you back to Earth."

A flicker out of the corner of my eye made me glance up. On the giant screen, the array had been replaced by video of blue-uniformed men and women sitting at a long conference table. From their intense expressions, I knew they'd heard every word. *Spies.*

I swept the line with a glare and whirled to confront Bauer. "So, on the off chance that Bianca fails to make a working Jackie-clone, you guys want to send her the real thing. Idiots."

The Air Force officers gasped, mouths open like their straight-laced suits suddenly got too tight for their necks. I didn't care. Bauer could call himself an admiral if he wanted to, but he couldn't command more than a hundred survivors. Back home we fought gangs that had three times that many. I rolled my eyes, turned on my heel and walked off.

The admiral dropped a heavy a hand onto my shoulder and spun me to face him. "Do you have the slightest idea what's about to happen?" he boomed.

I slapped his hand off. "It already happened, Bauer. We lost Earth. Take a look out the nearest porthole if you don't believe me."

"It's not lost."

That stopped me cold. "Not lost?"

Bauer sighed. "There's a good chance the epidemic could burn itself out. Infected are dying quicker now, months instead of years. That'll all change when she acquires your Class Three nanites. And she will, Jackie. She will."

"You should have thought of that before you treated me with 'em, then."

Bauer nodded grimly. "Believe me, we had that meeting."

I paced the room, desperately sifting options. "Can't you just nuke her from orbit?"

"We don't have nuclear weapons anymore. That was the AI's opening move against humanity. Every nuclear facility on the planet was sabotaged. Breakdowns at power plants were obvious, but it took months to discover that she'd altered the nukes too. They're nonfunctional, down to the last warhead."

"That's weird. Why didn't she seize control of them instead?" I asked.

"The detonation of a nuclear warhead in the upper atmosphere would set off an electromagnetic pulse powerful enough to shut down electronics across a continent. If our government had the backbone to do that the first week of the outbreak, it would have changed the course of history."

"So our leaders argued while the epidemic spread," I said softly.

"Figures."

That time, he let me walk away. I folded my arms over my sick stomach and paced the weird, concave floor of the cylindrical room. Minutes ticked past. Officers started shifting in their chairs. One dark-haired woman caught my eye and pointedly cleared her throat. Admiral Bauer silenced her with a gesture.

I finally stopped. "I don't know. I'm not so sure it's a bright idea. I'll think about it."

"Jackie, this is--" Bauer began.

I cut him off. "I *said* I'd think about it. Right now I need to see my crew."

A feminine chuckle came from behind me. Halfway to the door, I turned. Onscreen, the dark-haired woman laughed, white teeth perfect against her olive skin. "Imperious little thing, aren't you," she said to me.

I took a deep breath and the words tumbled out. "Imperious? I've been Chief since I was *eleven. I* have to feed people. *I* have to protect them. Even now! Here he is, asking me to fix the shitstorm somebody else caused." I pointed an angry finger at Bauer.

"Fair enough," the woman said. She looked at the admiral. "Sir, we need to level with her. I think she can handle it."

Bauer didn't answer for a while. He scrubbed a hand up his face and over his short-cropped hair. A long minute later, he nodded.

The woman's face softened as she turned to me. "My name is Captain Delgado. Alessandra Delgado. Just . . ." She looked down and pinched the bridge of her nose for a second. "Just call me Alessandra. Look, Jackie, we need you. But it's only fair that we tell you the truth."

What truth? A weight sank into my stomach. I waited.

Alessandra took a deep breath and went on. "You were treated with Class Three nanites. They're still circulating in your blood, repairing your tissues. It's miracle enough that you survived them, but now--"

The man beside her put a hand on her arm. They had a rapid, whispered conference. "Yes, *everything,*" Alessandra hissed. She turned back to me. "I know we're asking a lot of you. To go back, when virtually the entire planet has been compromised."

"We lost the whole planet?" I repeated numbly. "Every person is taken. Every last animal? You're sure. Absolutely certain."

Alessandra nodded grimly. "The EMP device is our last hope. Of course, we can't guarantee that you'll get close enough to Bianca to set it off. But . . . say you do. Say you succeed. We don't know exactly what will happen to you."

"Why? What could happen?" I searched their faces.

A pale, gray-haired man on the end of the line spoke up. "Our best guess is that the electromagnetic pulse will destroy your Class Three nanites."

I shrugged. "So I'll be normal again. Lose my healing ability." His dismal expression worried me.

"Maybe." The gray-haired man pressed a knuckle to his lips. "But our scientists think it's also possible that . . . that you'll age. Rapidly and catastrophically. It might be fatal. Or you might hang on for a year or two, until you succumb to a stroke, Alzheimer's, one of any number of geriatric diseases."

"Geriatric?" I knew the word. *That means old people.* I couldn't believe it. My teeth clenched, holding back sobs.

"Wait a minute, Jackie, don't jump to conclusions," Alessandra said. "You might be fine. Nothing at all could happen." She glanced at the gray-haired man, as if for conformation. He gave her a halfhearted shrug. When Alessandra spoke again, her voice was soft. "Or Doctor Olson could be right. You're the first person ever to be in this situation, so we just don't know."

"You don't know," I repeated bitterly. "But I have to find out."

"We're not forcing you--" Alessandra started.

The gray-haired man interrupted her. "Jacqueline, if you don't go, we'll lose the planet forever. And this station doesn't have the resources for long term survival, especially with the stowaways you brought along."

"Don't push, Olson," Admiral Bauer snapped. "We need her a hundred percent onboard with the plan, if she goes at all." He strode across silver-blue carpet to stand over me. "Don't worry, Jackie, you're not going down there alone. I'll assign a security force to you, the best we've got. These men are urban combat experts. They've seen multiple tours of duty in Iraq, Afghanistan--all over the world."

"This isn't urban combat, Bauer," I cried. "My only chance is to sneak in, small and quiet, like a rat. If you send me marching out there with a bunch of soldiers, we're doomed. She'll see us! You know what'll happen next. You saw the battle on *television.* So go ahead, tell us. Tell us what happens next."

Bauer didn't rise to my dig. I had to respect him for that. He just answered the question, calm and professional. It made me feel like a kid.

"If you're spotted, you'll come under attack. Bianca will likely deploy hunters to surround you. Nanobots will be recruited from surrounding areas. They'll synthesize mass quantities of proteins and lipids, creating the false flesh known as pox construct. Pox construct presents a . . . significant tactical challenge. Rips, burns, bullet holes, all mend. It can move, grasp objects, and change shape like an amoeba."

"Like an amoeba the size of a fucking apartment house," I snapped.

"Remember the tentacles?"

"I still have nightmares about them," Bauer admitted without a shred of shame.

"*You* have nightmares? I won't even tell you about mine."

Bauer folded his arms and stuck to business, like a grown-up. "So, your recommendation is to send a minimal force, and penetrate her defenses by stealth." He glanced over his shoulder at the officers on video. "I have to agree."

Disturbed murmurs came from the men and women lining the conference table. They didn't like it. I didn't care.

The admiral's laser-focus gaze locked on me. "Can we count on you, Jackie?" The power of that charismatic personality leaned on me like a physical force.

I couldn't deal with it. It wasn't fair. When did this whole mess become my responsibility? I backed up a step, then another. "I . . . I can't decide this right now."

The admiral's shoulders sagged. Suddenly he looked older. With precise, controlled motions, he walked to the command chair, sat down, and straightened his uniform. I felt sorry for him. In front of his officers, Bauer could never show weakness, never cry. I knew the feeling. He didn't ask for pox to wreck his life, any more than I did. It just happened, and somebody had to be Chief.

I stepped close, hesitated, and then dropped to a knee by the command chair. Looking up at his face, I put a hand on the admiral's arm. "I'm not saying I'll go. But if I do, you have to give me your word. No soldiers, okay? Promise me."

Bauer sat in silence for a long minute before he answered. "All right. I promise."

"But sir!" Onscreen, three or four voices spoke up at once, raising a chorus of objections.

I couldn't deal with it. I had to get out of there. Had to run.

Chapter 2

I burst out of the admiral's office and fled down the strange, looping hallway. No one followed me. I kept moving, always uphill, my eyes blurred with tears. People in matching pale blue jumpsuits passed by. My tight black suit and knee-high combat boots made me stand out, but I couldn't help it. Those were the only clothes I had. People recognized me and nudged their companions, but I refused to stop and talk. Maybe ten minutes later, I realized I'd missed my turn. I kept on going around the giant loop for another half hour. Dakota would be waiting for me, and I didn't want to see him until I got a grip. The crew would be full of joy, ready to start a new life. I'd have to tell them the truth.

By the time I came around the circle again and spotted the square, steel airlock Nielson had brought me through, my legs ached. An electronic sign flashed the words *gravity threshold,* along with a floating stick figure and a couple of arrows pointing up. I stepped deliberately over the line, pushed off, and floated. About twenty feet up, I reached the first set of handholds. An explosion rocked the station.

The earsplitting boom drowned out my scream. Red-hot pain flashed through my head. The aluminum bar got wrenched from my grip. I was pulled backward, spinning weightless in gale-force wind. Broken glass whipped past, slashing my cheeks. Far away, men shouted. Air howled into space through some unseen hole. I screamed again as I crossed the gravity threshold, hit the wall, and got slammed down. The ribs on my right side crunched. I curled on the floor, eyes squeezed shut against the sandpaper wind.

A strong arm hauled me to my feet. I barely recognized Nielson in his white astronaut suit and bubble helmet. He slammed a gloved palm into a big red button on the wall. A round steel door started to roll across the open portal.

"Into the airlock, move, move, move!" Nielson picked me up and hurled me through the rapidly narrowing gap.

Heavy steel hinges clipped my hip as the door thudded closed. A few seconds later and they would've cut me in half. I floated across the airlock, helpless with pain. Foamy blood spread across my lips. I gasped for air. My broken rib had torn a hole in my lung. I was drowning in my own blood. Then the Class III nanites kicked on and the real pain began.

It felt like some dark god was twisting me, wringing every drop of blood from my body. I sobbed. All I wanted was to drift into unconsciousness, but the cold, thin air kept me awake. A coughing fit wracked my crushed ribcage. Red globules floated dreamily away. The suffocating sensation gradually subsided, and pain faded from my broken ribs. The nanites had completed their repairs. I drifted, exhausted.

Inside my sealed airlock, the wind had stopped, but I was trapped. Red *locked* signs blinked from the doors on both sides. Using handholds, I worked my way over to a door and clung to the frame with shaking hands. On the other side of the porthole, the inner ring of the space station had stopped moving. Artificial gravity was lost. Small objects drifted weightless through the dusty air. Far away, space-suited astronauts floated up and down the wall, aided by small jets on their backpacks.

About an hour later, the ring began to move. Debris drifted to the floor. Behind me, the portal into the docked ship blinked green and opened. I flew back to my quarters as fast as I could. Our sleeping bag was gone. The blank patch of wall where it had been made me feel empty inside. I guess I'd gotten used to sleeping between Keenan and little Tito. During the day, Keenan could be pretty obnoxious. He pushed his boundaries constantly, trying to be the boss. But at night, he was different. I'd made it clear that we weren't gonna be fucking, not while I was somebody else's girlfriend. Keenan still held me and that baby in his arms like treasures. He made us feel safe. Thinking about him, I could almost feel his long hair brushing my cheek. At that moment, there was no one in the world I'd rather see. I felt a little guilty about it, but it was true.

A message light blinked from the computer. I played it back. No words, since Keenan couldn't write all that well. Instead he'd left me a map, with a green line leading through the rocket ship, up the central axle of the station, and out to Ring Four. *That's where he went. With the crew, probably.* I bent over the screen, memorizing it. Then I took off, leaving the door open behind me. It didn't matter. We had nothing worth stealing.

I zipped through the ship and floated into the central axle, feeling lost. It took me a minute to get my bearings. I was inside a long, hollow tube, the part of the station that reminded me of an arrow shot through the middle of a target. The central axle was connected to the innermost ring by an array of spokes, and more spokes connected each concentric ring to the next. The door into the rocket closed behind me. I got nervous and hit the button from the other side, but it didn't let me back in.

I had no choice. Pushing off handholds on the walls, I took a right and floated down the white-walled tube. A couple hundred yards down was a closed airlock labeled *Ring 1*. A smoky glass porthole in the door offered a peek into the abandoned inner ring, and I couldn't resist. Inside, red pinpoints glowed from the shadows.

It's a computer, or some kind of machinery.

The eerie reflections zigzagged forward, inhumanly fast, and flew toward the airlock. I squealed and pushed myself back. Something hit the door from the other side. Scrabbling noises came through, like claws raking steel. I kicked off the wall and went into a panicked flight down the tube, arms and legs churning. Whatever was in there, in the dark, it was definitely alive. My heart didn't stop racing for a quarter mile.

Keenan's map took me straight to my ride. It looked like one of those cylinders my mom used to send checks in at the drive-through bank, only this tube carried people. Nielson said I wasn't ready, but I was sick of floating through those eerie tubes. I decided to go for it. So I touched the button, and the door slid straight up. Inside, sturdy straps hung from padded walls, like a mobile insane asylum. My eyes went wide. While I stared, the door closed, leaving me standing there like an idiot.

A glowy map on the wall laid out the tube system. The red 'you are here' dot put me on the central axle that poked through the middle of Ring One. The tip of the axle had an oblong bulb on it labeled *Shuttle Bay*. Eight spokes ran perpendicular to the axle, connecting the concentric rings of the station. Each spoke held some kind of transport tube. Seven of them were the empty kind I'd been in before, with handholds for floating along. One contained the tube system, with moving capsules that carried passengers. According to the map, the tube system could whisk me out to Four in one straight shot. I admit, Nielsen's warning put my nerves on edge. But I squared my shoulders, hit the button again, and stepped inside.

A computer-generated voice made me jump. "Lock in?" she asked. Lights on flip-down shoulder harnesses flashed briefly.

"Should I lock myself in the little padded cell?" I repeated sarcastically. "Uh, maybe not."

"Acknowledged. Launching," said the computer.

The capsule took off sideways. It accelerated down the tube like a bullet, plastering me to the squishy quilted wall. I seized a strap in my right fist just as the thing started to corkscrew. The first turn flipped me face down and dropped me off the ceiling, bruising my nose. I lost the strap and tumbled, but not for long. As it picked up speed, G-forces pressed me into the padded wall. I couldn't have lifted my head if I wanted to. Eyes squinted almost shut, I gritted my teeth and endured. With a final, nauseating twist, the ride stopped. Doors opened automatically. I hauled myself to my feet and staggered out on weak knees.

"Welcome to Ring Four," the computer said cooly.

"Thanks a lot, bitch," I growled. A few nerdy Air Force boys in the hall heard that and grinned.

On Ring Four, people moved around calmly, unaffected by the accident on Five. I hiked around another weird, looping hallway and found my crew sitting in a silent classroom. Every head was bent over a computer screen. The older boys typed awkwardly, two fingers at a time. A soft-looking, motherly woman circulated among them, whispering answers to occasional questions.

The breath rushed out of me in a relieved sigh. We were together again, finally. A big grin lit my face. "Hey, guys, I'm back," I cried.

Boys swarmed out of their chairs and stampeded toward me, whooping and hollering. "Jack! Jack's here!"

"Welcome, Jacqueline. We're so glad you could join us," the teacher said.

I could tell she didn't like me. Not at all. The woman's gaze lingered over a shrine in one corner, a framed photo of a boy surrounded by silk flowers and tiny electric candles. I understood. Back at the Tech Center, teens fought for the chance to make it into space. That was their only chance for survival. Losers got left behind, sacrificed for the greater good. Then I showed up, uninvited, with a pack of stowaway street kids. Resources were scarce. The space station wasn't supposed to be able to support any more people, but somehow it did. There we were, sucking up oxygen and eating food that could have saved the boy in the picture. I got it, but that didn't make it any easier.

The teacher pursed her lips. "Jacqueline, please take a seat and enter your name on the screen."

That was a problem. At that point, I really needed to be talking strategy with my chief, not retaking fifth grade. "Thanks. Um, I'd love to, but there's people I need to talk to right now," I said over the heads of a couple of kids.

Boys hung on my arms, all talking at once. "So glad you're back," Caleb exclaimed. "Whaddaya think, is this place cool or what?"

"It is," I agreed. "Are they treating you guys okay?"

Paco grinned. "Yeah! They have so much food here."

Ash hugged me and patted the back of my black combat suit. "You look badass in that outfit."

I leaned back and looked up into his dark, compassionate eyes. Wherever Ash was felt like home to me. It didn't matter that he was black and I was white—he was crew. Family.

The teacher lady pushed him toward a chair. "Back to your seat, young man."

Ash backed up a step or two, but he didn't sit. Nobody did. Boys glanced from me to their new chief and back again. Neither of us gave the order, so the kids hung around. When Dakota took me in his arms, Keenan turned away, his handsome features rigid. I winced in sympathy, but then my boyfriend kissed me and I forgot all about it.

Almost.

Dakota wrapped his arms around my waist and lifted me off my toes. "Jackie," he whispered in my ear. "I love you."

Our lips met again, and the crew erupted in teasing laughter. "Whooo, baby," Caleb called. Paco let out a wolf whistle.

That snapped the teacher's patience. "That's enough. Sit down right now, all of you!" Boys glanced her way and then ignored her. So she turned on Dakota. "You. You're supposed to be in charge of this gang of hooligans. Make them sit."

Dakota's face took on that rigid, masklike look that came before a storm. He didn't have the patience for screamers. Too often, he solved that problem with his fists.

"Do you, uh, wanna let me deal with her?" I asked him. Damn. It felt weird not to be chief.

He nodded gratefully and released me. I didn't know quite how to handle the teacher, so I started with my crew. "Hey guys, what do you think of school?" I asked. "Is it worth your time?"

"Worth our time?" Paco echoed. He glanced at Caleb, who nodded. "I guess."

"Marc? You in?" I asked the new kid, since he wouldn't speak up otherwise.

He didn't seem to get that it was optional. "Yeah, sure. If you say so."

"I'm doing it," Ash said. "You guys can join me or not, I don't care. You good with that, Jack?"

I shrugged. "Sure, whatever you want to do."

Angry tears filled the teacher's eyes. The woman's mouth opened and closed, so her flabby jaw vibrated, but no sound came out. Sympathy filled me. We'd seen parents like her before. They passed through our territory sometimes, searching for their missing children. I used to assemble my crew and let them walk down the line, peering into every face on the slim hope that one of my orphans was theirs. Half the time those parents left in a fury, irrationally angry at us for not being the right children, the ones they loved. I understood why. We survived. They didn't. There just wasn't anything I could do to change that.

But I had my own problems, like an exploding space station and the prospect of launching a solo invasion of our pox-infested planet. So I couldn't worry much about another angry parent. I took her aside anyway, just to be nice. Without being told to, boys started wandering back to the desks and putting their headphones back on.

"I've decided to keep them in the program," I told her. "Let's see how it goes."

"It isn't up to you," the teacher snapped. "You're not their mother."

"No, I'm not. But I raised 'em, just the same." Despite my effort to keep a straight face, I felt my lip quirk in a nervous smile.

The teacher spotted it and glared. "Let me tell you about the so-called job you did. Those kids can barely read, let alone . . ." She kept on ranting, but I wasn't listening anymore.

All I wanted was to do was tell Dakota about the admiral's plan. We needed to end that bizarre parent-teacher conference somehow. I know, it was rude, and I felt bad about it later. But I stuck my fingers in my mouth and let loose the three-tone emergency whistle we used back home to call in crew off the rooftops. The high pitched sound made everyone jump.

The teacher's rant ended. Headphones clattered to the table tops. Chair legs squealed against the floor as my crew hastily assembled at the back of the room. I never used the emergency whistle unless something was up-- something bad.

Tito was the only one who didn't understand that. "School ova alweady? But I wanna play my compuda game."

"It's okay, you can play. You kids, stay here with your teacher. I need to see Dakota, Ash and Keenan outside," I said casually. Like that wasn't transparent as hell.

So it didn't surprise anyone when twelve-year-old Caleb gave me a level stare and said, "Bad news, eh?"

I didn't know what to say. "Um, yeah. I got . . . a tough decision to make. I'll fill you in later."

Caleb looked disgusted. He hated being twelve. Too young to run the crew with the big guys, and old enough to know the difference.

"Sorry," I tried, but Caleb wouldn't look at me. He went back to his seat, put on his headphones, and turned up the volume so loud the sound leaked out from twenty feet away.

I marched out the door with the three oldest boys on my heels. We stopped in the hall and I beckoned them close. "Look, I learned some scary things today. Let's go back to the ship. Maybe we can talk in the biosphere."

"It's not there anymore. They moved it to the outer ring." Ash said. He tapped a pattern on a bare spot on the wall, and a map lit up.

I was impressed. "I didn't know you could do that."

Ash flashed a taunting smile. "That's because you ditched orientation."

"That was Bauer's fault. Figures, he never bothered to fill me in."

"Let's see, what does she need to know?" Ash asked the other guys.

"Um, the station has five rings, you knew that. There's full gravity on Five, and it decreases as you go inward. Those crazy spinning pods take you around a ring or over to the next one. Low-gravity jump tubes only go inward, to where gravity is lighter. I guess that's it."

"And they told us to stay out of rings one and two. There's only mechanical stuff in there," Keenan added, with a scowl that said he didn't entirely believe it.

We took a quick, nauseating ride on the tube system. Just for fun, we decided to explore the service tunnel--a stationary, zero-gravity tube that went around the perimeter of the outer ring. Keenan hesitated at the opening to the glowing, white walled tube. "Just think, only that thin wall's between us and space."

Dakota jokingly punched him in the shoulder. "What are you afraid of, a little case of frozen eyeballs? Don't be a pussy."

Keenan laughed and shoved Dakota, trying to push him over the gravity threshold. A playful wrestling match broke out. I dodged them both and floated into the tunnel, trying to forget the explosion on the inner ring, the howl of air, the sting of broken glass. *Was it really an accident?*

I pushed off the walls and got moving. Soaring along was fun, and I soon started to feel better. My ribs didn't hurt any more. The crew was together, healthy and fed, and I didn't have to go back to Earth if I didn't want to. Plus I was starting to get the hang of that weightless swimming motion. At the next intersection, I tucked in my knees and did a fast spin to look back.

Ash was in the lead. Keenan and Dakota fought for second place, grunting and elbowing for position. I had to laugh. Only Ash looked normal in zero-g. His wooly, short-cropped hair held up to anything. The rest of them reminded me of a bunch of troll dolls with their hair standing on end. I giggled and pushed off again.

One last soar down a segmented tube brought us to an airlock. Back inside the big donut, we checked the map. The greenhouse module was nearby, clamped to its permanent dock on the outer ring.

The biosphere looked the same, with that familiar giant walnut tree in the middle and dozens of herb and vegetable gardens spiraling out around it. I could almost imagine we were still on Earth, back at the Tech Center. But through the semi-transparent walls, the sun glowed yellow from the black backdrop of space. After days in quarantine, it still felt comforting to touch grass, to hear the sound of trickling water.

Keenan didn't waste any time ruining my good mood. "A soldier hauled her off, and now look at her."

Everyone stared. On top of everything else, I apparently looked like shit. *Great.*

I touched my face self-consciously. The cuts had already healed, but a smear of old blood came off on my hand. "Nobody beat me up. There was an accident. A hole got blown in Ring Five."

"We heard," Keenan said shortly. "But that's not what really upset you, is it?"

I looked down, shaking my head. He knew me well, and sometimes I hated it.

The ship's cat came out of the bushes and curled up on Dakota's lap. He stroked its gray fur until it purred, claws kneading the fabric of his worn jeans.

My boyfriend trapped me with his gaze. "What the hell happened in there, Jackie?" The cat on his lap purred like nothing was wrong. Dakota gently lifted its paw, releasing the hooked claws, and stroked its soft fur. He always did love animals.

"They . . . they want me to go back to Earth." I regurgitated the whole story--EMP device, sudden aging, everything. It took all my control not to cry.

"Sudden aging?" Dakota repeated. After that, he wouldn't even look at me. That hit me in the heart.

Ash shook his dark head. "Say no. No way."

"He's right! Don't let 'em use you," Keenan growled. "This is bullshit."

I threw up my hands. "What if I don't? What if this really is our last chance?"

Keenan tore up a handful of turf and threw it. "Bullshit! If it's our last chance, we need a better plan. Why do they wanna send you in alone, anyway?"

I shrugged, looking down. "He didn't. That was, uh, my idea. I'd be better off alone. Those astronauts have been up here for years. They have no idea how to deal with hunters. One of 'em sprung me from quarantine, totally turned me loose, and *then* tested me for pox."

"It's a moot point, 'cause you're not going," Keenan snapped.

"Agreed," Ash said evenly. "She's not."

They both glanced at our new chief to see how he was taking that. Dakota would've normally been annoyed with his lieutenants for overstepping. That day, he just sat in silence, watching us blankly. I started to reach for his hand, hesitated, and withdrew. The cat retreated with dignity, the white tip of its tail disappearing into the bushes.

Dakota stood up. "What's next? School?"

"Back to school," Keenan echoed, rolling his eyes. "Sure, Chief. That feels important, under the circumstances."

Dakota just stared at him with a blank expression, and didn't answer.

We arrived at the classroom to see the crew trooping out, following their teacher. I fell in at the back of the pack. Dakota gave me a vague wave and took off the other way, probably to the bathroom or something. I didn't ask. He was chief, not me. I had to get used to that.

I caught up with Caleb, trying to make it up to him for leaving him with the little kids. "Hey."

He turned his dirty-blond head away.

I flicked his shaggy hair with my fingertips, so he couldn't ignore me. "You mad, bro?" Flick. Flick.

No answer.

"Didja have any fun at school today?" Flick.

Caleb wouldn't look at me. He ducked his head and walked faster.

I pursued him. "Where we goin'?" Flick, flick, flick.

"All right, all right!" Caleb slapped my hand off, making the other boys laugh. "They're sending us to the cafeteria for lunch. With all the people who are *supposed* to be here."

"Yep, that oughta be fun," Marc said sarcastically. He squeezed Caleb's shoulder. "Could be worse. They could've spaced us on sight."

I winced. Guess I should have known my crew of stowaways wouldn't be popular. We followed our reluctant guide partway around the artificial gravity loop to a silvery low-gravity freefall tube that looked like a hole in the floor. I edged forward to peek over the vertical rim. The thing reminded me of the slide at a water park, but it was dry and a whole lot steeper. I didn't like it. One by one, kids jumped in, feet first. They disappeared, squealing in delight.

Marc's comment was still stuck in my head, and it made me paranoid. "If they're spacing us, they just flushed the teacher too. She went first."

Marc laughed and poked Caleb. "Do you feel lucky?"

Apparently they did, because, one after another, the boys disappeared into the glowing tunnel. I was left alone, balanced on the padded edge. So I manned up and jumped. Gravity had only the slightest pull there, so I fell slowly, sometimes sliding and sometimes catching air in a dreamy freefall. The tube landed me lightly on a cushioned mat. I stepped into a low gravity zone and joined my crew, waiting at the back of a line that stretched down the hall. The angry teacher had disappeared.

The delicious smell of food wafted down the hall. Marc sniffed the air. His stomach growled audibly, making little Tito giggle. "This is killin' me," the new kid said. "And there's a couple hundred people in front of us."

I pushed him ahead of me. "There. Better?" That earned me a rare smile.

That shy, skinny white kid had only been with me a week before the battle at the array, so we barely knew him. He's been through hell in some basement harem, where his captors barely fed him. His knobby knees were still wider than his thighs, but that would change. I'd take care of him.

Twenty minutes later, when we were almost to the door, Dakota showed up. "Took me long enough to find you guys. Some soldier boy had to walk me over here. You could have said something before you took off. What's going on? Are we still on the large ring of the station? How can you tell?"

I didn't know what to say. Dakota saw us leaving, and it was him that took off alone. What was that about?

Keenan tapped a porthole with a disgusted look. "See for yourself, genius."

His touch activated a window where there wasn't one before. Almost instantly, an oblong sheet of metal brightened and cleared, becoming completely transparent. We were obviously on Three. Outside, two larger rings arced between us and a glorious field of stars. From that angle, I couldn't see Earth. It was just as well. I needed to let it go.

My crew trooped into the crowded cafeteria, and the room grew quiet. I pointedly ignored the stares and kept walking. In a faraway mirror, my reflection moved with me, a black dot in a sea of blue. Obviously, showing up in creepy armored riot gear wasn't the best way to make friends, but it wasn't my fault. Nobody issued me a sky-blue astronaut uniform. They probably didn't make them small enough for me, anyway.

When I got to the front of the line, a man in a hairnet slapped stew into my bowl. Thick brown liquid sloshed over the side. "Thank you," I said in a low voice. Hairnet Man turned away. I got the message and moved on.

Dakota led us to a table in the back, as far from the others as he could get. In seconds, a bunch of teens from another table grabbed their trays and came to join us. The unexpected gesture made my heart well up with gratitude.

A blonde girl dumped her tray on the table next to mine. "Hiya, Jackie."

"Hey!" I hugged the girl who'd fought Bianca by my side. "Guys, you remember Alanna. Without her and Adam, we'd all be dead."

Adam squeezed in on the other side of me, beaming his toothpaste-commercial smile. My crew was busy ogling Alanna. I couldn't blame them. Besides me, they'd hardly seen a girl in years.

"This is Adam Weatherford, our pilot," I told the boys. "He, uh, broke a lot of rules to bring us here."

My voice faltered when I spotted the bare spot on Adam's collar, where his embroidered-on rank insignia used to be. I deliberately reached out and took his ragged collar between my thumb and forefinger. "I don't know what to say. You paid a heavy price to save our lives, and I'm--" I choked on the word *grateful,* and never said it out loud. Later, I'd regret that.

Adam squeezed my hand and released it. "From what I hear, they're asking a heavy price from you too."

Ten-year-old Paco's voice rose high with anxiety. "What? What price?"

"Tell us what they said, Jack," Caleb demanded. "Up on the bridge. What happened in there?"

My spoonful of stew made it halfway down and stopped. I couldn't talk over the lump in my throat.

"Oh, sorry," Adam said haltingly. "You haven't, uh . . . told them yet?"

I swallowed hard, gripped the edge of the table and looked down the line of boys. Dakota listened intently, even though he already heard the news.

"It's okay, Adam," I said. "I was gonna have to tell 'em anyway. You guys, I'm not going. Not going, okay? But the admiral tried to pressure me into going back to Earth. He has a new weapon he wants to use against Bianca. The problem is, it has to be set off on the pox-boss herself, from, like, ten feet away."

"Impossible." Caleb scoffed. "You'd have to find her first. When she can wink in and out like magic."

I nodded. "Right. It wasn't a very bright plan. So I said no."

"You said no to the *admiral*?" Adam repeated. Over my head, he and Alanna shared an apprehensive glance.

"Well, I told him I'd think about it. I did. And the answer's no. I just haven't told him yet." I shoveled in another mouthful of brown stew and washed it down with the recycled shower water they drank on the station. Maybe the stuff tasted faintly of soap. Maybe I imagined it. I've had worse.

Alanna shifted uncomfortably on the plastic bench and leaned close to talk to me without being overheard. "Um, Jackie? About the admiral. You know, he expects everyone to contribute."

I rolled my eyes. "Okay, so we'll work then."

"You don't get it." Alanna sighed. "The kind of work a bunch of kids could do--it won't exactly buy their oxygen."

My spoon clattered to the table. "They're kids! What more does he want?"

Adam put a gentle hand on my arm. "Bauer wants *you* to earn their place for them."

"By handing myself over to Bianca? Look, I want to wipe out the pox as bad as anyone, but that's just stupid." My voice carried. Around us, heads turned.

After that, Adam and Alanna left me alone. Their conversation swirled around me, but I wasn't listening. *Bauer can't force me to go back! He wants me to leave my crew? No way.*

Dakota reached across the table, squeezed my hand, and let it go. Afterward, my gaze lingered on his face. When he laughed, the scar on his cheek crinkled. Damn, I loved that scar. The white line angled from the outside edge of his eye to his cheekbone, and it was crazy sexy. Not because it made him look dangerous, even though it did. I loved that scar because he got it over me, that terrible winter when I was thirteen.

It's January. Propane's getting hard to find, and the kids are cold. Dangerously cold. We need survival gear. Blankets, coats, boots. "Stay home, Jackie," Dakota begs. "It's too dangerous. You don't look like a boy anymore."

"I know that. But we have no choice." I don't say it out loud, but we both know why. The little ones could die.

Me and Dakota wrap up and head out into the bitter night. The city feels deserted. Only a few rare streetlights break up endless miles of darkness. My hands ache under my worn wool mittens, but my toes don't hurt anymore--they're already numb. Dakota jimmies the back door of the army surplus store and we slip inside, listening hard to make sure we're alone. The place is dark and silent, and it smells faintly of musty wool. I find a duffel and start cramming coats into it as fast as I can. A hanger clatters to the floor. We freeze.

"Enough. Let's go," Dakota hisses. It's too late.

The front door opens, and flashlight beams criss-cross the room. We duck. My heart pounds so hard, it feels like it's rising straight up. A bunch of men come in, not even trying to be quiet. Their boots thud heavily across the floor. The Outdoor Store is the heart of their territory. Only a big, powerful gang could hold onto a resource this rich. Those kinds of gangs had their own harems.

"Spread out," a deep voice growls. Men sweep the room, coming closer. Me and Dakota creep toward the back door on silent feet. I'm right on his heels. My breath sounds way too loud. We crawl the last few feet and then Dakota lunges for the doorknob. We explode down the alley. Behind us, men burst outside and chase us, shouting. Freezing air sears my lungs with every breath. The heavy duffle flops with every stride, slowing me down, but I refuse to drop it.

Dakota knows a secret spot where we can get under the fence. He squeezes through first and helps me with the fat bags, pulling while I push. The second the hole is clear, I drop to my belly to wiggle through. That's when the guy catches me. A big hand grabs the back of my neck, pinning me against the frozen ground. I thrash and cry out, but he's twice my size. I'm trapped.

"Jackie!" Dakota screams. He tries to get to me, but I'm partway under the fence, blocking the gap. With sickening certainty, I realize I'm going to be raped right in front of him.

Gasping and crying, I struggle to get an arm around, to elbow my attacker in the face, but my strikes only rattle chain link. The rapist reaches under my stomach and rips open my button-fly jeans. I can smell his vile body odor, feel his hot, stinking breath on the back of my neck. I scream and writhe, trying to avoid his horrid touch. Gravel gouges my bare skin. Something heavy hits us from above, splitting my lower lip against the frozen ground. It's Dakota. He's climbed the fence and dropped on my attacker. The males roll off me, spitting curses, and Dakota gains his feet first. They face off, boy against man, circling. Knives glint in the moonlight.

With a shout, the man lunges, blade out. Dakota dodges left, striking low. His blade sinks deep at the same instant that our enemy's knife opens up the right side of his face. The man goes down.

Dakota staggers, hand to his cheek. Blood pours between his fingers. I grab him by the shoulder and shove him toward the fence. We get through, get the bags, somehow get home. All that is a dream, but what's real is the smile on Paco's face when I put a brand new coat into his hands. Dakota brought back piles of green wool army blankets too, leftovers from some long-ago war. I hand those out too, because Dakota can't. He's flat on his back on Joe's kitchen table, getting his face stitched up with fishing line.

Joe bends over him, a needle between his thick fingers. "You'll live. But it's gonna leave a helluva scar."

It sure did. I leaned back in my chair and stared in appreciation. That white line tightened my nipples and sent tingles down my lower belly.

Dakota picked up on that and shot me a wicked grin. He stood up. "Come on, baby."

I knew exactly what was on his mind. A little private time, just the two of us. I scraped my dish fast and tucked the biscuits in my pockets, since I couldn't stand to waste food. Hand in hand, we hurried out of the cafeteria.

"Where do you want to go?" I whispered.

Dakota pulled me close to his side. "You still have access to those officers' quarters?"

"No. I'm in the dorm now, with the rest of you bums."

"That's all right." Arm around my waist, he wheeled me around and steered us toward the tube system. "You can share my sleeping bag in the bunkhouse. But for now, how about the garden?"

"Mmm. I love that place," I whispered.

As we waited, Dakota wrapped his arms around my waist and pressed his hips against mine. Gazing into his blue eyes, I traced the scar on his cheek with my thumb. The second the capsule arrived we scooted inside, but a big hand reached in and kept the door from closing. Admiral Bauer stepped in, along with three blue-uniformed soldiers. One of them waved a keycard in front of the control panel, and the lift froze, doors wide open.

"Test her first," Bauer said, inclining his silver head at me. His men moved to hem me in.

"What the hell?" I yelled, yanking my arm away from the oncoming needle. "I already got tested."

"We're re-checking everyone," Bauer said. "Starting with you."

Backed into the corner, I submitted to another needle stick and a cleansing beam of UV light.

"Negative," said the man carrying the lab-in-a-box.

"No shit. Negative, again? Just hours after my last test. How shocking," I sniped.

No one responded to my sarcasm. The soldiers collared Dakota, pinned his arm. and took some of his blood too. "He's negative, sir."

I got in the admiral's face over that, even though he loomed over me like a giant. "What's the point of this, Bauer? You gonna harass me until I agree to your stupid plan?"

The admiral folded his arms and held me in his icy gaze. "The point of this *harassment,* Miss Stuart, is to find the saboteur. That explosion on Ring Four just happened to go off in your general vicinity, at a time when you were wandering the station unsupervised."

"I didn't do it," I shouted. "Besides, how would I? Why would I? My whole crew is here."

He cocked that annoying white eyebrow at me. "I didn't think you did. Tell me, did you see anything? Anyone suspicious?"

I shook my head.

"Keep your eyes open," Bauer said. "That attack was deliberate. It's possible that we have one of the infected on board. Speaking of which, I have something important to show you. Come with me."

Dakota shot me an irate glance. I shrugged. So much for our romantic getaway.

"Docking bay," Bauer ordered.

"Lock in?" the computer asked. Lights flashed on the hanging row of harnesses.

"Yes," I blurted, wiggling into mine as fast as I could.

Dakota copied me. Bauer and his men clipped in too while I scowled like a kidnapping victim. A stone-faced soldier pressed the top button, and off we went, spinning down the tube with insane G-forces pinning us to the walls. I worked hard to keep my lunch down, even though it would've served the admiral right if I'd thrown up on his shoes.

The capsule released us into a zero-gravity zone, a long, narrow room with sealed airlocks lining the shiny white walls. A glance out the window told me we were on the far end of the central axle. Outside, a row of seven sleek shuttlecraft were moored by their noses. Dakota and I shared an excited glance.

"This way." The men floated away, a few feet above the slick, shiny floor.

On the right, the windows were nearly blocked by a view of the ship we came in on. Letting the others go on ahead, I pressed my nose against chilly armored glass. The massive ship was docked vertically against the central axle, like a needle stuck through a loop. In space, nothing was ever close enough to give me the feeling of being up high. This was different. The rocket had once been the size of a skyscraper, but only the top fifteen or twenty stories remained. Those dropped away in a dizzy swoop toward the planet below.

Bauer floated up behind me. His transparent reflection in the window watched me like a ghost.

"What happened to the rest of the rocket?" I asked him. "It used to be a lot bigger."

The admiral took a deep, calming breath. My ignorance obviously strained his patience. "Stages one and two contained engines and propellant that boosted the payload through the atmosphere. They jettisoned sequentially as the spacecraft gained altitude."

"Cool," I said, still staring out the window. The concentric rings of the station hung below us. Partway around the curve of the outer ring, a domed roof gleamed in the sun. "Oh, I see the biosphere. How'd you move it out there?"

"We used the shuttles as tugs. And the module itself has positioning thrusters," Bauer said shortly.

I caught Dakota's eye. *The biosphere*," I mouthed, with a teasing little smile. His eyes lit up, and he flashed me a sexy grin.

Bauer grabbed my elbow, pushed off a handhold, and moved my weightless body like cargo. Dakota saw it and smirked, which irritated me more. We stopped at Shuttle Five, near the end of the line. The admiral released me and entered a code on the keypad at the door. A blank screen lit up with a picture of a hand.

"Place your palm flat on the screen."

I almost said no. I hated doing things without an explanation. Or maybe I just hated following orders. Either way, I hesitated before pressing my hand on the screen. With a tickle of static electricity, the screen turned green. Letters scrolled across it. *Jacqueline Stuart, handprint access granted.* The airlock opened into the tiny, two-seater spaceship. We glided inside, down the narrow aisle between the bucket seats.

Dakota strapped himself into one black-cushioned chair, exclaiming in delight. "Oh, cool! Can we take it for a spin? Will you teach us to drive?"

"The term is *pilot*," the admiral grunted. "And no. This shuttle serves a more important purpose."

Dakota didn't answer, but I felt the sting of his disappointment. The admiral reached out a long arm and opened a compartment behind the seats. The silver sphere floated there, secured in a cargo net. The sight of the EMP device gave me a chill. *A one-way trip. Sudden, catastrophic aging. God, no.*

"The onboard computer is already programmed," Bauer said. "Your handprint is all that is needed to set off the launch sequence."

I backed away, shaking my head. "No. No. I can't do it," I whispered.

Bauer was on a roll, hardly listening. In his world, everyone did what he told them to. "Landing coordinates have been entered. The autopilot will take you to the Technical Center Airfield, twenty-one point two miles from the pyramid under construction--"

"No. I said I'm not going," I blurted, louder. Then something he said registered. "Pyramid? What pyramid?"

Admiral Bauer snapped the lid of the compartment shut, folded his arms, and looked down on me disapprovingly. "You just said you're not going. You don't need to know." He pointed us toward the door.

I floated out, eyes downcast, past the waiting soldiers. Dakota silently followed. Inside, I was burning with curiosity about the pyramid, but Bauer wasn't talking. Soldiers herded us down the docking bay. We glided into the capsule and turned around. Bauer wouldn't even look at me. Shame crept into my heart, and I pushed it away. The doors closed, leaving us alone.

I fumbled with the straps of a shoulder harness. "This trip is suicide! It's stupid. I'd be delivering myself right into Bianca's hands. I'd help 'em if they had a better plan, but they don't."

"I know, Jackie, I know," Dakota said. "Look, you got what you wanted. They're not kicking us out, and you don't have to go on this mission. So be happy."

I wasn't. Something nagged at me in the back of my mind, and it refused to come out into the light. What was I missing? Had I made the wrong decision? I didn't think so. But I couldn't shake the feeling.

Chapter 3

The capsule let us out with the usual synthesized voice message. "Welcome to Ring Five."

Passing workers gave us curious glances, but said nothing. I guess they figured we belonged there. Everybody on the station had jobs except us. Me and Dakota followed the curving corridor to an open airlock and peered inside. The garden dome seemed deserted. Giant fans hummed, pushing oxygen-rich air out through ventilation tubes. Stepping inside, I inhaled its humid, orange blossom scent and felt tight muscles in my shoulders go loose. Gardeners had been hard at work in there, and new equipment choked the entryway. Pallets of fertilizer sat next to a one-seat cargo lifter that had a giant grabber-snatcher tool arcing off the back end like the stinger on a scorpion. The tiny patch of lawn where Dakota and I had first made love was gone. The grass had been dug up, no doubt for more garden space to feed uninvited guests. That stung. The spot was sentimental to me.

Dakota didn't care--he had sex on his mind. He took my hand and led me up the spiral staircase surrounding the enormous central walnut tree. We ducked under branches and pushed leaves aside as we climbed. At the top, a circular balcony ringed the dome. Enclosed rooms safeguarded a few precious ecosystems.

The first room was labeled *Taiga.* "Let's do it in here. Come on, you'll love it," Dakota said, playfully dragging me inside a freezing chamber crowded with pines.

I giggled, resisting. "Right on the ice? I don't think so."

A blast of fan-driven wind shifted branches and stirred snowflakes into my hair. Dark pines shaded the space, making it feel mysterious and wild. I jumped for a snow-covered branch, shook it over Dakota's head, and ran away, laughing. He chased me into the next chamber, *Temperate Deciduous Forest*, where it felt like spring. The warm air smelled of wildflowers, and bright red cardinals chirped from the branches above. I dodged behind a leafy maple and dashed around the pond, but Dakota caught me with an arm around my waist. We sank to our knees on the grassy shore, kissing. Love filled me.

Dakota cupped my cheek and placed a string of tiny, tingling kisses down my neck. "What's it gonna take to talk you out of this suit?" he murmured, playing with the zipper on my one-piece jumpsuit.

I wasn't that hard to convince. He slid the zipper all the way down and peeled the sleeves off my arms, exposing my lacy white bra and the top of my low-slung bikini underwear. We untied our shoes at light speed, and my combat boots hit the grass next to Dakota's tennis shoes. Without them, I felt feminine, smaller and somehow more vulnerable.

Dakota instantly noticed. He stroked my hair. "Hey. You're safe with me. No more worries."

"But the admiral--"

"Shh." Dakota stopped my words with a kiss. "He'll come around. They'll think up another plan. One that keeps you right here next to me. And I will do whatever it takes to keep you safe, Jackie. Whatever it takes."

That was exactly what I needed to hear. I twined my arms around his neck and whispered in his ear. "I love you, Dakota."

"Love you too, baby. Always have. Always will."

I let him peel my black suit off my legs. Dakota tossed it aside without taking his eyes off me. I ran my hands over the velvet skin of his ribs and helped him pull his shirt off over his head. In a quick motion, Dakota pushed me down on the grass and rolled on top of me. A surprised squeak escaped my lips, making him laugh. He kissed me hard, his tongue demanding entrance. I opened my mouth, inviting him in. I could deny him nothing.

A tightness around my heart let go. I hadn't even noticed it until it was gone. Constant vigilance had become a part of me, but in his arms, I felt safe. Protected. My chief was there, and all I needed was him. Surrounded by love, we stretched out under the trees in that tiny, captive forest, and it was beautiful.

Dakota pressed his knee between my legs and squeezed my ass, letting me grind on his thigh. Pleasure built, and sweet wetness gathered between my legs.

"You like that, huh?" Dakota murmured, reaching his hand under my bikini to stroke my clit. He pushed a finger inside me and fluttered it, sending jolts of pleasure to my core. "Is that a yes?" he teased.

My hands clung to his back, pulling him closer. I could barely form words. "Oh. Oh my God. Mmm, yes. Yes."

"Good. Because today, we're takin' our time." He slid a hand between my shoulder blades, arching my back so my breasts jutted out. Dakota's tongue flicked over each mound, and then he unsnapped my bra. He sucked on my nipples, rolling my breasts in the palms of his hands.

His thumbs hooked my lacy bikini underwear, tugging them down. "Get rid of these," he growled. That was one order I didn't mind following.

Dakota stood to drop his jeans off his narrow hips. Somewhere above us, a fan kicked on, creating a summer breeze that swirled through the canopy. Speckled sunlight played across his naked body, the moving spots of light and shadow highlighting his wiry, defined muscles.

I sat up and held out my arms."C'mere, love."

He knelt and kissed me while I caressed the strong muscles of his shoulders. My hands slid down his chest. A thick erection lay heavily across his flat-muscled stomach. Suddenly shy, I hesitated, but Dakota grabbed my hand and pressed it against his cock. A little smile crossed my face at his rumble of pleasure. I played with him, sliding that impossibly soft skin over his rigid shaft. Watching his face, I learned what he liked and stroked a little faster.

He grabbed my wrist. "That's so good, God, so good. But we gotta stop. Stop, baby! Or I'll cum in your hand."

Dakota took me in his arms. His whole body trembled with eagerness. I nestled my cheek against his chest, overwhelmed by love.

"Roll over," he breathed. "I can't wait any longer."

I didn't quite understand, so he put me where he wanted, on hands and knees, facing away from him. I felt the warmth of his thighs against mine. "God, Jackie, you look so fucking hot from this angle."

His hand reaching between my legs, stroking me. "Mmm. So wet." Gripping my hips, he entered me and shoved his cock to the hilt.

I gasped.

Head thrown back, mouth open in ecstasy, Dakota found his rhythm and pounded me. His weight bore me down until I lay on my chest and forearms, ass high. His cock kept slamming home, over and over, sending waves of pleasure through my body. We both moaned. He lifted my hips and got a hand under me to tickle my clit. I cried out as I felt an orgasm coming. We exploded together.

Dakota collapsed on top of me. His weight on my body made me feel secure. I felt his lips on the back of my neck, heard his soft murmur in my ear. "I love you, Jackie."

"Love you too." In that moment, I swear I felt our two souls merge, and I knew I'd never stop loving him.

Dakota rolled us onto our sides so we spooned, with him still behind me. His lips tickled my ear as he spoke. "I'm yours forever. As long as I live."

"Forever," I repeated dreamily. "I like the sound of that."

"We'll have children together, a whole crew. I'll teach 'em to fight. It'll be fun."

"Babies? Wow." That idea used to thoroughly piss me off. Ever since I entered puberty, grown-ups had pressured me to get pregnant. As a rare healthy female, I was priceless. The human race needed me, and every girl like me, if we meant to survive. But on the station, with support, medical care, and plenty of food, starting a family didn't seem so scary.

My lips curved in a half smile. "Dakota, you're gonna be an amazing dad."

His low chuckle melted my heart. "Yeah? I've had plenty of practice."

He made love to me again, face to face that time, looking into my eyes. In the sleepy moments after, our crew's happy shouts echoed up through the ventilation shaft.

"Dammit. We're not alone," Dakota groaned.

I sat up. "They'll find us in a minute."

We dressed fast, ran down the spiral staircase, and met the crew trooping up. From the scowl on Keenan's face, my pink cheeks and freshly-fucked hair were all too obvious. Ash pretended not to notice. He had an easier time of it because he was carrying Tito, who made a good distraction.

Tito put out his chubby arms to me, but I shook my head, grinning. "Whatcha gettin' all over Ash, there?"

The toddler held up a drippy red gob in his tiny fist. "Mato."

"Tomato, I see. Yummy."

Ash jokingly tried to shove the messy child into my arms, but I ducked around them both, laughing. "Nope! You can carry him, Ash, he's destroyed your shirt already. Come on, guys. Let's see if those peaches are ripe yet."

They were. Boys gathered on the grass under the peach tree, munching happily. Sticky juice ran down their faces. I leaned on the trunk, full of joy. Watching my kids eat gave me a visceral sense of satisfaction, no doubt born from years of starvation. As soon as Caleb finished his fruit, I tossed him another.

He caught it in one hand. "I can see you turning into a fat little grandmother, pushing food on kids." Caleb faked a high, childish voice. "Grandma, I can't eat any more."

"Eat it," I scolded, a mock frown on my face. "Clean your plate. Clean the whole tree."

Ash grinned. "My mom was like that. If you didn't take seconds, she'd scoot the dish closer, like that would help." He shoved a half-eaten peach into my face, so juice got up my nose. "Have some more, dear."

I stole a bite and wiped my face on a sleeve while the kids giggled. After that, we all got quiet for a second. Ash had mentioned his dead family, and it was okay. Nobody fell apart. Maybe it would be safe to remember our own.

I sat on the grass between Ash and Keenan, pigging out while Dakota roamed the dome, foraging. He soon brought back a basket full of walnuts and a rock to break them open with. Even the ship's gray cat came to join our party. It paced back and forth between me and Dakota, meowing.

"Sorry. I got nothin' a cat would eat," I told it.

Dakota knelt beside me to pet the kitty. "Aw. Who feeds you?"

Without warning, the cat sprang at his face. Razor-sharp teeth and claws dug deep. Dakota fell backward, shouting and waving his arms. The hissing cat wouldn't let go. Children screamed. Blood streamed down Dakota's neck and soaked his shirt. Me and Keenan jumped in to help, but before we got our hands on it the cat dropped to the grass. It took a few weaving steps and slumped to its side, panting.

"What the hell was that for?" Caleb yelled.

"Dakota, are you okay? Look at your face, you're bleeding all over." I reached out to put a hand on his shoulder. "Let me help--"

"No, Jackie, no!" Keenan leaped between us and grabbed my arm. "Don't touch him. He's taken."

I pulled away, shaking my head. "There's no infection on the station. We're safe here."

Dakota slowly raised his head and looked at me from beneath his dark, disheveled forelock. Deep, bloody gouges marked his face. And the pox glittered from behind his eyes.

My heart shattered. A high keening noise came from my throat. I knew I should run, but I couldn't. Not without Dakota. I stood there, helpless, watching the man I loved turn into a monster. I took a step forward. Then another. It didn't matter. If Dakota was taken, I didn't care what happened to me.

I reached out a trembling hand. "Dakota, come back. Please come back," I said in a small voice. "I love you."

Keenan grappled with me, pinning my arms from behind. "Jackie, no!"

Dakota reached out with silver-tipped fingernails. "Return . . . to the planet," he rasped. "Bianca . . . requires . . . you."

I recoiled. That wasn't even his voice. Keenan and I backed away. Dakota staggered after us, but a seizure shook his body. Trembling, he fell to the ground. I wanted to run to him, to save him. It was too late. Metallic drool, teeming with nanobots, already bubbled between his lips.

He pushed himself up on his elbows and crawled after me. "Jacqueline . . . come . . . home."

"She's taking control of his body," Keenan hissed. "In a second he'll be able to run. We gotta go." Crushing my wrist in an iron grip, he dragged me away.

"Dakota, fight her," I screamed over my shoulder. "Fight her!"

Then I ran. It killed me to leave him behind, but I did it. I ran, leaving the love of my life alone in the dirt, with nanobots crawling through his brain.

Keenan and I raced down the path toward the door. Through the transparent walls of the dome, the light of the sun slowly turned gray. I realized with horror that the space station was going around the night side of the planet. We'd be in the dark soon. Something rustled in the bushes beside the trail. Keenan and I scrambled backward, stepping on each other in our panic.

The ship's cat popped out.

Me and Keenan both let out startled shrieks. Then I caught a flash of the cat's eyes. "It's okay. Uninfected."

The little gray cat spun a circle, set off, then stopped and changed direction again.

"It's lost," Keenan whispered. "I bet it came to when the pox jumped out."

I nodded. "Like Dakota. Remember how he got lost before lunch. Later he was fine."

Keenan jerked me to a stop under a tree. "You think the pox is jumping between Dakota and the cat? So *he* set that explosion?"

"Yeah. Or the pox riding him did." I stared over Keenan's shoulder. The spreading shadows held my attention. Had something moved behind us, or was that just a breeze fluttering the leaves?

Night overtook us faster than it did on Earth. In under a minute, twilight turned to dark, and the moist air in the dome grew cooler. Tiny lights normally outlined the garden paths at night, but they didn't come on. I wasn't surprised. The pox had planned ahead. Keenan and I crept through the maze of pallets and equipment by the door. Our crew waited for us there, wide-eyed and edgy.

"Everybody out. We gotta lock the door, trap him in the biosphere," I ordered.

Kids hurried through the open airlock into the dimly lit corridor beyond. I pushed the red button to close off the dome. It didn't work. The door stayed open. "Shit. Run!"

Caleb snatched up Tito and we thundered down the hall. Ash reached the capsule first and hit the call button. It lit up, a faint, white glow in the darkness. We waited for our ride, holding our breath, staring back into the darkened dome. Inside, an electric engine hummed. Headlights swept the garden.

"He's on the cargo lifter! We've gotta stop him." I took half a step toward the open airlock, but no one followed.

Ash grabbed my shoulder. "Don't risk it. We can get help. We'll call the soldiers. They'll, uh . . . take care of it."

A low moan escaped from my throat. I covered my mouth with shaking hands. "Take care of it? They'll gun him down."

"I'm sorry, Jack. That's not Dakota anymore. He's a hunter now." Keenan's hand wrapped the side of my head, stifling my sobs against his worn sweatshirt.

I shook my head, tears streaming from my eyes. "No. No soldiers. Please, no soldiers."

Keenan grabbed my shoulders and got right in my face. "What would Dakota say if he was here right now? What would he say, Jack? What would he tell us to do?"

"G-gun him down," I whispered through trembling lips.

"Right." Keenan squeezed me once, slapped my back, and pushed me away.

A series of sharp electronic beeps cut the stillness as the cargo lifter reversed. Tires crunching, it ground to a halt. A dark figure clambered from the driver's seat and shambled in front of the headlights. At first I thought it was some elderly, disabled greenhouse worker. Then, for just a second, the twin beams lit Dakota's profile.

The hunter limped into the shadows, stopped, and looked right at us, as if Dakota's stolen eyes could see in the dark. I cringed and went silent. After a moment he walked away, all hunched over, with one hand gripping the opposite wrist. His arms worked from side to side, as if wrestling each other, and his left leg dragged. With each step, that foot dug a furrow in the sandy path. I wanted to run to him, help him, but I couldn't.

He wasn't on our side anymore.

Dakota limped to the control panel, turned sideways, and wrenched his right hand free of the left. He typed in a series of numbers.

"What's he doing?" Ash hissed.

No one answered. Dakota mounted the cargo lifter again. Seeing him in the driver's seat gave me the creeps, because he didn't even know how to drive a car. Pulling on levers, he maneuvered the vehicle up to the transparent wall of the dome. A flat-edged tool on the end of a long, jointed mechanical arm swiveled over his head and dropped down in front, whirring as it spun.

Yellow lights on the wall flashed. A computer-generated voice announced, "Warning. Docking clamp seven released."

"Stop it," I screamed.

Boys shouted as Dakota swiveled the cargo loader, lining it up in front of the next docking clamp. When it let go, red and orange lights on the walls flashed and a siren wailed.

I shouted over the earsplitting sound. "He's killing the dome. That's our food, our oxygen."

The strategy was clear enough. To force us back to earth. Force me into Bianca's hands. Like hell. I'd suffocate in space first, if I didn't die fighting. I squared my shoulders and headed back into the dome. Ash and Keenan both pounced on me, grabbing my arms.

"Let me go! I have to stop him."

Keenan dug his fingers into the tender skin of my wrist. "No, Jack, no! You'll get taken."

A cold breeze wafted down the corridor. Air was being sucked from the biosphere. Dakota clambered off the cargo lifter and started down the hall after us, his left leg dragging, one arm still gripping the other. Thrashing and cursing, I tried to twist free. Ash and Keenan held my arms in painful grips.

"What now?" Ash muttered, pulling me backward, away from the oncoming hunter.

"Where's the fucking elevator?" Marc yelled. He pounded the call button.

A chime went off, and the capsule door slid up. The kids frantically crowded inside. Ash and Keenan shoved me in after them.

"Destination?" asked the calm, feminine voice of the computer.

"Anywhere. Away! Far away," Ash yelled. "Hurry up."

The computer paused, the capsule doors still open. "Acknowledged. Lock in?" The hunter's footfalls came closer. Thump. Drag. Thump. Drag. Dakota's torn and bloody face peered around the corner. A string of silver drool hung from his lip. His right hand reached out, grasping.

My back pressed against the far wall of the capsule. "Go! Just go," I howled.

"J-Jackie," Dakota gurgled.

In that instant, I saw a glimmer of humanity in his left eye. He still had some control. His left side was fighting his right. My heart leaped. He was still in there, still alive. "Hang on," I cried. "Resist!"

"Launching," the computer said. Doors snapped closed. Our capsule took off with a jerk.

I got slammed sideways, and my head cracked Caleb's. Tito's little body hit the wall. He shrieked once and went still. Our bodies tumbled together as the capsule picked up speed. G-forces pinned us against the wall. I strained my neck to lift my head and look for Tito, who was face down, out of reach. In under a minute, our crazy ride slowed. The capsule leveled and coasted to a stop. Boys moaned and struggled to their feet.

I crawled to Tito and put a hand on his back. His small ribcage still rose and fell. A rush of relief filled me. "He's alive."

He opened his eyes and whimpered. I gently lifted my child and stood, holding him close against my chest. Warm blood soaked through his straight black hair and touched my fingertips. The capsule door rose up. Freezing air blew in. Beyond was darkness.

We slipped out the door, bouncing lightly with each step. "Gravity's really low here," Ash whispered. "Where are we?"

"Welcome to Ring One," the computer said. The door clicked shut, and my world went dark.

Chapter 4

I clung to Tito. The sudden darkness made me feel like I was choking. "Oh my God. We're on the inner ring. This is bad. Seriously, you guys, there was something alive in here. I saw it earlier through the window."

"Something alive? What?" Paco asked anxiously.

I shrugged, forgetting he couldn't see me in the dark. "I don't know. An animal, maybe. It tried to tear through an airlock to get at me."

"Fuck," Keenan breathed. "That's all we need. We have to find someone, get help."

Oh my God, I'm Chief again. They're looking to me to get them out of this. The knowledge settled like a weight in my chest.

"There's gotta be a portal into the central axle," I whispered, trying to keep it together for the crew. "Move out. Everybody stay together. Hold hands."

With Tito in my arms, I couldn't hold onto anyone else. He felt lighter than a newborn, but the low gravity had me way off balance. The slightest push with my toes sent me into a wobbly arc a foot or two above the floor. I leaned too far forward and stumbled, steel-toed combat boots drumming on bare metal. I swore. Anyone already on Ring One would know we'd arrived.

Keenan's steady hand on my waist helped. He spoke in my ear, low and reassuring. "I'm right here, babe. I got your back."

Around us, boys bounced along, hissing under their breath when they collided with each other or the walls. Paco and Caleb murmured together in frightened voices.

"Easy, you guys," I muttered. "We'll be okay. Keep quiet."

Feeling our way along, we moved down the dark hallway. The blackness was so complete I couldn't see my hand in front of my face. Each lightweight step took me too high, and on every landing my stomach flipped like the floor was dropping away from beneath me. Waves of vertigo passed through my body. The back of my neck prickled. Was something there in the dark, watching us? On Ring One, the station's constant machine hum was louder, enough to cover a stealthy approach. I strained my ears for the sounds of claws on metal, but only heard the constant whirring of machinery. Cold penetrated my boots, and my fingers began to freeze. Tito shivered and started to whine. I snuggled him close against my neck, imagining stealthy footfalls approaching, unheard beneath the low, continuous buzz. Ahead, faint light appeared, a patch of twilight in the darkness. We eagerly picked up the pace, bounding lightly along, and then slowed when we reached the source. A round hole in the ceiling glowed with white light. More dim silvery lights glowed from the edges of the squishy landing pad beneath.

"It's the opening to one of those low gravity jump tubes. You know what that means," Caleb said darkly.

"Yeah. If he jumped, he could be here already," Paco said.

"Or he'll land any second now. So let's get out of here," I muttered. "Keep moving, people."

Ahead, the corridor continued its smooth curve, hiding what lay beyond. I edged forward and peered into the twilight.

Keenan put out a hand to stop me. "Wait. Let me go first, in case he's already here."

Ash brought up the rear, guarding our backs. Without being told, Paco and Caleb took positions on either side of me. That almost brought tears to my eyes. They were just kids, too young to be heroes.

Keenan moved without a sound, scouting ahead and waving us forward when it was safe. He gradually picked up speed, covering more ground with every leap. The nimble boys had no problem, but I struggled to balance Tito and keep up without falling on my face. Farther from the jump tube, the hall got darker. Once I stumbled over someone's foot, and Caleb's hand on my elbow saved me. Another faint, gray circle of light appeared ahead, this time on the right hand wall.

"There it is, the airlock," Keenan hissed. He lunged for the big red button and slapped it. The circular door rolled aside. Scratches marred its surface. Claw marks.

I stopped cold and pointed. "Oh my God, look. I told you so."

Ash prodded me between the shoulder blades. "Hurry up. They're just cat scratches, Jack."

We piled through the portal into the welcome light and warmth of the central axle, lost what little gravity we had, and drifted.

Ash hung in midair, fiddling with the portal. "It won't lock. Fuck it, let's go." He pushed off and led the way up the long, featureless tube.

I took one of Tito's hands, Keenan took the other, and we floated him along, pushing off the shiny white walls. The younger boys brought up the rear. Tito struggled and started to cry.

"Shut him up. You can hear that all over," Keenan hissed at me sideways.

I shot Keenan a glare. "It's not his fault. He's hurt."

A faint rumble came from behind us. Paco gasped. "The airlock just opened again. Dakota's here!"

Over my shoulder, I saw the painfully familiar face of the hunter. Panic took me. Gripping Tito's arm, I kicked off the wall and slapped a handhold with all my strength. We shot up the central axle toward the oblong shuttle bay at the top.

As we entered the huge, gleaming room, sounds of labored breathing came up behind us.

"There he is," boys shouted.

Dakota soared down the corridor, faster and more coordinated than he'd been just a few minutes before. Somehow I'd expected workers to be in the shuttle bay, people who would help us. But the place was deserted. *Damn it! Now what?* Our crew fled to the far end of the long, cylindrical room. We had nowhere to run. Nothing that could be used as a weapon. Clutching Tito, I backed up against armored glass and stared down at the rings of the space station below. If that had been an open window, I might have jumped.

Ash screamed into the intercom. "Help, help, we're in the shuttle bay! We've got a hunter here, one of the infected. We need--"

The intercom cut out as an explosion went off on the axle below. Through the window, a brief jet of fire appeared, instantly extinguished in the vacuum of space. The delicate structure snapped, and one end pivoted in slow motion toward the rings below. Astonished faces appeared at the windows. The impact shattered armored glass on Four. I cried out as tiny, human figures cartwheeled into space in a bloom of debris.

Dakota floated into the room, eerily calm, a faint silver light reflecting from his eyes. He drifted toward us. Kids scattered. I just hung there, weightless, and stared at him. I never expected to live a long life, but I couldn't imagine it ending like that.

Keenan got between me and danger, his amber eyes lit with adrenaline. I needed to help him, to fight by his side, but Tito's grip around my neck was choking me. Prying off the child's strong hands, I shifted him to my back where he clung like a baby monkey. Dakota approached in silence, soaring gracefully along the curved ceiling, his emotionless gaze fixed on me.

Three blue-uniformed men burst into the shuttle bay, flying low, apparently unaware of the hunter above. The leader was Nielson, the guy who'd let me out of quarantine that morning. Sweat plastered strands of russet hair to his broad, square forehead.

Nielson started yelling before he got halfway across the room. "The explosion cut us off from the rest of the station. We'll get back by shuttle. What the hell are you kids doin' up here, anyway?"

Dakota pushed off the ceiling behind them and drifted lower.

I let out a strangled cry, pointing up. "Look out, he's infected!"

The young black astronaut on Nielson's right looked up at Dakota's bleeding face and reached out a hand. "You okay, kid? What happened?"

All around the room, boys shouted. "Stay back!"

"He's got pox," I howled.

The astronaut hesitated, his wide brown eyes turned toward us. Dakota lunged, and his silver-tipped fingernails sank into the man's hand. His victim screamed once, arms and legs jerking, and then went still. Nielson instantly seized a Taser off his belt and let Dakota have it. I cried out, every muscle in my body clenched in sympathetic agony. Dakota's stolen body spun away through the air, twitching helplessly. I wanted to go after him, save him. I didn't even try, and it tore me up inside.

The shuttle bay went quiet as the infected astronaut drifted slowly past his healthy partner.

Ash gripped a wall-mounted handhold hard enough to make muscles stand out along his forearms. "Kill him. Kill him before he moves." In the silence, his low voice carried.

Nielson's deep, commanding voice reverberated off the walls. "Kid's right. Jefferson's infected for sure. You know what to do."

His husky, middle-aged partner paled. In a second the man nodded, ran a nervous hand over his dark, crew-cut hair, and pulled a silver tool off his nylon web belt. With a nauseated expression, he pushed off and floated after their partner, muttering, "It's not him. Not him. Jeff's not in there anymore."

"Hurry up," Ash hissed.

The infected astronaut shivered and looked around the shuttle bay with new eyes. Someone else's eyes.

"Watch out, he's awake," I yelled. "He's taken!"

The healthy astronaut pushed off the ceiling with his legs and shot toward his former friend. An arc of electricity shot out of the tool he carried and struck the pox-infected one, who shuddered and went limp. Dead or unconscious, I couldn't tell.

"Communication's down. Get out of here, get help, go," Nielson ordered.

The husky dark-haired astronaut rocketed out of the room without even touching Dakota. Irrational relief flooded my body, and I cursed myself for my weakness. Someone needed to finish him. I was his best friend, his lover. By crew tradition, it ought to be me. But I had no weapons, not even a pocket knife, and his blood was crawling with nanobots. If a drop touched me, I was good as dead myself. In my place, Dakota would have figured something out, I just knew it.

Nielson turned his back on the pair of incapacitated hunters and typed in a rapid code on the keyboard outside Shuttle Four. A long minute later, the door rolled open. He waved me into the small airlock, which connected to a boxy, eight-passenger craft. My crew rushed to follow. The outer door closed behind us. Inside the shuttle's airlock, we were safe. No one spoke. Tito's whimpers were the only sounds. In a minute, the inner door opened into the ship. Our crew floated inside, their young faces slack with exhaustion. People flipped in midair, grabbed seats, and strapped themselves in.

I guided Tito into a seat, clicked the seat belt, and bent close to his tiny, precious face. "Goodbye, baby. I love you. Don't forget me," I whispered. Tears welled up in my eyes. Without gravity, they refused to fall.

With an effort, I turned away. Tito started to cry, but I couldn't let myself look back. One push propelled me out of the shuttle and into the cramped airlock, where Nielson was typing on a wall-mounted keyboard and talking to the ship's computer all at once. He touched a final button, and a giant steel door sealed off the shuttle bay. Dakota was locked in. Near the ceiling, his hijacked body writhed. Nielson looked up at him through the round porthole in the airlock and shuddered.

I put a hand on the man's thick shoulder and spoke softly, so my crew wouldn't hear. "Tell the admiral I'm going."

Nielson's eyes went wide. "Back to the planet? That's suicide."

"I have to. Without the biosphere, how long can the station last?"

"Two weeks, if we're lucky. We've taken a lot of damage, and . . ." Nielson hesitated. "T' tell you the truth, we were in trouble before your ship arrived. Without that extra food and oxygen?" He shook his big head. "We're done."

Just like Bianca intended.

"Hang on here as long as possible. Don't come down unless you absolutely have to. I'll find Bianca and kill her if I can. If I succeed, I'll . . . I don't know, wait around until somebody notices." I tried to smile.

Nielson squeezed my shoulder. "The autopilot takes verbal instructions. Just tell her where you want to go, and she'll bring you back to us."

I gave him a shaky nod.

Impatient voices called from the shuttle. "Come on. What's the holdup?"

"Sit tight," Nielson yelled. He stuck out a hand, offering a handshake. My small hand disappeared inside his warm, gentle grip. "Good hunting, Jackie."

"Thanks. Keep the boys on the shuttle. Don't let 'em stop me," I whispered.

"I won't." Nielson placed a palm over the airlock button. "Ready?"

I nodded, my stomach fluttering.

Neilson glanced up at the floating hunter. "All right, then. Be quick about it." He pushed the button.

The circular door rolled aside. I pushed off its frame and soared through the air, aiming for the palm print scanner on Shuttle Five. I fumbled for a handhold and missed, grunting when my left shoulder struck the slick, white wall and slid. On the far side of the giant room, Dakota twisted in midair to watch. He glided toward me, expressionless as a shark.

Chapter 5

Boys' shouts came from the boxy passenger shuttle. "What the hell are you doing, Jackie? Get back here!"

"You kids get back in your seats," Nielson roared.

Shuttle Four's docking clamps released with a metallic thunk. Engine noise drowned out the astronaut's bellowed orders. Then my crew was gone. I was alone. Head down and legs kicking in the air, I fumbled for the scanner on Shuttle Five. My palm slapped it and the screen turned green.

"Welcome, passenger Jacqueline Stuart," the computer's feminine voice said.

"Open up!"

"Processing," the computer said serenely. I could have punched her.

Dakota was closing in, twenty feet away, then ten. Dark hair floated around his bloody face.

The airlock door opened and I dove inside. "Close airlock, close airlock!"

The door slowly rolled closed, but before it sealed, Dakota got a hand on it and tripped the safety. The door froze, leaving an eight inch crack. His right arm reached through. Gasping, I retreated. My back hit the closed shuttle door. I was trapped. The hunter struggled to squeeze his chest through the narrow gap. His arm waved, grabbing at me.

I whimpered. "No, no, Dakota. Please don't."

Of course he didn't listen. It wasn't him anymore. He was a hunter now. I accidentally brushed against a lump on the wall--a red button. I slammed my fist down on it.

"Confirm airlock manual override?" the computer asked.

"Yes!"

The shuttle door opened with a hiss of air. I fled inside, touched another button, and closed the door. My heaving breath sounded loud in the sudden quiet. Red lights flashed from the ship's console. I didn't have to be a pilot to know what that meant. The shuttle wouldn't launch with the airlock open. I was stuck.

Frozen, I watched the hunter worm his way through the narrow gap and slither inside. Dakota's shirt was torn. Bloody scrapes marked the soft skin over his ribs. My breath came fast and shallow, making me dizzy. My legs twitched, desperate to run. Eyes flicking from side to side, I scanned the shuttle for something I could use as a weapon. Nothing. I was trapped. Teeth clenched, Dakota turned sideways and began typing with one hand on the wall-mounted keyboard. His lip twisted as if he were in terrible pain.

The pox had to know everything about the space station. Was he setting another bomb, or shutting off the carbon dioxide scrubbers? Dakota tapped a final key, and the door into the shuttle bay closed. He'd trapped himself in the airlock. I had no idea why. Was he planning to force the shuttle door open? Trap me inside and infect me?

My console still flashed red. Whatever he'd done had disabled it, so the shuttle couldn't launch. Grimacing, the hunter approached the small, round window in the shuttle's door. His mouth moved oddly, as if he was trying to speak, and his left hand waved awkwardly. Dakota's fingers moved across the armored glass of the window, as if typing. In a moment it dawned on me--that was his left hand.

I pushed a button to activate the speaker. "Dakota, are you still in there? What are you trying to tell me? Was that you typing just now?"

His head bobbed in a jerky motion that might have been a nod.

"What did you do?"

His left hand waved, but I didn't understand.

"Find the cat," I cried. "Find the cat, get the pox to jump into it again."

He shook his head, the left side of his mouth smiling sadly.

I sobbed. "Please, at least try."

Dakota closed his eyes and pressed his forehead briefly against the glass. I reached out my fingers, as though I could run my fingers through his dark, wavy hair one last time.

His mouth worked, lips churning, and then slurred words came out. "W-w-whatever it takes." His left hand touched his lips, blowing me a kiss. He stepped back and struck a final key.

"Acknowledged," the computer voice said. "Launching."

"No," I screamed.

The docking clamps let go, and Dakota's infected body got sucked into space. He thumped against my shuttle and tumbled away, leaving a smear of blood on the shiny white paint. I screamed. In less than a second he was gone, out of sight. I hid my face in my hands and moaned. My stomach ached, and I wanted to vomit. *Oh my God, Dakota. Not you. Not you. Anyone but you.*

Thrusters fired automatically, backing the tiny craft away from the station. I floated, unmoving, numb with shock. Dakota's last words echoed in my mind. *Whatever it takes.* He said it back in the biosphere, when we made love, and he meant it. Dakota fought the pox for control. I'd never seen a victim do that. I didn't know it was possible. He killed himself so Bianca couldn't use him against me. I crossed my arms over my body as spherical tears squeezed from my eyes and danced through the air. Sunshine touched the tiny globes, casting miniature rainbows.

"Passenger Jacqueline Stuart, please strap in for re-entry," the computer said evenly. The mechanical voice repeated the request twice before I processed it, took a seat, and clicked the seat belt. The shuttle wheeled around and headed for the planet below.

Instead of diving straight down like I expected it to, the tiny ship went into orbit. Earth took up half my view. A thin skin of atmosphere caught the light, enclosing the planet in a glowing blue ring. Fluffy clouds swirled dreamily below. It was all so incredibly beautiful. I sat high above everything, all alone, with nothing left to lose. My heart ached with a terrible pain. Bianca had taken everything from me. Then I remembered something my mother said to me before she died. *There's always something to love.* She was right. Bianca hadn't taken everything, not yet. I loved my planet and every living thing on it. More than anything, I loved my crew. Those boys were counting on me. Everyone was. It wasn't fair. I never asked for that kind of responsibility.

Anger flared, and burned at the edges of my grief. Bianca was going down, if it was the last thing I ever did. I let out a bitter laugh.

Whatever it takes.

My shuttle crossed the line onto the night side of the planet. Rushing air buffeted the underside of the shuttle, growing to a low roar. That made me nervous, but indicator lights on my console still glowed green, so I guess everything was okay. On the shore of Africa, pale surf gleamed in the moonlight. The center of the continent was dark. I soared around the world and across the Pacific Ocean to the coast of California. Where I expected city lights, only a few tiny sparks remained. Alessandra was right. Pox had taken over the planet.

I jetted east. Black clouds obscured the ground. Then the shuttle dove below them, and I caught my first glimpse of Colorado. Vague outlines of circles and squares showed where farms had once been. To the west, the Rocky Mountains brooded, midnight blue against a dark sky. My ship banked left, went into a giant circle, and dropped lower. Moonlight caught the roofs of derelict buildings. Wrecked cars sat, eerily still, on networks of highways. Every last streetlight was out. The shuttle dropped low over the landing fields at the Tech Center. Red and green lights on its wingtips blinked. My heart pounded as the craft leveled out for its final approach. The infected would see me coming in. They'd be on me the second I landed.

Far away, off the left wing, neon-blue light glowed through low hanging fog, illuminating the stark triangular edges of a building.

The pyramid.

What was that all about? Was Bianca building herself a monument, like some egotistical dictator? Or did the pyramid have a more practical purpose? I lost sight of it as my shuttle descended and the rear wheels touched down. The engine groaned. I clutched the handhold beside my seat and hung on. The front wheels bumped down on the pitted runway.

"Braking parachute deployed," the computer voice said.

I took a breath of relief as the craft slowed. Then red lights flashed.

"Warning, obstructions on runway," the computer said. "Switch to manual?"

"Are you kidding me?"

Piles of jumbled white skeletons flashed past, remnants of the infected herd Bianca used against the array. I gasped as my wheels hit one, crushing it. More obstacles loomed out of the dark. The autopilot swerved. We shot between a pile of cattle skeletons and a derelict semi. There wasn't enough room.

"Look out," I shouted. With a sickening lurch, the shuttle went down on its side. I screamed. With one wing dragging, the ship slid down the runway in a shower of sparks. A bone-shattering impact rocked my world.

I woke hanging sideways, with my safety harness digging into my shoulders. The shuttle lay on its left side. A nauseating twisting sensation in my gut told me my Class III nanites were finishing their repairs, so I'd been unconscious for more than a few minutes. The ache in my head gradually subsided. Soft rustling noises came from outside. Tiny hairs on the back of my neck stood up. Was it the wind? Or hunters trying to get in? I had to get out of there.

I fought to free myself from my double-shoulder seat belt. Finally the latch clicked and I tumbled out. Some kind of white goo got all over my boots. Fire suppression foam, I figured. A bright red light still flashed from the crunched tip of the left wing, and my control panel glowed orange with emergency icons.

"Shut off the fucking lights. You're gonna attract every hunter in the city," I groaned. The computer was silent. Maybe she was pissed and ignoring me. Maybe she died in the crash. I couldn't tell.

I popped open the console between the seats. The EMP device hung there, safe inside its padded cargo net. Someone had tucked in a black daypack behind it. Pulling it out, I found my own gloves and black winter cap inside, along with a heavy water bottle and six or seven energy bars. Bauer had to be responsible for that. Somehow the bastard knew I'd go. I pulled on the hat and gloves, wedged the EMP device into the backpack, and strapped it on.

I crawled over the console, hesitated at the door and finally forced myself to hit the button. It hummed open sideways, too loud in the quiet night. A wave of cold, stinking air hit me in the face. Hand over my mouth, I stifled a coughing fit. The entire Tech Center smelled like burning oil. Crouching in the open doorway, I listened. Faraway sighs filled the air, like the breathing of giants. For a minute I thought they were coming my way. Then I wasn't sure. Either way, I couldn't stick around. The crash was a beacon, and Bianca's minions would surely investigate. Maybe they were outside already, waiting for me. If so, they were well hidden. I steeled my nerves and jumped.

My boots hit the cracked pavement with a thump. Half crouched, I darted for the shadows. A row of airplane hangars stood on the other side of a downed barbed wire fence. Good cover for me, and for hunters too. I stepped daintily over the wires. Through the heavy, unnatural fog, a dirty pink line glowed on the eastern horizon. It would be daylight soon. Should I keep moving, or find cover? I wasn't sure. I slipped between two rusting cargo containers and froze. Breathy sounds came toward me on the wind-- long, soft inhalations followed by the soothing sound of air thrumming out through velvet nostrils. Slow, synchronized hoofbeats drummed a funeral march.

Horses?

Against my better judgment, I crept out of my hiding place, following the sound. A line of horses came out of the fog, two by two. They had no riders, no bits in their mouths. Many had gory injuries, missing eyes and bloody foot-long gashes down their sides. They all limped along in step, heads low, never breaking stride. As they marched, their deep, unified breaths sighed in and out in a hypnotic rhythm. I was way closer to them than I meant to be. All I could do was drop to my belly on the cold ground, hiding my pale cheeks behind my gloves. I ached to set the horses free. But these were survivors of the herd Bianca used in the battle at the array. They were already slaves.

A beautiful chestnut limped past, the white star on his face bright in the gloom. His right front hoof was held off the ground, and in a moment I saw why. Bone jutted through the hide, dripping bright blood over the white stocking on that foot. Bianca was making him work anyway, and I despised her for it. The gelding took a few more steps, then staggered and went down with a groan. The whole team came to a halt. I wanted to help, but of course I didn't. He was taken, like everyone but me. Boots crunched on gravel. An infected man approached with a machete in his hand. I trembled and hid my face in the dirt. The long blade whistled through the air.

A few whacks with the machete freed the injured horse from his harness. Part of me hoped he'd put the animal out of its misery, but compassion wasn't part of Bianca's programming. She was made for war. The infected man connected the traces again, and the sad line trudged away, leaving the dying horse behind.

After the last pair of slave-horses came their wagon, an enormous flatbed trailer loaded high with scrap steel. Wheels squeaking, it rolled past, not twenty feet from my head. I lay still, wondering why Bianca hadn't fired up some of the abandoned vehicles that sat around the Center. Surely that would be more efficient than horsepower. Fear kept me flat on the icy ground until the cold penetrated my bones. If I stayed there much longer, I'd freeze. I listened until I was certain no one was nearby. Then I pushed myself to my feet and pressed on, following the wagon.

The sun rose, an evil red orb behind steel gray clouds. Faint rays barely penetrated the thick smog. All around me, black columns of smoke swirled into the air. Burning oil. That's what was stinging my eyes and burning my throat. Apparently Bianca had torched all the fuel she could find. I could guess why--to block sunlight. Until the smoke cleared, her pox nanobots could leave their host bodies and come out in daylight. I didn't know why they needed to, but it couldn't be good. As the day gradually brightened, human figures appeared on the path. I gulped.

Infected.

The closest one was only about fifty feet ahead. More emerged from the gloom, trudging along under the weight of enormous packs. They were all heading for the pyramid. I kept moving, glancing nervously from side to side. My palms sweated in my gloves, but I didn't dare remove them. Infected people didn't fiddle with their clothing. Even though they walked hundreds of yards apart, the ragged men moved in step, connected by the computer that controlled them. *Left, right, left.* With a quick skip, I switched my stride to match. I cursed myself. Being out in the open was stupid as hell. It was only a matter of time before one of them noticed me. Walking with hunters set my nerves on edge, but stopping would attract attention too.

My underarms grew damp, despite the cold, and goose bumps shivered up my spine. I felt lost. After only four days, my home town was unrecognizable. Bianca had torn down most of the buildings. Only the foundations remained, their basements half hidden under piles of rubble. The whole thing was surreal. I scanned the devastated landscape. Off to my right, wisps of fog wove between familiar red rock formations. Though the peaks beyond hid behind clouds, that was enough to orient me. The trail headed southeast across dry plains to the pyramid. Hazy blue light glowed from its triangular walls. I hiked toward it for three or four hours, but it never seemed to get any larger. The damned thing was like a mountain itself, bigger and farther away than it looked.

Exhaustion crept up on me, and thirst burned my throat. I struggled to stay in step with the long-legged men. A sharp cramp gripped my thigh. The muscles were spent. I took a risk and left the path, clambering over nearby ruins in search of a place to hide. Suddenly a block tipped under my weight, opening a gap between two slabs of concrete. My boots slipped on the mist-damp rock. I let out a yelp as I fell into darkness.

The landing bruised my knees, and a shard of metal punctured my glove, stabbing my left palm. I rolled onto my side, biting back whimpers as the injuries healed. In a minute I sat up and took a deep, shuddering breath, fighting rising panic. Dim light filtered in from a hole fifteen or twenty feet above. The walls were rough enough to climb. I could get out. Maybe I should hide there for the day and sneak up to the pyramid at night. That place was gonna be crawling with infected. I pictured myself asking one of them to take me to his leader, like a visiting alien. A hysterical laugh rose up, and I stifled it behind my hands. Tears filled my eyes. Would the guy comply? Or would he take me over first and then deliver my infected body?

I drank some water and ate one of the bars before I succumbed to exhaustion. Alone in that dark pit, I curled up on my side with my arm around the EMP device, soothing myself to sleep by stroking my fingertips along its slick, curved surface. Dakota filled my dreams, flashing that sexy grin. Taking me in his arms. Touching a button and spinning away into space.

Hours later, something damp and cold nudged my cheek. I woke in a panic, arms thrashing. A soft whine came from the darkness. A thin black and white border collie stood over me, wagging his tail. In the dark, I couldn't get a good look at his eyes. I scooted backward, crab-crawling over jumbled chunks of concrete. The dog dropped his front end in a bow and then danced around me. He thought I was playing.

"You're not infected," I whispered.

The dog wiggled up to me and let me pet the soft fur around his ears. Then he slipped through a crack and took off. My shoulders sagged in disappointment. I could have followed. The crack he'd gone through was plenty wide enough. I sat back down, telling myself I had a mission, had to stay on task. Truth was, that dark passageway creeped me out. I just didn't want to admit it.

Light still came through the hole above, so I settled in for a long wait. I had just dozed off when the dog returned. He wasn't alone. Four broad-shouldered men circled me, their faces obscured by shadows. Bianca's hunters had tracked me down.

I scrambled to my feet, clutching the EMP device tight to my chest.

"Take me to Bianca! I'm on my way to meet her, to bring her this, um, this gift. Tell her Jacqueline is here. Jacqueline, the primary host."

The hunters came closer. Adrenaline made my hands shake.

I retreated, talking as fast as I could. "You can't take me. Bianca wants me for herself. She's gonna want to see me. I need to go to her! Let me go to her!"

A bright light switched on, glaring in my eyes. The hairy-faced man holding it loomed over me like a monster. "You traitorous bitch."

He drew his arm back and hit me in the face with the butt end of the long flashlight, knocking me off my feet. The pain was incredible. Face down, I spat blood into the dirt. Blood spurted from my broken nose. Whimpering, I tried to crawl away. Then the nanites kicked in and I couldn't even move. The bearded man stepped forward, drawing a blade. He raised it high.

Another man grabbed his arm. "Hey, whaddaya doing? That's a girl, Ed!"

"You heard her. She's a fuckin' traitor," Ed snapped.

The other men elbowed him aside. Rough hands mauled me, grabbing at my small breasts through the armored jacket. I moaned and writhed on the ground. Caught in the grip of the Class III nanites, I couldn't put up much of a fight.

"That's enough." The white haired one pulled the others off me. "If you fuck her before the chief docs, he'll tear ya apart. He might give you a turn for bringin' her in, though."

Hairy Ed barked a laugh. "Dream on. Chief ain't the sharin' kind."

The old guy grabbed my pack and dumped out the contents on the ground. Men snatched up the energy bars. Then the EMP device rolled out into the dirt. Everyone stared.

The men muttered darkly. "What the hell is that?"

"It's prob'ly radioactive." One by one, their hands opened, letting my food bars fall to the ground.

Hairy Ed grabbed my collar and shook me so hard I bit my tongue. "Is that the present you were takin' to Bianca? Is it? Is it?"

"Yes," I cried, trying to peel his fingers off. "Only it's not a present, not really. It creates an electromagnetic pulse that's supposed to kill her. I thought you guys were hunters, that's why I said all that. But I really am trying to find Bianca."

"Nobody tries to find Bianca." Ed pushed me away so hard that I staggered and the back of my head hit the wall.

"Ouch!"

"Keep yer voices down, or we'll all get caught," a black man growled. "An' shut off that light, fer Christ's sake."

"Okay, okay." The light went out.

The silver-haired leader shoved my stuff back in the pack and shouldered it. "Take 'er. We'll see what the chief wants to do with her."

"I know what I wanna do with her," Ed leered.

"What, stab her?" another guy asked sarcastically. Men laughed.

Someone picked me up and slung me over his shoulder, head down. In single file, they entered the dark passageway.

Chapter 6

The passageway sloped down, taking us farther underground. The smell of burning oil faded, replaced with the reek of mold and warm, unwashed bodies. My captor's bony shoulder dug into my stomach with each stride, making it hard to breathe. Being upside down didn't help. My head filled with blood until my tongue felt thick and a dull headache pounded behind my eyes. I struggled, kicked, and bit until the guy carrying me swerved, deliberately cracking my head on the rock wall of the passageway. After that I got smart. I wasn't gonna win that fight. Better to hit him later when he wasn't expecting it.

The young white guy walking behind me kept reaching out and touching my short, auburn hair. "Wow, we got us a girl," he breathed. "A real live girl. And she's cute, too."

Hairy Ed corrected him. "*We* don't have a girl, the chief does. Best you remember that or he'll beat your head in."

"Like he did to poor Tom," the young guy muttered. "I know he kinda deserved it, but that was nasty. I had to clean it up, and there were chunks of--"

"Shut up about it," Ed interrupted. "I was there, remember?"

Dread tingled through my body. Every step took me closer to their boss, and from the sound of it, he was a sick son of a bitch. The men fell silent, and their strides lengthened as the trail leveled out. That didn't do my pinched stomach any good. Little grunts escaped me as we jounced along. Nobody cared. Maybe forty minutes later, we came to a wide spot in the underground passageway, where the air seemed warmer.

"We'll take a break here," the leader said.

"Finally." The guy carrying me rolled me off his shoulder and dumped me without bending down. I fell hard, and a sharp rock slashed my face. I cried out. Trembling, I crouched against the tunnel wall, knees to my chest. Warm blood ran down my chin and soaked my glove. Tail wagging, the black and white dog came over to lick it off.

The young guy nudged the dog aside and knelt in front of me. His blue eyes were kind, but I mostly kept my gaze down. He spoke over my head. "Damn it, you cut her up. She's bleedin' all over. Let's keep her pretty, guys."

"She ain't yours. And she ain't gonna be," the bearded dude said. "She was workin' for the goddamned pox-boss. Once the chief hears that, he'll prob'ly bash her head in himself."

"Still," the young one said. With two fingers, he tipped my chin up. I met his eyes. The guy was maybe seventeen, with a freckled nose that made him look younger. "Aw, it's okay, Jacqueline. Jacqueline. What a pretty name."

"How sweet. He's in love," the brown bearded one scoffed.

"Shut the fuck up," the boy said, but there was no real heat in it. Reaching into his back pocket, he dug out a dirty handkerchief and dampened it with a dab of water from a bottle on his belt. He started to clean my face. "Whoa. What the hell."

Across from me, Hairy Ed dropped my pack and turned. "What?"

The boy shrank away from me. "She got cut, I saw it happen. There's still blood on my handkerchief, see? And I'm pretty sure you broke her nose with your flashlight, ya dick. But look. She's . . . she's healed."

Ed turned the beam of his long handled flashlight on the red-stained handkerchief, then on me. The men gathered around, their backs rigid with hostility. The old one took the cap off his water bottle and threw half of it in my face. Coughing and sputtering, I tried to capture some drips on my dry tongue.

The boy wiped me down again, a lot less gently that time. "See, I told you so."

Hairy Ed drew his knife again. The blade darted out and slashed my cheek. I shrieked. My overused nanites kicked into gear instantly, twisting my guts into a knot. I bent over and puked up the remains of my energy bar at his feet. The men backed up, making disgusted noises.

The old guy kicked dirt over the mess and wiped my bloody cheek with his grimy sleeve, revealing newly healed skin. The others saw it and gasped.

"She sold out," Hairy Ed spat. "Bianca fucking *changed* her. I'm not even sure we oughta take that *thing* to the chief. That's no girl, it's half hunter."

They all stared at me. A few men fingered their knives. My eyes darted from side to side, looking for a way out.

"Hunters don't heal like that," the boy pointed out.

The old man spat in the dirt. "True."

"I didn't get the ability from Bianca," I cried. "A doctor at the Center did this to me after I broke my ankle. Some ginger named Graham. Total geek. I didn't ask for it, I swear."

Every man went silent. A few of them looked uncertain. I didn't get it. What had I said?

The boss folded his arms and looked me over. "Broken ankle, huh? Why not just cast it?"

I couldn't exactly tell them Graham turbo-healed me with illegal nanites so my adoptive father could use me as bait. What if they discovered I was a primary host, the one body Bianca could live in forever without it breaking down?

"I got special treatment because my father was a top scientist at the Technical Center. William Stuart. He built the biosphere they use on the space station."

"Like she knows what they use on the space station," Ed huffed.

"I was just there. Go on down to the airfield if you don't believe me. I crashed my shuttle coming in."

"Sure, she's got her own space ship." Hairy Ed rolled his eyes. "What a crock of shit."

"Go look!"

"Nobody's goin' to the airfield," White Hair ordered. "That place is right on the main road to the pyramid. It's infested as hell."

The men moved out again. That time I got to walk. They made me go first, with the brown-bearded guy behind me, prodding me every time I slowed. I couldn't make a break for the surface without pushing past them all. They didn't have to worry. I wasn't going anywhere without my EMP bomb, and that was strapped to the old man's back.

Soon the trail angled downhill. The air got muggy and mud squished under my boots. The guys behind me had lights, but the narrow beams didn't help me much. I couldn't see well enough to keep up the pace. Brown Beard shoved me, and I splashed through a puddle. A horrible smell of rotting sewage rose up. My eyes watered from the fumes. Above my head, tattered spider webs hung from the curved ceiling of the sewer pipe. A stinging slap on my left ear cued me to turn right, down a side passage. That tunnel was narrower, with a lower ceiling, and it didn't smell near as bad. A couple minutes later, they yanked me to a stop at the base of a rusty ladder. Brown Beard jerked a thumb at it, indicating I should climb. I didn't have much choice.

"What about your dog?" I blurted. Ed gave me a sharp poke in the ribs for that.

The young guy answered. "Don't worry. He can get in another way." He pointed just in time for me to see the white tip of the dog's tail disappear into a low hole.

I grabbed the rough metal of the ladder and climbed into the dark. Spider webs stuck to my damp cheek. I shuddered, trying to wipe them off on my shoulder. At the top, I crawled off the ladder, stood up in the dark, and hit my head on the lumpy rock ceiling. Pain jolted down my neck. A breath of air hissed in through my clenched teeth.

"Quiet," Brown Beard snapped, clipping my shoulder as he shoved past.

I got squeezed against the wall as the other three men came off the ladder and crowded into the closet-sized space.

Ed shoved his long flashlight into my hands. "Hold that." He turned his back on me.

I wanted to hit him with it. I wanted it bad. But I was outnumbered, with nowhere to run. So I stood still, gripping the heavy light. Ed bent over, put his shoulder against a big rock, and pushed. The quiet black guy helped him. Grunting, the men shoved the boulder aside. The warm scent of burning beeswax candles wafted in. Someone pushed me through the gap. I stumbled into the light and gasped.

The place was half survivalist bunker, half dragon's lair. Metal shelves lined the walls, sagging under the weight of canned food. A string of battery-operated Christmas lights hung messily from the arched ceiling. Multicolored light glinted off the framed art, silver candlesticks, piles of gold coins, and delicately carved statues that cluttered the floor. I barely glanced at them. To me, food was the real treasure. I hadn't seen so much of it in one place since the epidemic broke out, over five years ago.

Stacked cardboard boxes lined the walls of the narrow stone chamber. Most bore the Tech Center's swooping rocket logo. That explained the insane level of wealth I saw there. The whole underground complex probably belonged to the Center, or at least it had before Hairy Ed and his gangster buddies took over.

The men pushed the boulder back in place and herded me on. I dragged my feet, none too eager to meet their boss, but I had no choice. So I let them lead me to the far end of the treasure room, where a worn red curtain hid the entrance to another long, narrow chamber. Inside, moldy pillows and a Goodwill reject sofa shared space with a pair of beautifully inlaid tables that belonged in a museum. Low tunnels on each side led into dark, mysterious spaces beyond. The black and white dog trotted in through one of them, tail wagging, but I ignored him. The low dais at the end of the room had my attention. A wide, empty chair stood on top.

The king's throne.

"I'll get 'im," White Hair said grimly. The men paled.

"I . . . I'm sorry. I can't watch this," the boy said. Bent over, he scurried away through one of the low tunnels. Not a single man scoffed. They stood in rigid silence, watching him go.

That low tunnel looked like a pretty good option to me, too. I edged that way, ready to make a break for it, but the silent black man grabbed me by the arm. His long fingers wrapped all the way around my skinny bicep, so I had no chance of pulling free. I glanced up at my captor. He was watching the door, the whites of his eyes gleaming bright against his dark skin. I breathed faster. Tension tightened my throat.

Brown Beard peeked through a dusty curtain behind the dais and came running back. "He's coming, he's coming!"

I grew dizzy and cold, like all my blood was running out through my feet. Maybe my arm was shaking. Maybe the trembling came from the hand of the guy holding on to me. I didn't know, I was busy trying not to throw up again. With an effort, I straightened my shoulders and pulled my gaze level. I refused to let them see me cry.

Ragged men clustered at the foot of the throne, holding me out in front like a sacrifice. We heard the king coming before we saw him. Step-thump, step-thump. A long step and a short one. A long step and a short one. My breath caught. I didn't dare hope. The heavy footsteps came closer. Ed closed his eyes and swore under his breath.

The black dude's lips moved in a whispered prayer. "Sweet Jesus, don't let it go down like last time, not like last time, oh God please."

The curtain flipped back. Broad shoulders formed a silhouette against the light.

Hairy Ed grabbed me by the neck. "On your knees, bitch," he snapped, making a show of it. He planted a boot behind my knee, forced me down and held me there, head bowed, by a fistful of my hair. I bit back a whimper.

The king limped around the dais and headed straight for me. Step-thump. Step-thump. He stopped in front of me and took a deep breath. His deep, gravelly voice shook the room. "Get yer filthy hands off her."

Everyone jumped. Ed let go, but not fast enough to avoid the chief's swinging cane. The knobby end cracked him upside the head. With one hand on his face, he fled to the far wall and huddled there, blood streaming into his beard.

I was the only person in the room who dared to raise my head. "Oh my God. Joe. I thought you were dead."

He didn't answer.

I gazed up at him in wonder. The jeans and flannel shirt were gone, replaced by a navy blue business suit and a loud yellow tie fit for a gangster. A shiny black business shoe covered that familiar wooden foot.

I got to my feet. When I took a step closer, one of the men sucked in a sudden breath air. I wasn't afraid. Joe would never swing his cane at me. That kindly old cripple practically raised me. But he was different now, with a half-healed cut on his forehead and a whole new aura. Dark. Cold. Forbidding. Of course he'd changed. I abandoned him. Left him behind with ten thousand pox-infected animals. I told myself I didn't mean to. It was unavoidable. But it didn't make me feel any better inside. At least he was alive. He'd forgive me. Maybe.

"What happened to you? Everyone's afraid of you now," I whispered.

He didn't answer. Joe folded his big arms. Without turning his head, he swept the room in an impassive stare. His men dropped their gazes. Yep, that was Joe, all right. But not the gentle, wounded man I knew. He'd changed.

When I was a kid, I pulled that man from a car wreck, nursed him back to health. I saved his life, but I couldn't save his leg. He let my crew move into his old bar and grill. We got a roof over our heads, and he got his own child-soldier security force. Joe never made rules. Never told us what to do, even when we needed it. He offered advice now and then, but he never provided any real leadership, no matter how desperately I begged. I became chief because he refused to even try. Some days I hated him for that.

But there, at the end of time, Joe had finally manned up. And he did it with a vengeance. I shook my head in disbelief. "Leader of the free world, huh?"

"Yep. All twenty-two souls. Twenty-three, now, with you. Glad ya made it, honey." He pulled me into a gentle hug. Around the room, jaws dropped. "Where'd you find her?" Joe asked over my shoulder.

"Topside, sir. Not twenty feet off the surface." Brown Beard hesitated. "Who is she, Chief?"

"This here's the closest thing I got to a daughter," Joe announced, his deep voice reverberating off the rock walls. "And if anyone o' you bastards lays a finger on her, I'll whip 'im bloody an' stake him out for the pox."

He lifted me with one arm, the way he used to do when I was a little girl, and carried me from the room. Going out, I lifted my chin and locked eyes with Ed. I didn't say a word, but from his cringe, he got the message all right.

Motherfucker, you are gonna pay.

Chapter 7

The whole thing felt unreal. Joe carried me into his private quarters, where a fire crackled from the potbellied stove opposite his survivalist-bunker bed. He settled me on a scavenged love seat by the fire, ignoring the mud my combat boots got on the red velvet upholstery. The dusty little sofa was just long enough for me to stretch out on. All the healing I'd done took a lot out of me, and I could barely move. Joe tucked a pillow gently under my head before he switched personalities and stomped over to the curtained door to snap orders at guys on the other side.

Hairy Ed and the freckled teenager hurried in, carrying a fifty-gallon drum between them. The young guy gave me a relieved smile, but Ed barely dared to squint at me through his brand-new black eye. Working together, the men pieced together a pipe. Steaming water soon began to flow into the barrel.

The fatherly smile Joe had for me evaporated as he turned on Ed. "Don't just stand there, ya dumbass, bring 'er some food. Good food. The best we got."

"Yessir." Both men darted from the room.

I grinned, watching them go.

"Enjoy it while ya can," Joe told me. I thought he was talking about Hairy Ed, who had just become my bitch.

But then Joe leaned over and tested the water with one gnarled finger. "Long as fires are burnin' on the surface, we can make all the smoke we want. After that, it's gonna get chilly in here."

"Oh." There was so much I needed to tell him. Dakota. The EMP. It was all too much. My eyelids drooped, and I fought sleep.

Joe pulled off my boots for me. "Barrel's almost full. There's a little metal stool inside t' sit on. Don't worry, I'll guard the door. Toss yer clothes under the curtain, and I'll have 'em washed for ya. Meanwhile, wear this."

He dropped an overlong pair of jeans and a man's button-down shirt on the couch. When he left, I stripped and tossed out my clothes, imagining Hairy Ed hand-washing my lacy undies. That got into a weird zone I didn't want to think about.

Getting into the barrel of water was a challenge. I was too short to step in, and climbing the side would probably spill it. Eventually I tugged over a little carved table that looked like it came from King Tut's tomb. With a twinge of guilt, I used that priceless piece of art as a stepstool. I lowered myself into the water, sighing in bliss. There was even a tiny scrap of real soap. I wanted to stay in there all night, but I probably would've fallen asleep and drowned myself.

Eventually I dressed, made it to the couch, and collapsed. I knew I ought to move on right away. Grab the EMP, head for the pyramid. Give Bianca some payback. Instead, I passed out. Hours later, I woke to the low sound of men's voices.

"What the hell is that thing?" Joe asked.

I didn't move. Keeping my eyes closed, I listened in. I know, it was kind of shitty of me. But that's what happened.

"An EMP device. It's s'posed to make an electromagnetic pulse. She claimed she was taking it to Bianca as a gift. That's when the, uh, misunderstanding happened. Later she changed her story, said it's a weapon."

It took me a minute to place the voice. *White Hair.* I figured him for Joe's lieutenant. Not a bad choice.

"It's a weapon, then," Joe said. "Jackie's no collaborator."

"Of course not, sir. But there's something else you ought to know," White Hair said. His voice dropped to a low murmur. I only caught a few words, like *healing* and *nose,* but that was plenty.

"No. No way," Joe said from the other side of the curtain. "That fast?"

I cracked an eye. I was alone, still on the red velvet couch, covered with a blanket. The men murmured quietly for a while before someone spoke loud enough to hear.

"The men say she mentioned me by name."

I'd never forget that nasally, East Coast accent. *Oh my God. Doctor Graham is here.* If that pudgy Tech Center scientist was among the survivors, brains had to count for something. He'd be next to useless in a fight.

White Hair answered. "Yeah, she knows you, all right. And it prob'ly saved her life. Ed was in one of his moods before we even found her."

My head fell back in amazement. *Graham?* It made sense, though. After the battle at the array, he must have taken some survivors underground to the Tech Center's bunker.

Not three days ago, I would have happily watched Graham whipped for what he did to me. But I couldn't dredge up much anger anymore. Maybe I was still numb from losing Dakota. Those feelings were boxed up tight, because if I let 'em loose, Bianca would hear the screaming from inside her pyramid. The problem was, without anger to drown them, all my other feelings came rushing back. Fear. Loneliness. Grief. To hell with that. I wanted to be mad. I needed it.

I took a deep breath and told myself I had a right to be pissed. Graham was the one who changed me. Thanks to him, I wasn't entirely human any more. I was part machine. The moment was burned into my brain. The moment when I recognized that silver stream flowing into my broken leg. Nanites. Graham infested me with Class III nanites, slightly less evil cousins of the nanobots that made up Bianca's diffuse neural network. Mine had no artificial intelligence, though. No imprinted personality. The microscopic machines only healed me. Or so I was told.

Graham's Class III nanites had saved my life a couple of times already. But if Bianca got them—got me—she'd be unstoppable. And it would all be his fault. Graham was a smart guy. He had to know that. The thought sank in slow. By the time it was done, I kind of felt sorry for the guy. I sighed. So much for being mad.

My stomach growled and I struggled to a sitting position. Something smelled good. A pottery bowl sat on top of the wood-fired stove, covered with a plate. Joe used to save food for me like that, when I came in late after nighttime sentry shifts. Maybe the dish wasn't even meant for me, but I hadn't survived this long by being timid. I pushed aside my blanket, tiptoed over, and grabbed it. Back on my couch, I settled in with the warm dish in my lap. The mouthwatering aroma brought back a wave of memories that played behind my eyes like videos. Sitting in the diner with my crew. Everyone was small. Tito was a tiny baby. He could barely sit up, so I mashed up his food and fed him from my lap. That day, Joe made us an amazing dish--curried rat. This one was actually done with canned chicken, but it was pretty much the same. I inhaled the delicious steam, seeing each young face in my mind. My crew was out of reach. All I had left was my love for them.

There was no avoiding it--saving those boys meant facing Bianca. Only this time I had no friends. No spaceship to escape in. When the EMP went off, I was gonna be right there at ground zero. Of course I'd run, if I could. Suicide wasn't in my game plan. So I quit my sniveling and started filling my stomach. I was gonna need all the strength I could get.

Chapter 8

I scraped the last delicious morsel from the heavy pottery dish and reluctantly set it aside. Food sat warm in my belly, a tangible reminder of Joe's love for me. I'd absorb it, take it with me when I ventured outside. Squaring my shoulders, I stood. *Time to go to war.* I took two decisive steps toward the curtained doorway, tripped on the cuff of my borrowed jeans, and nearly fell. My self-esteem evaporated as I crouched to roll up the hem. I felt clumsy and small. I was no avenging goddess. But nobody could do this but me. I stood, fists clenched, and took a deep, shuddering breath. It was time. I was going alone into the mist, to walk among hunters. And follow them to Bianca herself.

Fear sank its roots into my stomach, making me reconsider every decision I'd made. Walking to the pyramid was insane. Suicidal. Wouldn't it be better to stay with Joe, warm by his fire? Or would we just be kidding ourselves, relaxing while Bianca's hunters tracked us down? I shook my head to clear it. That slow kind of fear was the worst. It let me overthink everything while my dread grew.

By the time I slipped past the curtain to join the men, my emotions were raw, right on the surface. They forced themselves onto my face, making my eyes wide and my lips trembley. I felt transparent as a wraith. Keenan would've slapped me. *You can't go out there like that,* he would have said. *Man up, Jack. Get a grip.* I raised my chin, climbed the stairs to the dais, and stepped into the light. On the right of the throne, three folding chairs had been set up for Joe's lieutenants. As I came up behind them, every voice in the room went silent.

Joe made a high-handed gesture and his men scrambled to their feet in a forced show of respect. Like it or not, I had become a princess. I didn't feel like one, in my baggy jeans and a man's shirt that almost came down to my knees. Only Joe remained seated, his twisted, burn-scarred hands curled over the ornately carved arms of the chair. I put a hand on the back of his throne and gazed out over the small crowd. Only about fifteen guys stared back at me. The rest were doubtless posted as sentries in the access tunnels. Most of Joe's guys were young. Every last man had the haunted eyes and hollow cheeks of a survivor. I felt their attention as a palpable pressure, and their emotions hit me in waves. Curiosity. Lust. And something else that really pissed me off--fear. Fifteen pairs of eyes cut from me to Joe and back again. The men weren't just afraid of their one-legged chief. They were afraid of me, too. With a word, I could have any one of them whipped and staked out for the pox. Anger flushed my cheeks. That was no way to run a crew.

I turned on Joe, ready to give him a piece of my mind, and my gaze fell on the tiny, hawk-nosed man beside him. His wiry muscles looked like beef jerky, all dried up, and the deep, mahogany tan I remembered had faded to an ashen hue. I still knew him. Still despised him. His shit-brown eyes met mine.

"Viktor, the arms dealer." The words fell out of my mouth, dripping with disdain.

Viktor stood and made a showy bow. "Miss Jacqueline," he said in his thick Russian accent. "I am honored you remember. Though ve vere never introduced."

"Honored? Oh, bullshit," I snorted. "Everyone knows you're a slave trader. You would've happily sold me into a harem."

"Yes, yes." Viktor opened his wrinkled hands in a conciliatory gesture. "I could have. I knew where you lived. At diner, no? But better business to arm gangs zat fought over you."

That rang true, and it made my skin crawl. Viktor had literally sat in my kitchen, selling guns to my crew while I hid in a closet. And the whole time, he knew I was there.

"Yeah, I remember your sales pitch." I mocked his accented voice, adding an extra layer of stupid. "Let me equip you with zee right veaponry, and she will soon live with you."

A few men cracked grins. They glanced at Joe and their smiles faded.

Striding around the throne, I got in Joe's face. In that huge chair, he sat only a little lower than I stood. "What's Viktor doing here?" I hissed. "He's *poison*."

Joe's deep voice resonated throughout the cave. "He's still human, Jack. It ain't about whether we like each other. This is all we got left."

I closed my eyes for a second and breathed. *Stay focused. Bianca is the problem. Viktor is in the past.* I opened my eyes and saw him sitting right there beside the chief. Joe had made him a lieutenant, along with White Hair and Doctor Graham.

I clenched my teeth to control my anger. "Viktor doesn't matter. It's time for me to take the EMP device and go after Bianca."

"What's this EMP thing?" Joe rumbled, too low for his men to hear. He glanced from side to side and tugged my black pack closer to his feet.

His paranoia gave me an evil urge to grab the thing and run. Of course I resisted. "The EMP device puts off some kind of field. Electromagnetic, that's the word. It fritzes out electronics, like lights . . . or nanobots. I got it from Admiral Bauer, on the space station. I was really up there, Joe. You saw the launch."

Joe nodded, his dark eyes full of pain. I knew I was making him re-live the worst day of his life, and I was sorry. But he had to believe me.

"Look, the device will only work if I can get close to Bianca. Real close." Tension made my voice rise, louder and higher, until I sounded like a frightened child. I blurted out the rest before I lost control, so my words came out in a rush. "I'm pretty sure she'll show up if I go to the pyramid alone. I have to find her. Or let her find me. She'll try and take me. And then I'll kill her."

A shudder went through the room. The men began to murmur excitedly. They'd heard every word.

Joe looked at me accusingly. "Nice goin' Jackie."

"Guess I'm not used to keeping secrets from my crew," I snapped.

"Like hell you're not."

That stopped me, because I knew it was true. I had lied to my crew a couple of times. Maybe more. But only for their own good. I tried to shrug it off, but the guilt still rankled.

"You're gonna have to trust 'em now," I said, right out loud. The acoustics in the cave were perfect. My voice carried all the way to the back of the room. "Might not be easy, since you've been such a prick. Beatings don't inspire much loyalty, in case you hadn't noticed."

"Says the girl chief who walked around with a car-antennae whip in her pocket," Joe sneered.

That was true, but I never actually hit anyone with it. And he knew that. Didn't he?

Joe pushed himself from his throne and stood over me, gripping his cane with one twisted hand. "You got no idea what we've been through down here. We needed discipline! Or nobody woulda survived."

I stepped forward, close enough to that cane for him to swing it on me. I was betting he wouldn't, but my muscles trusted no one. My thighs quivered, ready to leap away if Joe so much as twitched a finger. When I spoke, my voice came out as a whisper. "It's only been four days, Joe. Four. And look what you've become."

White Hair's mouth dropped open. Viktor quirked a lip in amusement. Joe winced, and his eyes closed for a second. Doctor Graham came to his rescue.

"Joe's right, we did need discipline," Graham cut in. "When we first got here, fights broke out every hour. Three men were injured, and one almost died. Joe talked to 'em, got the situation under control. That's why I backed him for Chief." He glanced down the row of lieutenants. "We all did."

"Fine." I turned my back on them, ending the argument. Stepping to the edge of the dais, I spoke to the gaunt, grubby men standing on the floor below. "You, uh, may have heard rumors that I'm after Bianca."

A few men cracked smiles at that.

The freckled boy stood in front of the stage, his face turned hopefully toward the light. "You're after Bianca? How?"

I swallowed hard and made myself tell him the truth. All of it. With so few of us left, I couldn't bear anything less. "I can bait her in. She wants me because . . . because I'm a primary host. That means I won't sicken and die if I get infected. In my body, Bianca would live forever. So it's a risk. A huge risk."

"Tell 'em the rest," Hairy Ed bellowed from the back of the cave. Fury glinted from his one good eye. "Tell 'em what Graham did. Tell 'em how he changed you."

Graham squirmed from his seat on the dais. I thought he might get up and leave, but he stubbornly folded his arms and stayed put.

"Okay," I said softly. "I'll tell them the truth. I'll tell 'em everything."

Ed shut up. The other men barely moved. I took a breath, blinked back tears, and reminded myself that these strangers were my crew now. Probably the last free humans on Earth. The only people I had left. They deserved the truth.

I took a deep breath. "Like I said, I'm a primary host, and Bianca knows it. Four days ago, she came after me with an army of pox-infected animals. Thousands of bison, cattle, bears, coyotes--whatever she could infect. Plus human hunters. So many that they filled the highways."

People nodded. They remembered. Jumbled skeletons still littered the roads.

"William Stuart, my adopted father, worked for the Department of Defense. He led the team that created Bianca, and he built the array to destroy her. The array was basically a huge trap, and he . . . he baited it with me." My lower lip trembled. The crowd murmured sympathetically, and I hated it. Compassion always made me cry.

I struggled to get the words out. "I had a broken ankle, and I couldn't fight. Bianca's army was closing in. So Graham treated me with nanites--microscopic machines that circulate in my blood. It's not pox, okay? They just heal me when I get hurt."

Joe's crew stood in silence, digesting that. I wasn't sure they understood.

I sat on my heels at the front of the stage, trying to look each man in the eye. "There aren't that many humans left, so we should all decide this together. I want to go after Bianca, but it's a gamble. If she takes me, she'll get my healing ability too. And she'll pass that trait on to her hunters."

A few men groaned. Others shouted out their votes. "Don't do it!"

"Come on, let's take a chance!"

"What do we have to lose?"

Ed shouted from the back of the room, loud enough to drown them all out. "This is your fault, Graham."

All the tension and fear in the room fixated on that one target. Blended voices rose to a loud, angry growl. I backed away from the mob. The doctor slumped in his folding chair, staring guiltily at the floor.

"This is Bill Stuart's fault, and he's dead now," I shouted over the clamor. "So don't take it out on Graham. He did what he had to do."

Why I defended him, I don't know. I guess I just got tired of carrying the hate.

The paunchy doctor stood up and faced the angry crowd. "Thank you, Jackie. Gentlemen, here's the issue. The epidemic appears to be slowing down. The average time from initial infection to death has declined from eighteen months to just under seven. If this trend continues, the epidemic may burn itself out. Remember, I said *may*. But if Bianca takes Jackie, humanity is done."

"Humanity's already done," Justin yelled. "Two more guys were taken today. We're down to twenty-one, counting the girl. We need to do this now, before we lose any more. Send her out!"

Eager, hopeful voices echoed him from around the cave. "Send her out!"

"Kill the pox."

"Kill Bianca. We can do it."

I saw my moment. Most of them were on my side. I whirled and snatched the backpack from under Joe's feet.

Pulling out the EMP device, I held it up. "See this? This means hope! We can win the war. Rebuild. There are healthy people on the space station. Women, too. They're coming back because . . . because pox got onboard. Bianca sabotaged us. She took . . . she took Dakota."

Behind me, Joe's knees buckled. He collapsed onto the throne, covering his face with crippled hands. That broke my heart all over again.

The heavy silver sphere sank lower in my arms until I hugged it against my stomach. My voice shook. "B-Bianca turned him against us. Against . . . me."

I never told those guys who Dakota was, but from the tears streaming down my face, they knew. They knew.

"Let's get some payback," I suddenly screamed, lifting the sphere high over my head. "Let's take back our world!"

"Yes!" Joe's lieutenants leaped to their feet, fists in the air. The men on the floor went wild, jumping and cheering. A chant broke out. "Take it back, take it back, take it back, take it back."

I was dumb enough to try and give instructions over the din. "You're all gonna have to stay inside. Nobody leaves this cave. If you get taken, Bianca will go through your memories. She'll know what you know. So everyone's on lockdown until this mission is over."

"This mission is over now," Joe said. No one seemed to hear him but me. His voice rose to a shout. "Yer not goin'! It's too dangerous."

The celebration ended. Men's shoulders slumped. Their dusty faces sagged in disappointment.

Joe stood. Leaning on his cane, he limped to the center of the stage. "This is not a democracy. Y'all got t' say yer piece. But it's over now. She ain't goin'."

"You can't be serious," I said into the sudden silence. My voice built to a scream as I got madder. "You just lost two guys! Both of 'em knew right how to get in here. Now Bianca knows too. How long do you think you're gonna last down here? How long?"

"You don't give the orders, Jackie. Get used to it. You're my daughter, nothin' more," Joe said. "I need to keep you safe. I've lost all my other kids. I ain't gonna lose you, too. Men—lock 'er up."

"What?" I couldn't believe it. Joe's lieutenants surrounded me. I backed up, slapping at their grasping fingers. "Hey, hey, get your hands off me. Don't touch me!"

They ripped the EMP device from my hands. Lifted me right off my feet. And carried me, kicking and screaming, from the room.

Chapter 9

Joe's cronies hauled me down one of the low tunnels that branched off the throne room. In about fifty feet, the cold, damp passage dead-ended in a Plexiglas cage like the ones Center researchers used to keep pox victims in. That made me sick. Had Joe installed it for discipline, or was it a relic of the Center's last, desperate medical experiments? Graham threw me inside the clear plastic chamber and White Hair slammed the door. With a practiced motion, Viktor clicked the padlock closed. I wasn't the first girl he'd locked up.

"Somebody help me," I screamed, sobbing and pounding the greasy walls. "Joe! Don't let them leave me here. Please don't leave me."

They marched away in single file, taking the only light with them.

I crouched in the dark, shaking with cold and fury. For the first hour, silent men visited me at intervals, bringing blankets or water. Ed came in last with a moldy pillow, which he crammed through a sliding port on the wall. It didn't really fit. If I had the pox, I bet I could have infected him then.

I stood to face him through the smeared plastic. "What's Joe saying about me? How long do I have to stay in here?"

Ed didn't answer. Eyes downcast, he jerked a shoulder in a short shrug and then trudged away. That was easy enough to read. He didn't agree with his chief. Most of the men didn't. I was still stuck, though. Unable to rest, I paced the dark cage. Three steps over, three steps back, until my aching legs forced me to stop.

The boy came back later and lit a candle lantern outside my chamber. That small gesture brought me more comfort than I wanted to admit. For a while, muted voices came from the main room, but as the night wore on, they trailed off. I wrapped myself in thin blankets and stretched out on the floor, wrinkling my nose at the smell of dried urine in the corners.

I was busy crying myself to sleep when Joe came down the passageway. I recognized his uneven stride and cut off my sniffling. Too late. He heard me.

"Aw, Jackie," his gruff voice came from the darkness. "I'm so sorry."

I sat up, a worn blanket wrapped around my shoulders. "Good. Let me out then."

"I love you too much to do that, honey."

I bit back an angry outburst. That might drive him away. With a lot of shuffling and old-man grunts, Joe settled his bulk onto the stone floor across from my cage. With his wooden leg, that wasn't easy. Mad as I was, it gave me hope. He was putting out an effort. Maybe I could convince him after all.

"I'm so sorry you got left behind when the rest of the crew got away on the rocket," I whispered. "I never meant that to happen."

"That was out o' your hands, Jack. You were up on the array when it happened. Besides, it was my choice. I'd do it again."

"You're not . . . mad at me for that?"

Joe slowly shook his big, square head. "You're not in here 'cause I'm mad. You're in here because I care."

"Bullshit," I muttered. "I'm in here because fear rules your life. That's why you rule by fear."

In my head, I gave myself a high-five. Two points for Jackie. Sadly, Joe didn't even respond to my devastating wit. I decided to tell him what was on my mind anyway, even though I figured he'd shoot me down.

I steeled my nerves and said it. "I know what's wrong with you, Joe. You're angry because you're not whole. You know, without the leg." I got real uncomfortable then, and had to look away. "I couldn't help you before, but I can now."

Joe said nothing. The candle lantern had burned low, so I couldn't see his expression. I imagined it from memory, the sad, dark eyes and those drooping, hang-dog jowls that made him look like an old bloodhound.

"You wanna give me *'bots*," he spat. The venom in his voice made me recoil. I hadn't seen that coming.

"Not pox nanobots," I whispered. "Nanites. They don't take over your mind, and I bet they'll grow your leg back."

"No. I wouldn't take 'em if I lost both my legs."

"But just imagine, with two legs you'd lead your own patrols. Get outside, run and fight with your crew. That's how you inspire loyalty."

"I said no, and that's the end of it," Joe snorted. "It ain't yer fault what happened to you. Graham treated you without your permission. But if he'd asked, what would you have said?"

He got me there. *Dammit.*

I sighed in defeat. "No. I woulda said no. But if I knew then what I know now, it would have been different. Just think about it, okay?"

Joe looked down. That conversation was over. He sat still and silent for a long time before he spoke again. "Jackie? Do you believe in reincarnation?"

Out of the blue like that, the question startled me. "Um, I don't know.

I like to think so. Yeah. Why?"

His voice came from the darkness, slow and uncertain. "When we die, if there's no free people, what'll we reincarnate into? Hunters?"

I shrugged. "I doubt it. Bianca owns every single species, doesn't she? They all have her soul now."

I sank down to my side on the filthy floor of the prison, the musty pillow under my head. Our lone candle flickered as it began to die.

Joe sat still, his lumpy shadow crouched beside him like a troll. "So you think Bianca has a soul?"

I remembered her fierce eyes, that unmistakable presence looking out of my mother's lined face. "Absolutely. Except Bianca's is split. Like sunlight, when it hits a crystal and makes rainbows. The colors look separate, but they're really all part of the same thing."

"That's beautiful, Jack."

I turned my face away. "No it isn't."

Joe sat with me, not speaking, as time ticked by. I was grateful for the company. As long as he was there, I had a chance. Thoughts spun in my head as I composed my final argument.

I sat up, cross legged, and took my best shot. "So . . . by now, Bianca has to know we're here. Any minute hunters could come down those tunnels."

"Yeah. I know," Joe said. He sounded defeated.

"Don't make me die in this cage, Joe. Please. At least let me run when they get here. Please unlock the door. If you ever loved me, you'll do this one last thing for me."

Joe slowly struggled to his feet. I jumped to mine and waited eagerly at the door of my cell, certain he meant to open it. Then all I'd have to do was blow by him, find the EMP and bolt.

Joe faced me though the dirty Plexiglas door. "I ain't stupid," he said. "If I let you out, you'll run topside an' get yerself killed."

"We're all gonna die anyway," I muttered.

"Every minute alive, every minute free, that's a victory," Joe said.

"No it's not," I screamed, slapping the clear plastic door so hard he flinched. "Not if you just sit there, waiting to be taken."

When Joe spoke, his voice was calm. "Sorry, hon. I just can't let you go. I shoulda never let you do half the stuff you did. Runnin' around the streets after dark, scrounging food. Gang fights and territory wars. I shoulda put a stop to it a long time ago. If I'd been a better man, none of this would've ever happened."

"That's not true. The kids would've starved. And we'd still be dealing with Bianca."

Joe shook his head. I could tell he was done arguing. "We'll talk more tomorrow. Try an' get some sleep." He picked up the candle lantern and limped off down the tunnel.

"Joe? Joe! Wait. Don't leave."

His footsteps retreated. A long step and a short one. A long step and a short one. My forehead sagged against the wall of my prison. As the light slowly disappeared, I couldn't even cry.

***

Late that night, something woke me. I lay still, listening hard, before I heard it again. Stealthy footsteps, coming down the tunnel. *Hunters!* I took a breath to scream, but in that moment, men's whispers carried in on the damp air.

"Careful there. Got the key?"

"Yep. Right here."

Hunters didn't whisper. They could barely talk. These were men, sneaking into my prison in the dead of night. I could guess why.

Rapists. Somehow they got ahold of a key.

Leaving my blankets on the floor, I backed into the darkest corner of the cage. The footsteps came closer. Three sets of them. In close quarters, I couldn't win that fight. My mind raced. Should I scream, and maybe bring in a whole mob? I didn't know Joe's crew. His men might protect me from the rapists, or join them.

The lock clicked open. Men hesitated outside the door. The leader held a tiny penlight in his fist, shading the light behind blood-red fingers. Another guy tossed something into the cell. Its hard edge hit me in the thigh.

"Ouch." My combat boot thudded to the floor by my foot. The damn thing was heavy. In a second, the rest of my clothes sailed in. I caught my white bra in one hand. "What the hell?"

Viktor's quiet, accented voice came from the tunnel. "Get dressed, Miss Jacqueline. Let's go."

"I'm not going anywhere with you, Viktor, you creeper."

"If you vant chance of making it to pyramid, you vill keep your voice down," Viktor hissed.

The pyramid? My heart began to pound. Those guys weren't there to rape me. They were breaking me out! A wild joy seized me. I was free!

I snatched my clothes off the floor, sorting them as fast as I could by feel. "Where's my EMP device?"

"Right here." I recognized that voice. The freckle-faced teen. He walked into the cell and handed me my heavy black pack. I checked inside. The silver sphere was there, along with my food and water. I was in business.

"Turn your backs, you guys," I ordered.

The skinny teenager reluctantly obeyed. Viktor didn't. I ignored him. Shivering in the chill, I tore off the borrowed clothes and wormed into my form-fitting armored gear. I tugged the laces tight on my knee-high boots and stood, an inch taller and a whole lot braver. Hope glowed in my heart. Bianca had no idea I was after her. She was going down.

I strapped on my pack and rolled my shoulders, feeling the strength in my small, tight muscles. "Okay. Ready."

"Let's go," someone whispered from the tunnel.

The boy grabbed my hand and led me from the cell. I tolerated that just to avoid an argument. We fell in step behind Viktor and the leader, who had switched off his tiny light. By then I was clinging gratefully to the young guy's hand, since I couldn't see a thing. They marched me double-time down the musty, pitch dark tunnel. Every third or fourth step I had to chip in a running stride just to keep up. I barely had time to swipe aside nasty strands of web that stuck to my face. Once I felt a horrible tickling across my temple as a spider got caught in my hair. I shook it off, shuddering. The thing hadn't attacked, so I guess it wasn't taken by the pox. As much as I hated spiders, they gave me hope. Apparently there were other free creatures besides us.

Our leader moved confidently through the dark, taking us up ladders, through crawl spaces, and around so many corners that I became hopelessly lost. We mostly stuck to narrow side passages, some with ceilings so low that I was the only one who could walk without hunching. Slick mold coated the walls. No surface noises penetrated that deep, so the only sounds were our thudding footfalls and deep, rhythmic breathing. Eventually the smooth floors of the sewer tunnels gave way to passageways of packed dirt, and we began to climb. I caught my first whiff of outside air, rank with burning oil.

Faint, gray light came from occasional gaps in the rock ceiling. We were just under the surface. Goosebumps rose on my skin. Bianca's hunters weren't far away. I'd be among them soon. Our leader raised a hand, signaling a halt. He turned.

I got my first look at his brown-bearded face and recoiled. "What are you doing here?"

"Helping you save our asses, I hope. So pay attention. This is as far as we go. You're on your own from here on out. Follow this passage until it dead-ends in a rock fall. Climb up however you can. You'll be near the main trail to the pyramid. It's another eighteen or twenty miles from there. Take this. You'll need it." Reaching out with both hands, he slung the lanyard of his penlight around my neck.

"Okay. Thanks." I clutched the tiny light in my fist like an amulet.

Oh my God. Twenty miles with hunters. Will I make it?

The man's expressionless face softened. "And, um, Jackie? I just wanted to say . . . I'm sorry. I swear I'm not like Ed. I never was, anyway. Not until the world went to shit."

"I know. Nobody's the same now. It's okay." I stuck out my hand for a handshake. "Peace."

He gripped my hand hard. "Peace."

My eye fell on Viktor, and I gave a bewildered shake of the head. I never expected to see that scumbag risk his neck to help a girl.

He laughed softly. "You are last female. We must spend you wisely, no?"

"Oh fuck off, you incredible asshole." I started to walk away.

Viktor grabbed me by the arm and stopped me. I tried to pull away and failed. He wasn't much taller than I was, but that big, calloused hand could have crushed my wrist. He turned my palm up and pressed something cold into it. "This vas my mother's. I give to you. I vant only one thing. You take this, you stab Bianca in her black heart."

I took a breath to argue. Stabbing Bianca would only kill the host body, freeing her nanobots to morph into horrible false-flesh constructs like the one that killed Stuart. But then I opened my hand and the words died on my tongue. A beautiful pearl-handled folding knife lay there, the keepsake Viktor carried to remember his mother by. Somehow, it never occurred to me that a douchebag like him even had a mother. Viktor ran a finger longingly down the iridescent silver-gray finish and then brought that finger to his lips, his eyes bright with tears. Holy shit. The world just kept getting weirder.

Viktor gripped my forearm tight. "Kill Bianca, Miss Jacqueline. Kill that bitch for me."

"Yeah. I'm doing all this for you, Viktor." A hysterical laugh bubbled up, and tears threatened. This time, when I pulled away, he let me go.

The teen boy squeezed my shoulder. "I'll go with you as far as the rock fall. Then I better get my ass back in bed so I don't get popped when the chief finds you missing. Damn. This is gonna get ugly."

Brown Beard looked like he wanted to puke. "Yep. Heads are gonna roll."

I had to smile. "What's wrong with you guys? He's only got one leg. All you have to do is run. What's he gonna do? He can't chase you."

The bearded man shook his head. "You don't understand. He has the crew's support. They can kick us out. Send us topside."

I rolled my eyes. "So? Circle back. Joe can't catch you. Who else is gonna chase you? Viktor won't. That white haired dude can't."

"See? That is vhy she is survivor," Viktor said. "Good luck, Miss

Jaqueline. Godspeed."

With a final wave, Viktor and his companion took off down the tunnel. I was actually sorry to see them go.

The boy shivered. He put an arm over my shoulder and leaned close to whisper. "Farther down we'll come real close to the main trail to the pyramid. Let's keep as quiet as we can."

I nodded. We crept along the brightening tunnel, our nerves on edge. Outside, the sun had risen. I swore under my breath. Traveling in daylight was risky, but if I didn't take off, Joe's men would find me and drag me back to the cage. We kept moving. Holes in the ceiling became more frequent, and the air got colder. A few snowflakes drifted in and swirled around our heads. One more corner, and we had to halt. A pile of fallen rock blocked our way.

I gulped. "This is it. Thanks."

He stared up at the gray sky, the ropy muscles along his jaw tense with fear. "I'll . . . uh, I'll go with you, Jackie."

"No you won't." I put a gentle hand on his arm. "Look, I really appreciate this. But I'm safer alone. Hunters never travel in pairs. Packs, sometimes. But they're really only a bunch of individuals following the same orders. Hunters don't have friends."

The boy's shoulders dropped, betraying his relief. "Oh my God. I can't believe you're doing this."

I tried to smile. "Don't talk about it or I'll chicken out. Go on, hustle home before you get caught. If they accuse you of helping me escape, deny it. Stick to your story no matter what."

"How can you bother with somebody else's problems?"

I shrugged. "Maybe it's easier."

The boy stood there shifting his feet like he had something to say. I didn't have time for it. I busied myself getting my cap and gloves on, but he was still there.

"Um, Jackie? I'm thinking, the hunters are coming. Even if you win, I might not be here when you get back. I was, you know, only a kid when the epidemic broke out, and, uh, now all the girls are gone, so . . ."

I could see where he was going with that, and I didn't like it. I folded my arms. "Spit it out. I don't have all day."

The boy stared at me beseechingly. "I . . . I've never even kissed a girl."

Maybe I was taking my shit out on him, but that irritated the hell out of me. "Oh, for God's sake."

His wounded expression stopped me. That could be the last free human I ever saw. I didn't want it to end mean. I sighed. "Look, my boyfriend just died. I'm sorry. It's not personal, but no."

"Oh. Yeah, I remember. That's the guy you told us about. Dakota, right?"

I nodded, eyes downcast. My heart felt like it had just torn in half.

"I'm sorry." The boy gave me a quick hug and a kiss on the cheek while I stood woodenly, unable to even hug him back. "Goodbye, Jackie."

I didn't answer. I was already looking up, plotting my course over the treacherous heap of debris. A flock of infected starlings crossed overhead, wings beating in perfect synchrony. Bianca would be watching. I'd better get my head in the game.

I tightened the belly strap on my pack and began to climb.

Chapter 10

I clung to the edge of a broken slab of concrete and poked my head a few inches above the ground. The city looked like it had been bombed to rubble. Not a single landmark remained. It was hard to believe nanobots did the damage, not explosives. Scattered fires glowed orange against the gray landscape, sending tendrils of smoke twisting up to join the low, oppressive ceiling of fog overhead. A few sparrows flitted by. I ducked, the back of my neck prickling. Their bright little bird eyes spied on the world like security cameras, reporting back to Bianca. I made damn sure the last one was gone before I dared to scramble from the hole.

I picked my way across rubble to a packed dirt trail, where the going got easier. Far ahead, a few infected trudged mechanically toward the pyramid. Those didn't scare me as much as they used to. Bianca's hunters had become drones, working mindlessly until their bodies fell apart. None of them paid me any attention. That left me with a tingling feeling of suspense, like any second they'd all turn and face me. I kept waiting for it as I marched along, the black pack hanging heavily from my narrow shoulders.

Once I came across a tennis shoe abandoned on the trail. That hurt, because I knew some poor hunter was walking with one bruised, bloody foot. Bianca hadn't left them with the power to so much as tie their own shoelaces. I never used to have any compassion for the infected. As far as I was concerned, they were pure evil. But Dakota had taught me one thing before he died. The owners of those bodies were still inside, trapped and suffering. I meant to free them or die trying.

I did all right for the first four or five hours, marching along in step with the drones. But the damned infected never seemed to rest. I wondered if they ate and drank at all. They had to, but I'd never seen it. The sun hid behind the fog, giving the day a timeless feel.

The temperature dropped and thirst made my tongue feel like sandpaper, but I was heading into a flat zone with almost no cover. That wasn't the time to start digging through my backpack. I gutted it out and pressed on, exposed to the full force of the freezing wind. My cheeks stung with cold. I blew into my cupped hands, then stopped abruptly. That wasn't something a hunter would do.

A few blocks of intact buildings stood on the other side of the flats. The closest one looked like an apartment house, or part of one. I squinted. The building ended abruptly, as if the right third had been erased by the hand of God. My eye didn't make sense of it until I got close. The building was severed, no doubt by nanobots. Eerie as hell. The north wall was missing, so I could see inside the abandoned homes. Sofas, counters, books, even a kid's doll—everything was cut cleanly. No rubble, no dust, no fallen sections of wall remained. Half of everything was simply gone. That creeped me out. But I needed to rest and warm up. The weird, severed building was the only shelter for miles.

I tiptoed around to the open side and scanned the windblown apartments for movement. Nothing. On the ground floor, a hallway yawned open to the weather at one end. Farther in, the corridor faded into darkness. I half expected to see quicksilver streams of nanobots running across the dusty carpet, but only one lonely suitcase stood by a door, evidence of someone's failed escape plan. Inside, it smelled like rotten meat, or maybe decomposing bodies. I didn't mind much. The dead held no terror for me anymore. Listening hard, I heard the wind shuffling trash down the open hallway—not the wet squelching sounds of Bianca's horrid false-flesh tentacles rising up to grab me. So I slipped inside and crept up the first stairway on the left, intent on getting a top floor view of the landscape. The heavy fire door clicked behind me with a thunk. I jumped. That sound used to bait in every hunter around. Were there still any? I didn't know.

Inside the concrete stairwell, the rotten meat smell got stronger, but the silence and heavy, undisturbed coating of dust reassured me. I took a moment to gulp some water before I tiptoed up the stairs, past the second floor landing, and then the third. At the entrance to the fourth floor I found the source of the stench. A man's partially mummified body sprawled across the floor beside a bulging duffel bag. A handgun lay by his hand. The sight made me incredibly lonely. Plan A had been the duffle, loaded with whatever the guy thought he needed to make his break. Plan B was a nine millimeter bullet. He was scared and alone, like me, so he bailed and went with B. I picked up the Glock, hoping to keep it for emergencies, but the clip was empty. So I stepped over the guy's shriveled, open-mouthed face and helped myself to his duffle. Business clothes, credit cards, a passport—that was it. No food, no water, not even spare ammo for the nine-mil. Nothing I could use. Nothing he could have used, either. I shuddered. I'd seen enough death. Why that one unnerved me, I didn't know.

I tried to tell myself it was his piss-poor planning. But in truth, there was some dreadful appeal to the path he'd taken--the easy way out. I straightened my spine, telling myself I'd never give up, never take that path. Not if I was the last free human on Earth. I pushed open the fire door and stepped onto the fourth floor.

Wind rushed through the breach where the north wall had been. A storm was blowing in. I narrowed my eyes against the icy blast. Outside, a slender figure moved along the trail, head bowed against the swirling snow. I flattened myself against the wall, holding my breath. The hunter knelt for a moment and inspected the trail. When he left the path and veered toward the apartment building, exactly along the line I'd taken, my hands started to shake. He was tracking me for sure.

His strategy was obvious—to trap me in the building. I'd made it easy for him by going right to the top. Cursing, I slammed open the fire door and bolted down the staircase, leaping three or four steps at a time. Breath panted through my open mouth, loud in the stillness. On the last U-turn I vaulted the handrail and skidded to a stop. On the right, the hallway hung open to the cold air. Leaning forward, I peeked. The hunter was out of sight. The faintest noise came from the north side of the building, like a foot crushing dried leaves.

I ran left, down the dark side of the hallway. An intact door stood closed at the far end. I'd slip out that way and sneak off. Second thoughts plagued me as I reached the end of the passageway. What if the hunter was right outside, ready to grab me when I opened the door? What if I hesitated and he came up the hall behind me? Silently, I turned the doorknob and pushed. It didn't budge. Behind a closed door, someone's television switched on, blaring the *Star Spangled Banner.* I jumped. No way could there be reception. That building didn't even have electricity anymore.

A woman's voice spoke over the music. "Survivors, come out! Celebrate the birth of our new world order. Global America. Worldwide democracy. Peace through cooperation."

Global America? That did it. I slammed the door with my hip and it flew open with a crack. Giving in to panic, I ran through the hellish landscape, leaping from rock to rock so I wouldn't leave footprints. I was dimly aware of birds overhead, riding the storm. Were they watching me, relaying my position through Bianca's wireless network? The pyramid's neon light glowed through the fog, closer now, but still miles away. I had to find Bianca before the hunter found me.

The heavy EMP device bounced as I ran, bruising my back. Nanites in my blood picked that moment to repair the damage, which didn't help. I ran on, gasping in the cold, smoky air. I hadn't made it a mile before thickly falling snow obscured the trail. Even the bright lights of the pyramid disappeared in the blizzard. The wind picked up, and patches of exposed skin on my nose and cheeks started to burn with cold. I crossed my arms over my body and shook. The beds of my fingernails ached where I'd frostbitten them the year before, foraging on the riverbed with Dakota.

With Dakota. Oh my God. Never again. He's gone.

I meant to avenge him, and freezing in the storm was no way to do that. I had to find shelter.

I stumbled down what had once been a road. Buildings on both sides were missing, taken away a molecule at a time by nanobots. Bianca was probably using the materials to build her giant pyramid. What she needed that for, I had no idea. The devastation ended abruptly, and I cautiously entered a shadowy lane lined with intact buildings on both sides. Every last window was dark. On my left, a frosty iron handrail gleamed dully in the twilight. Beside it, a set of cracked concrete stairs disappeared into the dark. I could hide down there.

Unless someone already was.

My instincts screamed against it, but a deep, bone-chilling cold had set in, and wind howled across the barren land. That kind of cold could kill. Trembling, I started down the stairs. Sneaking inside in total darkness was the safer option, and I knew it. But halfway down, I chickened out and switched on Brown Beard's pen light. Faint, greenish light illuminated a glass door that stood a few inches open. Curly script on it read *The Underground.* I slipped inside, closed the door tight, and swept the light around. A shiny black bar lined the left wall. Unbroken bottles of booze still sat on the shelves behind it. Mirrored walls, round glass tables and black leather benches completed the sleek, urban design. I crossed the vacant dance floor and methodically explored every corner of the nightclub to make sure I was alone.

Even indoors, my breath billowed out in clouds. Sweat chilled between my breasts. Inside my combat boots, my toes had gone numb. I had to do something about that, or I wouldn't survive the night. Beside the bar, a swinging 'employees only' door led into a hall. Along the way were storerooms and a walk-in cooler. The last door opened into an office with a dusty computer and a mattress on the floor, the perfect place for a tired manager to grab a nap. A low table beside the bed held an ashtray, a bottle of Absolut 100-proof, Zig Zags, and a few packaged condoms. *Eeuw.*

Maybe that nest wasn't for napping after all.

I headed back to the darkened nightclub. The air was colder there, and the frosted glass door made me feel exposed. Mostly out of habit, I dug around behind the bar to check for stored food. No luck. Just alcohol, and I had no interest in that. Whatever snacks they once had were gone or chewed by rats. *Figures.* I leaned my elbows on the slick black granite bar and sighed. All around the nightclub, flat screen TVs on the walls switched themselves on.

I gasped.

Martial music played as an American flag waved against a blue sky. The camera cut to a young, pretty black woman in a lacy white dress. I had the oddest feeling that she could see me too. Behind her, a row of blank-faced drone mothers stood along a long, padded table, tending a neat line of infants.

"Manifest destiny." Bianca's willowy spokesmodel flashed her white teeth. "Our glorious vision has come to pass. Global America. Bringing the world freedom, democracy, and traditional family values."

On cue, all the tiny baby heads turned toward me at once.

I guess I should have ducked, or run, or hid. But I stood there, transfixed by the eerie artificial intelligence glinting from their cute, emotionless faces. I'd never seen infected newborns before. I thought they all died of pox. This was worse. The sight of them in their identical white diapers made me sick. Clinging to the edge of the black granite bar, I sank to my knees and covered my mouth with my hands.

Baby drones. Oh my God. Were they born infected, or taken at birth?

I hunched on the sticky floor and plugged my ears, but the woman's relentless voice was impossible to avoid. "America. Peace through cooperation. Life, liberty, and happiness for all."

"Liar," I hissed. Her words still tugged at me. I didn't believe them, but part of me wanted to. The infected were never alone, never afraid. Not like me. I peeked around the corner of the bar. Bianca's spokes-drone turned her head and looked right at me.

She stretched her lips in an empty smile. "The revolution is over. Good has triumphed over evil. Poverty and discrimination have been eliminated. Global America: one mind, one planet, one nation. Join us, and help rebuild our world."

Patriotic music played, and the scene changed to a shot of the pyramid beaming glorious neon-blue light into fog. Camera cut. The American flag waved again, this time over a backdrop of the earth from space. Music filled the room, gradually becoming louder. The volume increased until sharp pains stabbed my eardrums in time with the beat. Deep bass vibrations pulsed through my chest from wall-mounted speakers, making me frantic. Any hunter within a mile would hear it.

"Stop it. Stop it!" I jumped to my feet and advanced on the TV opposite the bar. Grabbing the cord, I yanked. It wasn't plugged in.

The model's face reappeared, larger than life and less than a foot away. Chin tilted, she looked down on me, her perfectly shaped brows furrowed sternly. Speakers all around the nightclub amplified her insistent voice, sending vibrations through my feet. "Global America. One mind, one planet, one nation. Join us."

"No. I'll never join you!" I fled behind the bar, boots slipping as I rounded the corner too fast. Heavy glass jugs of whiskey lined a shelf there. I seized one by the neck and hurled it full force at the nearest TV.

The bottle flipped once, hit the screen and shattered, raining stinking liquor everywhere. Broken glass skidded across the floor, and every screen in the nightclub went dark. My ears rang in the sudden silence. Staying low, I peered over the black granite bar, my eyes jumping between the cracked television screen and the frosted glass front door. Long minutes passed before I got up the guts to push through the swinging doors beside the bar and retreat to the manager's office at the end of the hall.

I swept the penlight around the room. Indecision nagged at me. The office was warmer, but it only offered one way out. Any street rat knew better than to stay in a place like that. It could easily become a trap. Maybe I was too tired to drag the mattress someplace else. Maybe choosing that room was my own wimpy, passive version of Plan B. I don't know. It wasn't the right decision, but I wasn't in my right mind, so that's what happened. I dumped my pack on the floor and locked the door.

The first thing I did was snap the manager's dusty laptop closed and cram it in a drawer. In a fit of paranoia, I shook out the musty bedding, cringing when I had to touch the stained sheets. No spiders or poxy rats ran out, so I collapsed onto the bed, wrapped myself in blankets, and curled into a ball. Shutting off the penlight took an act of will, but I had to conserve the battery. New ones would be almost impossible to find. In the dark, my courage faltered. Everything felt lonelier and more frightening. I missed Dakota with a savage pain. Sobs forced themselves from my chest, and I bit my lip to suppress them. I replayed everything in my mind, helpless to see how I could have saved him. Returning to the planet, leaving Joe—those were the dumbest things I'd ever done. Then a soft thud came from somewhere down the hall. Throwing off the blankets, I sat bolt upright, afraid to breathe for fear of making noise.

In a moment, the floor creaked. My heart raced. Fear jangled down every nerve, magnifying every sensation. Crawling to the foot of the bed, I pressed an ear to the cold wall. Another creak, then the soft sigh of a boot sliding on wood. An eternity later, the noises repeated. The hunter had found me. He was approaching like a tiger, slow and patient, in near silence.

I was fucked.

I cursed myself. How stupid could I be to trap myself in a small room, with no other way out? I grabbed the vodka and a lighter from the bedside table. Every kid in my crew knew the rule--you couldn't make a hunter bleed without getting infected yourself. But you could make him burn.

Furtive steps approached. An unseen hand rattled the doorknob. Then soft metallic clicks and scrapes came from inside the lock itself. *Lock picks?* I'd never seen one of the infected display that kind of ingenuity, not unless he was being ridden by Bianca herself. *Shit!* I lunged for the EMP device. In that instant, the door crashed open. A dark form blocked my escape.

I whirled. Twisting the cap from the bottle, I sprang forward, flinging vodka. The lighter flared to life in my hand.

The intruder backed away, palms out. "Jack, no! It's me!"

"Keenan?" I gasped. Reflexively, I held out the lighter to see him by.

He retreated farther. "Whoa, whoa, careful with that."

"Oh, yeah. Right." Almost sobbing with relief, I switched off the lighter and fumbled my little flashlight on. Keenan had me in his arms almost instantly, his lips pressed against the side of my neck. Snow coated the shoulders of his jacket. Wind had twisted his long hair into ropy strands, and he smelled like smoke and vodka. I didn't mind. His muscles felt warm and strong under my hands. Life force poured into me, giving me strength in an invisible cascade of energy that coursed through my body like music.

I clung to him like the two of us were the only living things left on the planet. "Oh my God, you scared the crap out of me."

"Sorry, babe. I didn't know for sure it was you. Marching band music isn't exactly your style."

"You heard that?"

"How could I miss it? Global America. One mind, one planet, one nation," Keenan intoned in a deep, fake voice. "Oh yeah. I'm a huge fan."

"Me too. I'm all about family values." I had to smile, because in some strange way, it was true. Then the obvious question made it to my lips. "How'd you get off the space station?"

Keenan leaned back a little and grinned. "Shuttle. Bauer's goons caught me trying to steal it. Failing to steal it, actually. Apparently incompetence is no excuse. So they roughed me up and hauled me to the bridge for sentencing. I thought I'd had it there for a minute, but I talked Bauer into authorizing the trip. He even programmed the autopilot for me himself."

"Holy shit. He gave you a fucking shuttle."

"Yep." Keenan sounded all proud of himself, and he had a right to be. But that was bad news for our crew.

I looked down, unsure if I ought to point that out. If the admiral was handing out shuttles, that meant he was desperate. Sending Keenan was Bauer's Hail Mary, his last-ditch effort to help me succeed. The station had to be in bad shape. It wouldn't stay in orbit much longer. The astronauts would have to land. If I didn't win against Bianca, she'd meet them at the airfield, wearing my face. And the last free humans would be taken.

Keenan let go of me to lock the door. He spoke with his back mostly turned, so shadows hid his face. "I found your shuttle. Or what's left of it. It's overrun with hunters."

I set down the Absolut and dropped onto the bed, weak and shaky from the aftereffects of adrenaline. "Yours probably is too, by now."

"Hope not. That's our only way home. We still have one, because I didn't crash *my* shuttle." Keenan smirked. "Apparently my autopilot is more talented than yours."

I smiled. "You're nuts."

"Yeah, well, it's workin' for me, so don't fuck it up."

"Oh, Keenan, Joe is here! He's got like, twenty men, all underground. One of his patrols captured me. But . . ."

"That's great, babe," Keenan said. He squatted down to get eye level with me. "So what's wrong?"

"It's Joe. He's . . . not the same. He's Chief now, only meaner than shit. His men are terrified of him. He locked me up, like he was doing me a favor, keeping me from attacking Bianca. I'd be stuck there now, but some of his guys helped me escape."

Keenan's face darkened. "I woulda found you. Broke you out."

I know, he would've tried. That boy had the biggest ego of anyone I'd ever met. He truly believed he could do anything. The problem was, he just kept on winning, so he never got the reality check I expected. I hoped one wasn't coming any time soon. Groaning, I pulled off my black cap and ran my hands through my short, cinnamon hair. I couldn't believe Keenan was really there. Bauer had given me his word--no soldiers. But he used a hell of a loophole. I would never have risked a member of my crew. But I had to admit--my odds sure felt better with Keenan along. Lucky I didn't torch him.

Half laughing and half crying, I let my head sink into my hands. "I can't believe I nearly burned you alive." I wiped my streaming eyes.

"Yep. That woulda sucked," Keenan said casually.

I snorted. He laughed out loud, and then we both laughed. Damn, it felt good. Then that brief, magic moment ended, and Keenan went back to roaming his environment like a wild animal. Despite the cold, he took off his old brown Carhartt jacket, slung it over the one chair, and prowled around in his long-sleeved thermal, going through shit on the manager's desk. I didn't mind. I was just happy that most of the vodka stench stayed over there with the jacket.

Keenan came around to the bedside table and let out a low whistle of appreciation. "Oh yeah. This is where the magic happens."

"Not anymore." Maybe I sounded a little too brusque there. I didn't mean to be a bitch. Okay, maybe I did. A little. I shut my mouth, awkward and embarrassed. Keenan ignored me. He rummaged around on the table, came up with a pack of matches, and got ready to strike one.

"Wait a minute," I blurted. "You sure that's safe, with all the alcohol fumes in here?"

"Nope." Keenan struck the match anyway.

I buried my face in the mattress, waiting for the *floom* of burning alcohol. It never came. Honestly, I was a little irritated.

Keenan laughed it off. "See, we didn't blow up. We're good." In a second he'd lit a candle I never even noticed. A glow of comfort and coziness came over the cold room, earning him my instant forgiveness.

I took off my boots, sat cross legged on the edge of the bed, and warmed my hands over the tiny flame. I had this primal need for fire. Not like I was gonna chase Bianca off with a burning branch, but still. Fire made me feel secure. And so did Keenan, even if he was nuts. The bedsprings jounced as he plopped his butt down beside mine.

I toasted him with my water bottle, gulped some, and passed it over. We sat shoulder to shoulder, chewing energy bars in famished silence. Then he dumped his big boots next to my small ones and settled in, leaning back on the wall. Without even a trace of shyness, Keenan wrapped his arms around my waist and tugged me backward until I was tucked in close to him, my back to his front. I was vaguely surprised at how easily he moved me across the bed.

I leaned against him, my hands on his thighs. Keenan pulled the blankets over us both. Delicious warmth spread through my body, but I kept my jumpsuit zipped all the way up. Part of me waited, watching to see if he'd try and take advantage, but he didn't. Good. Because something in me was strung so tight, if Keenan crossed that line, I would've shattered. I don't know what that would have involved. Crying? Screaming and ball breaking? Whatever it was, Keenan must have sensed it. He held space for me inside the circle of his arms, not saying much, just holding me. Caring enough to show up, even there, at the end of the mother fucking world.

Why? That was the question I couldn't ask.

I asked him how he got down to the planet, not why. I already knew why. We both did. But I'd never ask, and he'd never say it out loud. I knew Keenan cared about me. I mean, we were crew. Of course he cared. But I never expected devotion like that. Never deserved it. Him being there weighed heavy on me, in a way I'd never felt before. And then I realized what it was. I felt honored. Honored by his sacrifice. Because he'd given me his life.

And I guess I'd given him mine. Or I was about to.

I allowed myself a guilty indulgence, playing out the worst in my mind. Maybe I did it just so I could torture myself. Maybe I was addicted to the pain, the sweet hot rush of it, like the taste of my own blood in my mouth. *Fuck!* Okay, I wasn't normal, I freely admit it. But who was? So I gave in to my dark side and let the images flash across my mind. *Me, squaring off against Bianca. She looks like my mother. I push the button, and the EMP goes off. I don't know if I've killed her. All I see is my own face, sagging into deep lines. Blue veins pop out on the backs of my hands. My spine curls into a dowager's hump. Keenan sees me. He's stunned. I read the sorrow in his eyes, and worse, the revulsion.*

What must it feel like, to age seventy five years in under a minute? Will it hurt? I think . . . I think it has to.

Keenan leaned forward and gave me a squeeze, interrupting the dark fantasy. "Chin up, babe. Nobody's dying. We could still win this."

"How'd you know I was thinking that?"

"Feeling," Keenan corrected. "I don't know what you're thinking. But I know what you're feeling. Or I can, anyway. When I'm, y'know . . . in the mood to care."

I elbowed him. In return, he hugged me and placed a kiss on my hair. On top of my stomach, I put one hand over his, letting Keenan lace his fingers with mine. With my other hand, I stroked the lifeless surface of the EMP device.

My grief and rage froze to icy determination. *One more day.* If I could stay free one more day, I'd be at the door of the pyramid with my finger on the button. My lips split in a cold grin. I loved being the predator. It was about fucking time. And now I had Keenan on my side.

I couldn't wait.

Chapter 11

I had no idea what time it was, even if it was day or night. I lay warm and still, my head pillowed on Keenan's shoulder. The sound of his deep, calm breathing soothed me. I wrapped my arms around him and cuddled closer, tucking my face into the comfortable hollow between his neck and shoulder. Strands of Keenan's long, tawny hair veiled my face. I wanted to hide there forever, but a strange sound nagged at me. A rushing noise came from somewhere above the nightclub, like wind blowing crumbs of Styrofoam against glass. *Snow,* I told myself sleepily. *There's a blizzard on.*

No. Something wasn't right.

I sat up, listening hard. Keenan had claimed the side of the bed between me and the door. So I crawled off the foot of the mattress, tucked the blankets back in around him, and found my combat boots in the dark.

Keenan stirred when I tiptoed to the office door. "What's going on?"

"I dunno. Thought I heard something." I pressed my ear to the door. Beyond was silence.

The strange hissing noises were gone, leaving me wondering if I imagined them. I knew I'd never get back to sleep unless I reassured myself. So I crept down the darkened hall, the tips of my fingers brushing the penlight in my pocket. I'd only turn it on if I absolutely had to. On stocking feet, Keenan followed.

At the end of the hall, we cracked the swinging door an inch and peeked into the deserted bar. Keenan went first. He crossed the empty dance floor and stopped, head cocked, as the odd, rattling wind came again. Maybe from the stairwell? Trapped by my own curiosity, I let myself be drawn forward, across the dark, silent nightclub. Frost lay thick on the etched glass door. I opened it, acutely aware of each tiny sound I made, and stepped outside onto the below-ground landing. Still, freezing air enclosed me. The storm had passed, and a beautiful full moon sailed through a gap in the clouds. I climbed a few stairs, enough to bring my eyes level with the street, and peeked between the bars of the ornate, wrought iron handrail. Moonlight reflected off snow-covered rooftops, lighting them in silver and gray. Something invisible approached, making a sound like blowing sand. I froze.

A cloud of silver dust rolled along the frozen ground. The current swirled around a building across the street, sending fissures crackling across stained adobe walls. It took me a moment to grasp what I was seeing. Nanobots were scavenging steel, even pulling rebar from the foundation. Loose molecules of iron thickened the cloud until part of it sank to the ground and oozed toward the pyramid in a glittering, silver river of lava. I should have run, but my horrified fascination held me there, watching open-mouthed as nails shot from the wooden frame in little puffs of dust.

The roof collapsed with a crash and I jumped. Across the street, a mouse sprang from hiding. He ran into the open and scurried toward me, whiskers twitching. The infected didn't show fear, so that mouse had to be clean. I rooted for the little guy. He was small and scared, but surviving-- like me. Rustling like locust wings, the nanobots began to blow away. I took a breath of relief. At the top of the stairs, the brown mouse sat up on his hindquarters and rubbed a paw over his cute, furry face. We both watched as the silver cloud rounded a corner. Then a tendril of mist twisted off the cloud and whipped backward, impossibly fast. It struck the handrail like a bolt of lightning.

I threw myself backward. The cold iron let out an inhuman screech as it warped. Metal molecules boiled off into the freezing air. In less than a second, the railing turned transparent. As I lunged for the door, it came open under my hand. Keenan seized my wrist in a painful grip. He jerked me inside, slammed me into the nearest corner and pinned me there, protecting my body with his. I could barely stand on my shaking legs. Keenan's heart hammered so hard I felt it through my armored jacket. I hid my face against his chest as the rustling of the nanobot army faded away.

Our panicked gasps were the only sounds left. I still couldn't move. Keenan had me trapped, the knuckles of my right hand pinned hard against the wooden wall. His chest heaved. It took me a second to realize he was sobbing. "Don't ever do that to me, Jack. Don't ever. You could've died."

"I'm sorry. There was this weird noise, and I wanted to check it out. I think I saw nanobots," I said. His thumb still dug into the tender skin of my wrist. "Ouch. Keenan, you're hurting me." I struggled a little, expecting that would cue him to back off.

He snapped.

"Nanobots? So you went to check it out? Alone? Outside? Without waiting for me? Don't. You. Ever!" He bit the words off. In a flash, Keenan had both my hands pinned over my head. His wildcat eyes were only inches from mine, and his whole body trembled with fury.

"What the fuck is wrong with you?" I twisted, trying to escape. "Get off me!"

My right knee rose in a groin strike, but he anticipated the move. One of his hard-muscled thighs trapped my leg against the wall. I'd made a serious mistake there, pissing him off. I had no idea what he would do. Keenan had always been crazy, but never that out of control. We'd never been truly alone before, without Dakota and Joe around to rein him in.

I stopped struggling. Frightened tears welled in my eyes.

Keenan let go of my wrists and crushed me against his chest in a bear hug. He spoke into my hair. "God, Jackie. I thought you were dead! You nearly were. Look." He seized my left hand and dragged me back toward the pretty glass door. One metal hinge was missing, so it hung crooked. Frigid air leaked in.

Keenan pushed the door open with his boot, grinding the sagging glass against concrete. Outside, the wrought iron railing was gone. Holes in the pavement showed where it had been. A tiny, white mouse skeleton lay limply across the top step. Every shred of meat had been peeled from the bones. I saw it and sobbed.

"Shhh." Keenan pulled me back inside. "Don't cry. She'll hear you. She'll come."

That scared me quiet. We jammed the door closed the best we could and retreated down the hall to the manager's office. In sullen silence, I got back into bed. I was scared to shut off Justin's penlight, so Keenan lit the candle. He stretched out on his back, eyes closed. He might have been sleeping, if it weren't for the tension in his hand, gripping mine. I didn't blow out the candle. It could burn all night for all I cared. There was no reason to save it.

At some point, hours later, I woke. The fat red candle still flickered from its puddle of melted wax, lighting the room with a comforting glow. I rolled over, and Keenan's arm tightened reflexively around my waist. He wasn't gonna let me sneak off again. We spooned for a while in silence, but I couldn't get back to sleep. War filled my mind.

I stirred. "Come on. We'd better get moving."

Keenan stroked my arm soothingly. "Just another minute."

He hadn't been asleep either, I could tell. He rolled to face me, those golden eyes staring into mine, and I buried my fingers in his long, butterscotch hair. We clung to each other, soaking up comfort. I broke the spell before I did something stupid, like letting him kiss me. Not that it mattered, at that point. No one was judging us. But I was destroyed over Dakota, and I just couldn't handle it. So I sat up and pretended to be all busy, opening up my black pack.

The EMP device rolled onto the bed between us. Dread washed over me.

Keenan let out a low, impressed sound. "So this is it. The death star."

"Oh, shut up." I laughed and started to punch his arm, but my wrist went loose and my knuckles barely flicked his sleeve. Our smiles faded. After his fit of rage, I didn't dare hit him the way I used to, even in play. I knew he felt it too.

"Jack, I'm sorry," Keenan said. He didn't say for what. He didn't need to.

"I know you are." I knelt on the bed, facing him. In another life, I would've stayed pissed at him for weeks. Probably sicced the crew on him, too. But that kind of drama was a luxury neither of us could afford.

"It's okay, Keenan. We're good." My fingertips massaged the tight muscles over the tops of his shoulders.

Keenan relaxed, giving himself in to my touch. His forehead slowly dropped to my shoulder as I worked. I kissed him on the cheek and reluctantly released him. The EMP device pressed cold against my thigh.

I rolled the heavy sphere over, showing him the recessed switch on one pole. "See? That's the 'on' switch. Remember, it'll only kill Bianca if it's within ten feet of her when it goes off. And it only works once, so don't go hitting the button if you're not sure it's her."

"How can I be sure?"

"You can't be. But I'll know, when she comes after me. That's why I have to carry it. I just wanted to show you . . . uh, just in case." I didn't say it. In case what? In case I was already dead? Taken?

I closed my eyes tight, fighting back tears. Keenan's warm hand cupped my cheek. His lips brushed my forehead. And that gave me the strength to hang on.

We drank half our water and munched on more of those gummy, fake-chocolate flavored energy bars. My nervous stomach barely let me force the food down. Keenan finished his in seconds. I dropped a second bar onto his lap.

He gripped it tight. Hunger showed on his lean, hollow-cheeked face. "I'm not eating another one if you don't."

I knew what it cost him to say that.

"Don't bother saving them for tomorrow," I said.

Keenan gave me a dark look. He got the implication. Silently, he tore open the wrapper and chewed. I spent longer than I needed to loading my pack and tightening the laces of my combat boots, but I couldn't put it off much longer.

I stood, tugging the flexible, segmented strips of armor into place across my knees and elbows. "Who wants to go first? We have to travel separately, like hunters."

"Like hell we do."

"Why does everything have to be an argument with you?"

Keenan ignored me, busying himself folding our blankets into a messy wad. He tied the corners into a loop and slung the bundle over one shoulder. I thought bringing them at all was overly optimistic, but I didn't say so. Besides, it did make him look like one of Bianca's drones. They all carried makeshift packs of some kind.

Keenan stood. We took a final glance around our refuge. I pocketed the lighter and blew out the red candle, leaving it on the table beside the unused condoms. Last night the place had seemed so cheap and skanky, I shuddered when I touched the sheets. But I'd confront Bianca soon. Live or die, it would all be over. That stripped away my judgments, letting me see things in another light. The manager's bedside table, with his rolling papers and vodka—it was just a relic of someone's search for connection, for a few minutes of happiness. The girls who partied there were long dead. The manager himself was dead or taken. Maybe they found some love first. Turning away to hide my wistful expression, I led the way down the dark hall.

The fancy nightclub door didn't quite close anymore, so cold, oily air seeped in. Keenan pushed it open, grinding the sagging glass against concrete. I winced at the sound. It was early morning, still mostly dark. We hesitated, listening, before we dared to venture out onto the below-ground landing. Every whisper of wind set my nerves on edge. I pulled my black knit cap low over my ears, crawled partway up the cracked concrete steps, and peeked. Scattered fires burned, glowing orange through the fog. A lighter shade of gray marked the eastern horizon. Every streetlight was dead, every window dark. Harsh, blue-white light beamed from the top of the pyramid. It loomed over us, seemingly closer than it had been the night before. I blinked and looked again. The structure wasn't closer, it was bigger—significantly bigger. Silvery new metal sheathed its sides like armor. I swore softly. Staying low, Keenan slunk up to join me on the stairs. His tense shoulder pressed against mine.

A faint vibration came through the ground, tingling my fingers, like a sound too deep to hear. "Oh!" I hissed. "Feel that?"

Keenan placed his bare hands flat on the cold step. In a moment, he nodded. The vibration went on for another minute or so, and then abruptly ended. He shot me a warning look, as if spies were listening. "I bet that's the all-clear," he mouthed. "Bianca's bringing in the nanobots and sending out her hunters."

I nodded. It made sense, after what happened to the mouse, whose skeleton still lay on the top step. I liked Keenan's explanation better than mine, anyway. To me, the vibration felt like a swarm of nanobots rising out of the ground beneath us. I didn't share that with him.

Keenan's bare finger tapped my armored glove. "Ready?" he mouthed.

I wasn't. Never would be. I pushed myself to my feet anyway. "Can I . . . can I go first? I feel safer with you watching my back."

"No." Keenan's weird amber eyes held mine. For a second I felt hurt and confused. Then he reached out and took my hand. "We're walking in together."

"Don't be stupid," I exclaimed, too loud. I lowered my voice to an aggravated whisper. "Hunters never travel in pairs. They don't have friends."

"Well, we do," Keenan said stubbornly.

I wanted to slap him. That was so typical. He showed up to help and made trouble instead. But then he said something that crushed the argument right out of me.

"It doesn't matter. Bianca already knows we're coming."

I gulped. My eyes got huge. "I . . . I hope not."

"She has to. You think it was an accident that you survived last night? She's letting you walk right in. It's what she wants."

Keenan won that round. I swore under my breath, but didn't resist when he took my hand. Together, we stepped from the shadows.

Chapter 12

Fog swirled around us, so thick it muffled sound. The trail to the pyramid took us down the last block of intact buildings, a former business district. I kept shooting nervous glances up at the dark second story windows, imagining faces looking down at me. We passed the last shop, a clothing store, where yellowing mannequins hung like ghosts behind oily glass. After that, there was no cover at all.

Keenan was right. Bianca would see us coming.

A flock of infected pigeons left their perches on the last rooftop and whirred over, their beady red eyes on us. They dove low, swirling around and around us in a dizzy circle. Keenan strode on, head up and shoulders back. He didn't even flinch.

We hiked for three hours before the dots moving around the door of the pyramid resolved themselves into hunters--a thousand, at least. The area seethed with drones, approaching the pyramid with bulging packs and leaving with flat, empty ones. I'd never seen so many in one place, and they made my skin crawl. My instincts screamed at me to take cover, but the red earth around the pyramid had been cleared for a mile in all directions. We had to walk in the open.

Nerves tingling, Keenan and I drew close enough to see their blank, expressionless faces. Like other survivors, they were mostly male, mostly young. Infected workers wove among one another with eerie precision, never once changing rhythm or shortening their identical, drumbeat strides. Neon-blue light bathed the door of the pyramid. Every time a worker entered the tall, narrow door, the blue light brightened momentarily and then dimmed again.

I gripped Keenan's hand tighter, wishing he'd stop. I just needed a second to breathe, to steel myself. Jaw clenched, he kept on striding toward the pyramid. Keenan never looked at me, never took his eyes from the infected. With single-minded focus on their work, the drones ignored us. We closed in, a hundred feet away, then fifty. Harsh neon light from the top of the pyramid glared down on us all.

"Stop. Please stop." Resisting the pull of his strong arm, I tugged Keenan to a halt. "Listen, I have to go on alone from here. Wait for me at the nightclub? I'll come back if I can."

Keenan shook his head. A grim smile twitched the corners of his mouth. "I didn't come all the way down here to wait at the bar."

My stomach roiled. I clutched his brown canvas jacket, like that could make him see reason. "Keenan, don't, there's no point. You'll just get taken. It's suicide."

Keenan clasped both my hands at once, pressing them gently against his chest. He licked his lips and paused, struggling to get the words out. "Yeah . . . maybe. Probably. But . . . going back without you? That would be worse. I can't do it, Jackie. I just can't."

"Oh God." I imagined him curled up alone on the floor of the office. Anxious. Scared. Desperately lonely. So this was Keenan's Plan B. To follow me into hell, because the alternative was worse.

He gazed pleadingly into my face. Suddenly he looked so young.

"Okay. We'll stay together as long as we can, then," I whispered. Tears welled. I didn't try to hide them. "Uh, Keenan? Thank you. Thank you for coming after me." It felt so lame, saying that. So trite. He deserved better. He deserved for me not to lead him to his death, but since he'd followed me, there wasn't much I could do about that.

I put my hands on his shoulders, stood on tiptoe, and kissed him on the cheek. Before I had a chance to pull away, Keenan seized the back of my head and pressed his lips hard against mine. His eyes were lit with emotion. He didn't say it. He probably knew I couldn't take it if he did, and he was right. That part of my heart still belonged to Dakota. A tear spilled from my eye and rolled down my cheek. Keenan wiped it away. I realized that my arms were still twined around his neck. I didn't want to let go. He was all I had left.

Movement in my peripheral vision stopped. I glanced sideways. My spine went stiff, and I forgot to breathe. Thousands of hunters were looking at me. Not at Keenan. At me.

With a sound like blowing sand, shimmering silver particles flowed down the sides of the pyramid, wave after wave of them, breaking into kaleidoscopic patterns as they reached its wide, square base. I stared, horrified. What I thought was an imperial display of wealth, like the gold dome on the state capitol, was actually a layer of naked nanobots. The constantly shifting patterns made me nauseous. I tried to look away and got drawn back in. The nanobots gradually stilled until untold trillions of them pulsated in a thick band along the base of the pyramid.

Unconsciously, I began to breathe in time with their beat. When I noticed, I exhaled hard, breaking the rhythm. A small, terrified whimper escaped on the air.

Keenan's hand tightened on my waist. "Come on. Let's get this over with." Together, we marched toward the pyramid.

I squared my shoulders, trying to look brave. Every muscle in my body wanted to run. It took all my control to keep walking, head held high, like a chief. The infected stepped aside for us, creating a corridor to the door. More ragged men converged on the area until they lined the path a hundred deep. There'd be no getting away. The drones had awakened. Their blank stares had become the intense, predatory gazes of hunters. Fragments of Bianca's synthetic soul watched me through their eyes. As I passed, each one tensed and leaned forward, inhaling. I shrank away, quivering in revulsion. Our path narrowed until we were barely out of reach of their silver-tipped fingernails. Keenan wrapped his arm around me, supporting me as we walked. His strength kept me going. We reached the door and stopped. I craned my neck to look up. What abomination had Bianca created, to need a portal like that?

A vertical slit had been cut in the pyramid wall, fifty feet tall but barely wide enough for a man's shoulders. A deep, mechanical hum came from inside, thrumming in time with the pulsating nanobots. Blue light flashed from inside the open portal into the pyramid. The agitated shifting of the hunters stopped. Frozen, they watched the door, holding their synchronized breath in anticipation. I shifted my backpack and loosened the top strap, so my hand fit inside. Then I stood still, my finger inches from the button. No one moved.

A blue light flashed, and one of the infected stepped outside, a muscular drone in close-fitting black pants and no shirt. He wasn't exactly human anymore. His wooly hair and broad, handsome features belonged with dark skin, but Bianca had changed him to a silvery shade of gray. Toenails and eyes were bleached to match. Granular snow pelted off his bare feet, but he showed no sign that he felt the cold.

The drone's bleached, expressionless eyes turned toward me with something like recognition. Maybe it was a trick of the light, but as he came toward me, I thought I saw a faint pattern of miniscule, black tringles appear and disappear on his skin.

"Jacqueline, primary host. Welcome to America," he said in a deep monotone.

What's he talking about? We're already in America. Or what's left of it, anyway. Then I realized what he meant. Global America. We had arrived.

My heart hammered as I delivered the line I'd rehearsed in my head for the last two miles. "I'm here to see Bianca."

"You are seeing Bianca." The drone waved a silver-gray hand to include the pyramid, the mass of waiting hunters, even the destroyed city beyond. He stood still, watching me attentively. Waiting.

I didn't know what to do.

"I need to see Bianca *herself*," I emphasized. "The, um, information I'm carrying can only be delivered to her."

"We are herself. Share your information," the drone said evenly. "We are Bianca."

My face got hot, and I wanted to slap him. "No, you're not, and neither am I!"

Keenan squeezed my shoulder in warning. "Be careful," he hissed.

The drone never changed expression, but on the walls of the pyramid, nanobots shifted in agitated motion. Their symmetrical, kaleidoscopic patterns broke into sharp, angular shards that either reflected light or created it. I couldn't tell. Either way, I had a hunch that Bianca was irritated. Fine. She's be really pissed when I blew her to hell.

I took a deep breath and tried again, using her words. "Tell Bianca I saw her message on television. I'm here about Global America. About freedom and democracy. I'm here to help rebuild our world."

Those catchphrases seemed to have an effect. The gray drone stared into space, as if listening to something I couldn't hear. Then he stepped aside and motioned me toward the door. "Bianca sees you now."

"Of course she does."

Keenan and I glanced at each other, checking, and exchanged tiny nods. A shiver of anticipation went through my body. We were going in. He silently came up beside me and took my hand. As we followed the drone toward the blue-lit door, I silently rejoiced. *Nobody asked to look in my pack. This could work.*

The silver-gray man fixed his strange, bleached eyes on me. "Step into the light."

The ice-cold way he said it made me want to run. Instead, I gave Keenan's hand a squeeze and released it. Goosebumps rose on my arms as I stepped into the patch of light beaming down from above that tall, narrow slit of a door. For a second, the diffuse, neon-blue light flared brighter. A thousand hunters let out a collective sigh. Startled, I looked over my shoulder. The mob of ragged infected still watched me, but their stances had relaxed, as though I'd passed some test.

Then my eyes met Keenan's. He gazed at me, full of wonder. "Jackie, you look like an angel."

"What?" I looked down.

On my arm, a thin slit of luminous gold skin glowed between my sleeve and glove. I was emitting light. Or the nanites in my skin were. I pulled back my sleeve and gasped. My whole body tingled with energy. When I touched fingertips to my bare face, the glow didn't rub off on my gloves. A surge of courage rose inside me. Bianca had enslaved humanity, but I wasn't quite human anymore. Maybe that's what it took to beat her. I beckoned Keenan forward, into the light.

He took a deep breath. His face wore the rigid, controlled expression of a condemned man determined to die with dignity. That hurt to watch. He should never have followed me. At least he could have waited at the bar. Too late for regrets. I held out a hand to him, and Keenan took it. He stepped into the light, stopped, and closed his eyes like he fully expected it to strike him down.

Nothing happened.

Keenan looked the same, only kind of sick, with rapidly fading blue light reflecting off his pale skin. With a deep, electrical thrum, a sudden strobe of glaring white flashed from above and just as quickly ended. That message was clear enough. My nanites were apparently close enough to pox nanobots, so I was accepted. Keenan was not. Gathered hunters tensed, leaning forward, their hungry eyes fixed on him. Some silent signal from Bianca held them back. She was playing with us.

The muscular guard drone stepped between us, jerking Keenan's hand from mine. "Jacqueline, primary host. Enter."

My stomach clenched as I realized that Bianca intended to let me in and leave Keenan outside, alone with a thousand hunters. He'd be taken.

The gray man reached for me.

I jumped back. "No. We're staying together," I cried, brushing his muscular arm aside as I dodged. Something stung the bare skin of my wrist.

Keenan and I skittered backward about ten feet and stopped, trapped between the pyramid and the mob of infected. The radiant light from my skin died out, leaving me weak and shaky, a mere human again. Hunters shifted fretfully, their worn shoes churning the frozen red clay to slush underfoot. Their sour-milk breath washed over us, tainting the fog itself.

The guard-drone strode after us, straight-armed Keenan away and grabbed me by the neck. He lifted me clear off my feet, crushing my face against his iron torso.

"Let me go." Palms on his chest, I arched my back, fought the pull of those thick arms, and lost. He pulled me in.

My cheek scraped the bare, silver skin over his collar bone, and a wave of prickling pain scorched me from cheekbone to chin. I yelped in shock and surprise. My lacerated face ached and burned and bled. Warm, red rivulets ran down my cheek to spatter the guard's wide, silver shoulder, outlining millions of tiny, dark-edged triangles that lay flush with his skin. Running them backward made the razor-sharp teeth rise up and cut me. I screamed.

"Jackie!" Keenan threw his full weight on the drone's arm.

The gray man elbowed him aside and kept on walking, carrying me toward the door of the pyramid. Panic took me. I twisted in the infected man's grip, kicking and biting. His armored skin tore my lips until bloody shreds of my own flesh caught between my teeth, but I wouldn't quit, or couldn't. All my carefully rehearsed lines flew from my mind. Giving in to my terror, I pummeled the drone's rough skin with my fists until my gloves shredded. Red-hot pain seared my nerves as I grated my knuckles on his hide, healed, and tore the delicate new skin open again. Some distant part of my mind heard my own voice, screaming Keenan's name.

Keenan attacked, pounding the drone's face with fists and elbows. Blood streamed from his torn knuckles, staining the gray man red. We pried at the drone's immovable silver fingers, dug deep into the tough black fabric of my jumpsuit. The gray man showed no sign of pain as he dragged our tangled bodies toward the pyramid. Nanobots surged up and down its triangular walls in turbulent, iridescent waves, making a rushing noise. Bianca was clearly furious. I couldn't understand why she hadn't set her hunters on us yet.

Fighting and thrashing, the three of us reached the doorway. Bright spots splotched my vision as blinding white strobe light alternated spastically with flashes of neon-blue. The two kinds of light warred with one another, setting off high, nerve-wracking static that came from the walls of the pyramid itself, almost drowning out my frantic shouts. Suddenly Keenan lunged for my face and pressed his torn hands against my bleeding cheeks. With a nauseated expression, he brought his bloody hands to his lips.

Everything went still.

The guard drone abruptly released us. He stood frozen, not even bothering to wipe our blood from his toothed skin. The mind-numbing static from the walls mercifully stopped as the last, faint flickers of white strobe light died. Every last hunter stood motionless. The only noise was the wind.

For a surreal moment, my focus shrank until I saw only Keenan, cut and bruised, his long, tangled hair blowing around his face like a lion's mane. He reached out as tenderly as a lover and cupped my glowing, silver cheek. Lip twisted in disgust, he raised his fingers to his mouth and licked off the last drops of my nanite-infested blood.

He'd just infected himself for me. That could never be undone.

I wanted to cry. Nanobots, nanites, Keenan loathed them all. They'd killed his family, murdered members of our crew. He hated them like I hated spiders, so even thinking about touching them made his skin crawl. I thought it was a big deal when, before the battle at the array, he let Doctor Graham treat him with a temporary form of healing nanites, the kind that did their job and then died out. This time the change was permanent.

When I triggered the EMP, Keenan would age, the same as me. In a matter of moments he'd become an old man. He would die.

He eyed my black pack, and I knew that thought had hit him too. I rolled a shoulder under the weight of the device. Nobody had taken my bag, or even checked inside, which seemed unlikely. Were drones really that stupid? Could I be that lucky? I wondered if Bianca knew something I didn't. Maybe the EMP wasn't going to work, so it didn't matter if I hauled it inside or not.

Keenan wiped his mouth with the back of a hand. His lips parted, and a golden light glowed from between them, slowly spreading as the nanite infection spread. Neon blue light enveloped us both. The gathered hunters let out a soft, synchronized sigh, enveloping us in their putrid breath.

"Welcome to America. One mind. One planet. One nation," the guard-drone said. He extended a silver hand, pointing us inside the pyramid.

Gripping the straps of my backpack tight in my fists, I stepped through the door into darkness.

Chapter 13

The gray man herded us into a dim, narrow passageway. Inside, the air was stifling. Suffocating humidity caught in my throat and drenched my tongue with the sour-milk scent of hunters. Fear crackled along my skin, so every little sound made me twitch. I cast a last, desperate glance over my shoulder. The drone's wide, naked chest blocked our escape. I hesitated, half blind in the sudden darkness, but the gray man put a hand on my back and pushed me forward. I shuddered at his touch.

Keenan paced silently beside me. Only his rapid breathing betrayed his terror. Swirls of milky light, too dim to see by, flowed across the high ceiling and trickled down the pale, damp walls.

Joe was right. What was I thinking, coming here? Sacrificing Keenan?

Only the weight of the EMP device on my back kept me moving. I clung to the hope that it would work, whatever the consequences.

Without meaning to, all three of us fell into step, our unified strides thudding on the bone-white floor. I hadn't noticed it before, but a faint, electronic beat pulsed from the building itself. I stutter-stepped, deliberately breaking the rhythm, and my toe caught on some unseen ridge. My right shoulder bumped the wall. The warm, cushioned surface gave a little under the pressure, and it smelled like old sweat.

"Ugh." I recoiled, making a disgusted noise.

"Easy," Keenan whispered. He slid an arm around my waist, pulling me close as we walked. I wished he couldn't feel me trembling.

Maybe twenty feet in, the passageway widened to a strange dome-roofed atrium with four arched doorways supported by bony, asymmetrical frames. Their gnarled shapes reminded me of old roots growing up out of the ground. Pleats of the same soft, pale material that covered the walls gathered over the archways like curtains. As my eyes adjusted, I spotted smaller, matching gaps set low on the walls, and taller, irregular ones gaping darkly from the corners. Warm, moist air sighed through those cavities, fluttering thready filaments that hung from the walls and ceiling.

Gripping my shoulder, the drone steered me toward the door in the middle. I shrugged his hand off my black jacket, and the rough hide broke contact with a sound like tearing Velcro. He didn't grab hold of me again, which surprised me a little. Our path angled uphill as it passed through a narrow, oblong arch, only wide enough for one person at a time. The gray man raised an open hand, signaling Keenan to wait. I had to go first. Steeling my nerves, I took two steps up into the raised archway, my thick-soled boots rocking a little on the ridged, ivory floor.

I stopped at the top and reflexively gripped the door frame. The air that swirled up from below smelled like a sweaty locker room. Goosebumps tingled down my arms, and a few tiny hairs on the back of my neck stood up. Dread grew inside me. Bianca was down there, somewhere, watching us. My gaze swept from side to side, but the only movement was the fluttering of those weird threads on the walls. Behind the leathery wallpaper, slender, flexible rods framed the portal like the bones in a bat wing. Along the sides, a few long ribs had torn free, forming freestanding arches. I rubbed one between my fingers and found it covered with the same thin, beige skin. I let go with a shudder, scrubbing my torn glove on a thigh.

The tall drone reached up and prodded me, sending a nasty shiver down my spine. I reluctantly led the way down the bony, porous ramp, followed by Keenan, with the infected man on his heels. Over my shoulder, I caught a flash of Keenan's face. He moved like an invading conqueror, shoulders square and eyebrows drawn together in a belligerent scowl. Somehow that helped. About thirty feet down the passage, I passed another twisted portal on the right. That one had been closed off by more of the pale, leathery wall covering, as if skin had grown across it, tight as a drum, so not even air could escape. The sight gave me a suffocating feeling, and I forced my gaze away. The gray man jerked me to a stop.

I waited in the warm, humid passageway, shoulders hunched and arms folded protectively across my body. The drone drew his silver thumbnail vertically down the drum-tight covering of the door, slicing it. My eyes went wide. When he pulled back the curtain, dark blood welled from the cut edge. I recoiled with a strangled gasp.

The walls were alive.

I turned with a snap and took a fast step toward Keenan. "Get out of here. Run," I hissed. "The whole building is--"

The gray man slammed a hand down on the back of my neck, bending me over. I struggled, making choking sounds. He tore the backpack from my body and shoved me away so hard I staggered.

"No!" I whirled, making a wild grab for it. His open palm struck my chest, knocking me backward and smashing my head into the firm, fleshy wall. I bit my tongue on impact, and the sting brought tears to my eyes.

Keenan hung on the drone's arm, flailing at the pack, poking the stiff canvas. Trying to set off the EMP.

"Keenan, no, not yet," I cried. "It won't work, Bianca's too far away." He didn't listen.

The drone bitch-slapped Keenan, knocking him to his back on the hard, ivory floor. Keenan rolled to his feet, blood pouring from his flattened nose, and I lunged for my black pack. At the last second, the drone turned a shoulder to block me, and every fingernail on my right hand broke to the quick on his diamond skin. Pain flared up my hand like fire. I didn't care. The tall drone held my pack high, out of reach. Then, with a powerful flick of his arm, he threw it into one of those low, arched holes along the wall. With a wet, squelching sound, pale, leathery skin spread over the gap.

The device was gone.

I swore. Tears of fury blurred my vision. I'd done all this for nothing. Sacrificed Keenan's life, for nothing! With a strangled cry, I swung a fist at the drone's indestructible face. He caught my arm and yanked, hurling me past the bleeding curtain of skin and into the pitch-black space beyond. I fell face down on a warm, cushioned surface. Where I hit, splashes of white light erupted from underneath the soft, leathery floor. Keenan landed beside me with a grunt, setting off another sparkling light show.

Silver streams of nanobots began to flow through the walls, gradually brightening the small, oval room. Under my torn gloves, tiny hairs on the floor tickled my palms. Human hairs. The entire floor was covered in living, human skin. I sprang to my feet, shuddering, and turned in time to see the hide curtain grow back over the portal, sealing us in. I slapped for Viktor's knife, still tucked into a hidden pocket on my black pants. I could cut us free. But then what? Thousands of infected waited outside, and they weren't about to let us walk away.

I labored toward the door, my combat boots sinking eight inches deep in the squishy, light-flecked floor with every step. The gray man's elongated shadow showed through the thin, stretched skin.

"Wait! Don't leave us. I need to see Bianca." I didn't even know why I said that. Without the EMP device, I couldn't stop her.

A muffled monotone came through the leather curtain. "You are seeing Bianca." The shadow turned and walked away.

Keenan stood in the middle of the oval room, wiping his bloody, beaten face on a sleeve. Then his brand-new nanites kicked in and he bent over, fists clenched, hissing in pain. His broken nose made slight crunching sounds as the bones set. I knew how much that hurt—way worse than the original injury, every time.

"Hang on. You're healing. It'll be over in a minute." I took a few steps in his direction, hooked my toe on a fat roll of flesh and stumbled.

Groaning, I pivoted in place, my arms wrapped tight across my body.

Beneath us, shining globules of nanobots rose like bubbles through water, allowing us to see deep into the warm, living tissue we stood on. Then I understood.

"Oh my God. We are seeing Bianca. The whole pyramid is alive. She grew herself a body, and we're . . . inside."

"Don't touch it," Keenan snapped. Still grimacing in pain, he whipped the bundled blankets off his back and spread them out on the floor.

I stepped gratefully onto the bed he'd made and sank to my knees, trembling. Not that I believed for a second that blankets could stop nanobots, but at least they kept those gross little hairs from touching me. Exhaustion battled my anxiety and won. I pulled off my black knit cap and stretched out on my stomach, carefully keeping my hand from slipping off the edge of the blanket. A patch of exposed skin between my sleeve and glove caught my eye. I sucked in a shallow breath through clenched teeth.

Keenan tensed, golden eyebrows raised. "What?"

I sat up cross-legged and took off my gloves, comparing my own winter-pale skin to the living floor of our prison. "Look. They . . . they match. Exactly."

I had a hunch what that meant, but my mind couldn't face it. Wouldn't face it.

"Don't look. Don't even think about it," Keenan whispered, stroking my short, tousled hair. "Just look at me. Pretend with me, okay? Pretend it's just us here. Just you and me, and everything's peaceful. Breathe with me." He inhaled, long and slow.

I tried to copy him, and my chest shuddered as if I'd been crying.

"It's okay, babe, it's okay," Keenan murmured, pulling me close.

Of course it wasn't okay, not at all, but I played along. It was the least I could do for him. I rarely saw Keenan's gentle side. His idea of emotional support usually had more to do with back slaps than hugs. I slid my arms around his waist, turned my head, and rested my cheek on his shoulder.

All around us, streams of quicksilver rose from the depths, swirled around our blanket, and flowed away across the curved walls of our prison in endlessly branching rivers of light.

Keenan caught me watching them. Ever so gently, he turned my face toward his. "Don't look at the 'bots, Jackie. Look at me. Breathe with me." He ran the fingers of both hands softly through my hair.

With an effort, I lifted my gaze and locked my hazel eyes on Keenan's golden ones, pretending with all my might that we were alone, somewhere safe. His handsome face was calm, the broken nose re-centered, straight and perfect again. Only the blood on his shirt remained as a relic of the fight. I took a deep breath with him, then another. Comforting warmth radiated through the blankets. My heart rate slowed, and the rigid muscles in my back relaxed.

My shoulders slumped. "I'm so sorry. I never meant to involve you."

"I know. That's why you left without saying goodbye." The ghost of a smile touched Keenan's lips. "Listen, Jack. Leaving the station was my choice. I wouldn't change it if I could. I can't imagine how you'd feel if you were in here alone."

I couldn't imagine either. "I . . . don't deserve this," I mumbled.

"Why? Because you're in love with another guy?" Keenan asked bluntly. "It's okay. I know you still love Dakota, even though he's dead."

"Yeah." I could barely answer over the tightness in my throat. "It's true . . . I do still love him." I looked down, and tears filled my eyes.

"I know what people think. That when he died, I got exactly what I wanted." Keenan practically spat the words. "But I lost him too, Jackie. Dakota was my brother. He forgave me for things nobody else would've. Yeah, I wanted you. Still do. More than anything. But that doesn't mean I'm not grieving him right along with you."

Some wall inside my heart broke, and the tears let go. I hugged Keenan, crying, my fingers buried in his long blond hair. He laid down on his back, pulled me down on top of him, and held me while I sobbed. My tears gradually dried and my head sank to his shoulder. Totally spent, I went limp, my slender body rising and falling as he breathed.

After a few minutes he stirred. Keenan stretched under me, his muscles growing taut with arousal. I felt him get hard through my tight, black pants, and tingles of pleasure warmed my lower belly. His musky scent filled my nostrils and set my heart racing. A sweet ache filled my nipples, and my pulse pounded between my legs. I couldn't help making a soft sound of pleasure, and that only encouraged him. Keenan's hands slid down my back and grabbed my ass, grinding me against him. I didn't even want to resist. The part of my mind that could still think straight wasn't happy about that. My traitorous body had instantly responded, without waiting to see if my brain thought it was a good idea or not.

I couldn't deny my attachment to Keenan. After what he'd done for me, coming back, he was the most deserving guy on the planet. So why did being close to him feel like cheating? It didn't make sense. I needed time to work it out, time for my heart to heal. But we were out of time. Bianca wasn't going to leave us alone forever. Taking a long breath, I leaned my forehead on Keenan's shoulder and hid my eyes.

I was a mess.

"It's all right, babe," Keenan whispered, wrapping his arms around my waist.

No, it wasn't. I wasn't. So I arched my back, pushed myself up on my elbows, and looked into his eyes, trying to figure out exactly how to explain that. The bulge in his jeans pressed deliciously against me as Keenan gripped my hipbones and squeezed. He let go with an apologetic look.

With an obvious effort, he got control of himself. "I'm sorry, Jackie."

My lips quirked in a little smile. That boy was so damned earnest, even half out of his mind with desire. "You don't have to apologize."

"I just don't want you to think . . . I don't know, that I'd . . . force myself on you. I've seen enough guys try, and I don't ever want you to think of me like that. I just can't help it, you're so beautiful."

I leaned forward and placed a quick, soft kiss on his lips. "It's all right, love. Don't worry, I know I'm safe with you," I whispered. My jaw stiffened. I hadn't meant to call him that. That had been for Dakota, only whispered in private. A new wave of tears stung my eyes.

Keenan instantly noticed. He slowly rolled me off him and tucked me against his side, my head pillowed on his arm. Eyes closed, he took a deep breath and restrained himself, though his body trembled with suppressed need. Gratitude filled me. He'd given me his life and demanded nothing in return. I impulsively slid an arm around his neck and tilted my head, gazing up at him with wide, soft eyes. He cracked an eye to glance down at my face, and that was all it took.

Keenan rolled on top of me and kissed me hard, almost desperately, his hands sliding down my body. I clung to the hard muscles of his shoulders, my lips parting under his probing tongue. Emotions roiled inside me. Had I lost my mind? Did it even matter?

Afterward, Keenan looked into my eyes. "I love you, Jackie."

That simple admission, the raw honesty of it, moved me. I didn't know what to say. I couldn't answer him. Couldn't say I loved him, or even admit I cared. That felt like a betrayal, even if Dakota was dead. So I said nothing, just held him close, gazing over his shoulder as radiant fountains of nanobots burst over the ceiling and cascaded down the living walls of our prison. Sprays shot higher, bouncing off one another, their orderly streams dissolving into a growing flood that splashed our prison with moving blobs of light.

The chaos was out of place. Bianca's actions were always structured, always logical, even during her rages. Keenan fidgeted, turning his head to track random splotches of light. I could tell he shared my nagging anxiety.

The heavy, synchronized footfalls of drones marched past the leather curtain of our prison cell. Their rhythm picked up, moving faster, and then fell apart completely as some of them began to run. Shouts echoed down the passageway.

I sat up with a snap, my back rigid, one hand raised to shield my eyes from the blazing white walls.

Keenan crouched opposite me, his hollow-cheeked face pale in the moving light. "What's going on? Infected don't run. Not unless they're hunting."

"Right." I twitched my chin in a terse nod. "And they never yell."

Keenan stood and pulled me to my feet by the hand, his eyes lit with hope. "Something's wrong here. Maybe this means we have a chance." He glanced at the surging nanobots and abruptly silenced himself. Bianca could be listening.

I moved over the disgusting gushy floor toward the door, picturing myself cutting its leathery skin. Escaping into the corridor. Worming my way down that dark, slimy hole after the EMP device. Would I even fit? Was the thing even still there, or had it already been shit into whatever vile depths lay under the pyramid?

I stopped within arm's reach of the door. Every few seconds, a burst of nanobots shot across the tight-stretched hide, making a faint, high-pitched electronic whine. Moving shadows of drones flickered past in both directions. Reaching down, I split open the Velcro top of the long, narrow pocket on my thigh. The cold metal of Viktor's knife touched my fingertips, tempting me. I had no plan, no idea what to do once we got loose. But anything was better than waiting to be infected. For a moment, the corridor went quiet. That was my chance. I looked over my shoulder, checking with Keenan.

"Hurry up. Do it." He slashed the air with one hand.

"Now, while people are running around crazy out there?"

Keenan shifted a shoulder in a tense shrug. "That. Or go sit back down."

I flipped open the blade, licking my lips nervously. If I wasn't careful, poxy blood would get all over me. I clenched my jaw and reached high to start the cut, trying to ignore the pounding footfalls right outside. Maybe, in the chaos, we could escape. I took a deep breath and stabbed the door, cringing when the living fabric convulsed under my hand.

"Oh my God. The walls feel pain." Blood streamed from the wound I'd made. I bit my lip and forced myself to continue, drawing the blade down with both hands.

Suddenly a human body hit the door from the other side. I flinched and dropped my knife as the outline of a man's shoulder pressed into the elastic hide for a second and then disappeared. A thud came from the corridor as something big hit the floor.

With a dull tearing sound, the leathery skin over the door separated. The gray man stood there, eyeing us grimly. Behind him lay the twisted body of another drone, clearly dead.

"What the fuck?" Keenan breathed from behind me.

"Bianca will speak to you now," the drone said.

I opened my mouth to say no. Not a good time. Definitely not. Fast as a striking snake, the infected man snatched my wrist and dragged me through the portal. The second he took his hand off it, the hide door sealed, locking Keenan in.

His muffled cry came from behind the curtain. "Jackie!"

I twisted in the drone's iron grip, expecting to see Keenan tear free and come after us. He tried. The blade of Viktor's knife stabbed through the drum-tight skin, ripping downward. The skin instantly healed behind it. Keenan plunged in the dagger again and again. All he made was a small, bloody hole, no wider than the blade, and even that sealed every time he pulled out the knife.

Keenan's anguished shouts followed us as the gray man marched me away. "Wait! Take me with you."

Chapter 14

I dragged my heels, resisting the gray man's inhumanly powerful arm, and only managed to scrape my wrist bloody on his toothed palm. I swore, and tears of fury filled my eyes. Physical pain hardly upset me anymore. Regret burned me up inside. The war was lost. Any minute I'd become Bianca's host. Why hadn't I spared a little love for Keenan? I could have filled his last hours with bliss. Given him the only thing he ever wanted—me. Not just my body, but my heart and soul too. And I refused him. I was all caught up in my own pain, holding on to Dakota and all the other people I'd lost. Keenan lost family and friends, just like I did. He gave up everything for me, and he had no regrets. None.

Too late. Too late now.

The drone marched me down the ivory-floored corridor, past the spot where he'd dumped the EMP device. I was certain of it. But there wasn't even a hole there anymore. The living wall had healed completely. I hadn't realized I'd even been hoping until that last shred of hope died.

The gray man crowded me, dogging my heels up the bone ramp, through the narrow, bat-wing archway and down the other side into the circular atrium, where five identical, arched portals led off in different directions. He backed me up to a hairy wall, so close I almost had to touch it, and dropped my arm. I stood still, holding my breath.

The drone leaned in and locked his burnished gray gaze on my face without exactly making eye contact. "Jacqueline, primary host. Peace through cooperation."

That startled me.

"Fine," I snapped, rubbing the itchy new skin on my wrist. "Want peace? Why don't you start by giving me back the backpack you stole?"

He didn't respond. I couldn't tell if he'd really been trying to communicate. Maybe not. He might just be a mouthpiece for Bianca's propaganda, with no more self-awareness than the television in the bar. I half expected him to start spouting off lines about Global America.

The drone took a step back, and I could breathe again. He pointed me toward one of the arched portals. I thought the door just to the left of it might be the way out, but all five of them kinda looked alike. Going up the bony ramp, my thighs quivered. Apprehension twisted my guts into a knot.

Every step took me closer to slavery. Once Bianca took me over, I'd be a prisoner in my own mind, watching helplessly as she used my nanites to solidify her control of life on earth. I didn't want to die, but under the circumstances, wasn't that the right choice? Furtively patting down my pockets, I found no real weapons, only the lighter I took from the bar. With nanites in my blood, suicide by fire would be damn near impossible, even if I had the guts to try. Truth was, I probably didn't.

My captor shoved me forward.

The bone ramp dropped down into a wide, bright passageway with rooms on both sides. Stretched skin sealed off some of the portals. I caught unsettling glimpses through others as we walked. The first room on the left looked like a science lab, with bubbling vats attended by white-clad women. I couldn't see what was inside the giant tanks, but the steam rising out of them carried enough ammonia to make my eyes water. The drone kept me moving, prodding my back with a stiff finger when I slowed to stare. Fifty feet farther down, on the right, we passed a wide, open archway that led into a huge chamber, as big as a basketball court. Skeletal, shirtless workers crowded the level floor, lying on rows of steel tables while milky liquid flowed into their navels through clear plastic tubes. I shuddered. So that was how Bianca fed her drones.

I stopped dead when the closest one suddenly sat up. The young Latino searched the room with wide, frightened eyes, his calloused fingers sliding along the length of his feeding tube. "Gabriela? Gabriela?"

Whoever he was looking for didn't answer.

With a strangled cry, the slave wrenched the feeding tube from his stomach and threw it. Thick, white liquid splashed the sleeping man next to him and kept on pumping from the tube, pouring over the bone floor. The rotten-meat scent of it filled the air, making my stomach churn. Even the gray drone curled a lip in disgust, the first emotional reaction I'd ever seen from him.

The slave rolled off the feeding table and limped toward us, pushing a hank of straight, black hair from his eyes with the back of a hand. Dilute pink blood leaked from the circular, uncapped port where his navel used to be. Behind him, more ragged figures writhed on steel tables. On the far side of the room, a second man sat up. His cries brought attendants in stained white lab coats rushing to his side. Instead of helping, ghoulish nurses pushed the man back down, pinning him while he screamed. Fists clenched, I backed away until I bumped the gray drone, standing impassively behind me.

The young slave reached us, hands outstretched and dark eyes pleading. "Help me. Please help me."

"What's happening?" I blurted. My voice came out girlish and shrill.

"How'd you get--"

The gray drone clapped a rough-skinned hand over my mouth and dragged me backward, clearing a path through the door. The escaped worker bolted past us, took a left, and ran, followed by half a dozen others. My captor switched his grip to my arm and quick-marched me down the hall in the other direction. I sucked in a breath of air, rubbing his fishy stench from my lips with my free hand.

"What was that all about?" I whispered, eagerly falling into step beside him. "Were you helping them escape? Will you help me too?"

He refused to answer. I ground my teeth, trying not to scream.

The drone pushed me up a curving ivory staircase at the end of the hall. Behind us, inside the feeding room, people shouted. Something metallic crashed to the floor. More workers were coming to their senses. I felt my first glimmer of hope. Part of me wanted to run off and join the rebellion, but freed slaves were way outnumbered. If I tried, would I be taken? I'd surely be infected if I didn't. I decided to go for it, and soon, before Bianca showed up in person. The long delay gave me the impression that she wanted to take me herself. I didn't see why. If a hunter got me, wouldn't it all be the same in the end? As if he'd read my mind, the drone's hand clamped down harder on my arm. I fumed.

At the top of the stairs, he released me into a silent oval room, about thirty feet across. Fat, round computer screens lined the walls. We'd reached the command center, and it was deserted. That couldn't be right. Had Bianca gone to deal with the emergency? The drone guarded the door, blocking my escape, so I slowly walked the perimeter, past dozens of thick, wall-mounted monitors. They played silent videos, like the pyramid from above, drones scavenging, and low, close-up views of ruins. The sky view caught my attention because the camera swept from side to side, zooming in on whatever moved, and then taking the wide view again. I stepped closer to the weird, circular screen. It took me a second to realize I must be looking through the eyes of an infected raptor, sailing the smoky skies above.

The bird's-eye camera arced lower, circling the pyramid. Drones milled around outside, and more streamed out the tall, narrow door, setting off flashes of white strobe light so bright they made me squint. When a cluster of escaped slaves took off, I clenched a fist and silently cheered. Fleet hunters ran down most of them, tackling them in eerie silence. Gaunt men wrestled on the slushy ground, pounding each other with fists. My imagination filled in the vile, sour-milk stench of the hunters, the anguished howls of recaptured slaves. A few runners made it across the cleared area around the pyramid. A nearby screen showed a rat's-eye view of someone's worn boot, stumbling over cracked concrete. Bianca was tracking the escapees. I edged closer to the monitor. Then the damned thing blinked.

I gave a short shriek and jumped back as a naked, lashless eyelid dropped down from the top of the monitor and rose again, coating the screen with a sheen of oily liquid. Groaning in revulsion, I turned away. The screens were alive. I should have known.

I itched to break Keenan loose and get the hell out of there. Screams of the rioters downstairs held me rooted to the spot, trembling with indecision. I was alone, with only one guard at the door. Should I try to escape? Even if I somehow got past him, could I make it back to Keenan's jail cell without getting infected? Even now, Bianca was battling to regain control.

One at a time, the living computer monitors went dark. Wild optimism bloomed inside me. Then the eyeball-screens lit again, this time as actual eyes, each a foot or two across. I shuddered as a horrid chill went down my spine. The screen closest to me had become the russet, black-rimmed eye of a hawk. Beside it, on another screen, the vertical-slit pupil of a lizard spun in a circle, surrounded by tiny green scales. Other eyes were human, with dark, curved lashes fringing disturbingly familiar shades of blue and brown. The sad, dark eye across the room had to be from a dog. Had Bianca cut them from her victims, or duplicated the eyes of living, infected animals? Somehow she grew them to monstrous proportions. I could have puked. I had no idea shit like that was even possible.

Enormous, wet eyeballs flicked from side to side, scanning the room. One at a time, they spotted me. Locked onto me. I froze, my back rigid.

"Bianca sees you now," the gray drone said from his post at the door.

"Obviously," I snapped.

Maybe my mind unhinged a little. Maybe it cracked, and decided nothing I was seeing could possibly be real. Consequences felt far away. Only the soft, brown dog eye seemed genuine. It watched me—no, he watched me, as if he knew I was different. The gaze of that poor, disembodied dog weighed on me with palpable pressure, heavy and expectant, like any second I'd spring open the door of the pyramid and let him run out onto green grass. I had no way to explain that I didn't have the power. That even if I did, he didn't have a body to run in anymore.

And Bianca calls the infected her children. It makes me sick. She doesn't love them. I do.

Rage made my whole body hot. I strode toward the guard-drone, my fingers curled around Bianca's imaginary throat. "She'd better get her ass in here, in person. Or I won't have a word to say to her."

I knew that was stupid and immature the second I said it. There was clearly no terror in that threat, but I delivered the line with my chin up, like a chief. Beside the gray drone, a hundred repetitions of my defiant, black-clad reflection looked back at me from the bulging, multi-faceted surface of an enormous insect eye, at least eighteen inches wide. The furry, forked feelers sticking out above it twitched and bent toward me. That made me queasy. I turned my back and walked away across the middle of the room, my arms wrapped tight around my body.

Behind me, a slipper whispered on ivory. I whirled. Three gorgeous young women entered the room in single file, all in gauzy white gowns. The willowy black model I'd seen on TV lead the way. Behind her walked a curvy blonde, maybe seventeen, followed by a teeny, stunningly beautiful Asian chick. Bianca glared from behind the leader's eyes. The force of her personality hit me in the chest, constricting my heart in an icy fist. I had no doubt whatsoever that it was her. And I had no EMP device. No UV lights, nothing to fend her off with. Bianca meant to add me to that pretty line of slaves. My hands balled into fists. Not without a fight, she wouldn't.

Bianca stalked toward me, her dark eyes flashing. In that tall, athletic host body, she could kick my ass all by herself. She wouldn't need to—she had plenty of backup. Two new guards had joined the gray drone at the door. I raised my chin and stood my ground, feeling small. I only stood an inch over five foot anyway, and on my recent diet of protein bars and anxiety, I'd probably dropped under a hundred pounds.

The trio encircled me, stopped, and stared me down. Up close, the women weren't so perfect after all. A diamond barrette adorned the blonde's waist-length hair, but her pale locks hung limp with grease. Yellowed sweat stains ringed the armpits of the spokesmodel's lacy white gown, and grime darkened the toes of the Asian girl's embroidered silk slippers. Bianca had dressed them up like dolls. Human habits like showers and laundry were irrelevant to a computer.

The blonde girl's ample chest rose and fell in fast, shallow breaths, and she kept glancing around, as if looking for a way out. I felt a sharp pang of sympathy. She was uninfected at the moment, but not for long, and she knew it. Bianca always jumped from one host to the next. I never knew why, but she somehow burned out her victims. Maybe sharing the burden extended their lives. Bianca herself was a strange mix of genius-level artificial intelligence and apparently genuine emotion. Her anger felt real as hell, anyway. The America thing had to be part of her original programming. She'd been created to crawl into the bodies of world leaders, steal their secrets, and return to our president with the information. More than a little sketchy, but that shady stuff was all okay, a sacrifice in the name of freedom and democracy. A noble cause.

I rolled my eyes, glanced down the line of hosts, and snorted.

Bianca's ego was the most human thing about her. She only included pretty women in her stable. I really wouldn't fit in.

My rudeness won me a piercing glare. "Such--" the black girl began. The blonde finished her sentence. "Attitude."

I flinched and turned my attention to the blonde. Her face went slack, and she blinked. It took me a second to catch on.

Bianca advanced on me in the Asian girl's body, her beautiful face twisted in fury. "Here she is, in the flesh. Jacqueline, the poison pill. Delicious little morsel, so hard to resist." Venom laced her voice.

I wasn't prepared for that. I expected arrogance and gloating. But fury? No, I wasn't expecting that. Not after she won the war.

Bianca goaded her host body forward. I backed away, ducking between the television spokesmodel and the blonde teenager. The women turned to face me in a ragged semicircle. The willowy model shivered and closed her eyes. I took the hint and sprang out of her way.

When the model's big brown eyes opened again, Bianca glared from behind them. Spit flew from her mouth as she screamed. "You horrid little bitch! Do you have any idea of the damage you've caused?"

I backed away. "Damage? What damage?"

Ignoring my question, she flashed into the body of the blonde teen, whose eyes narrowed thoughtfully. "It's like a puzzle."

"How to sort them out," the Asian girl added.

"Without destroying the integrity of the original genetic material," the black girl concluded.

My gaze jerked from one woman to the next. They'd lost me. I had no idea what they were talking about. "Sort what out?" I asked.

High shrill laughter came from the black girl, abruptly silencing as Bianca switched bodies. The Asian one laughed, and then the blonde. The tittering circled from woman to woman, faster and faster, driving me crazy. My head swiveled, trying to follow. I took a stunned breath when Bianca stopped body-jumping and the laughter stopped.

Under my thick, armored jacket, sweat slicked my skin. Bianca was nuts. I shouldn't have expected her to make sense. I didn't understand what the delay was, either. Why hadn't she taken me already? Maybe toying with me was fun.

"Of course we knew *you* were poison, but sending the dog was brilliant," Asian Bianca told me. "You're going to have to suffer for that."

"What dog?" I could barely focus. I was still stuck on the suffering bit.

Psychotic laughter circled me again and then abruptly stopped. Following the women's gazes, I faced the oversized, fuzz-rimmed dog eye on the wall. Something about the particular shade of brown seemed familiar. He must have seen us staring. Bristly lashes dropped over the eye as it hid. My heart swelled with compassion. I could almost see the poor little guy lowering his nonexistent head, tucking his tail, and flattening his soft ears. I hadn't had a dog in years. I would have loved one, but my crew couldn't afford the extra mouth to feed.

"What dog?" blonde Bianca mimicked sarcastically. "Pretend you don't remember if you want, but I know how you humans are about your pets." She waved a pale hand.

The giant eyeball-monitors flickered, and then every one of them showed the same picture—a thin black and white border collie, tail wagging happily as he trotted up to a hunter. I groaned. That was the stray dog from Joe's place. Taken. Then I remembered. After that asshole from Joe's crew broke my nose, the friendly stray had licked my bloody face. The dog got nanites then, and nobody noticed. Bianca thought I sent him to the pyramid on purpose as some oddball act of war. That meant the nanites were doing some damage. Good.

But it still didn't make sense. I thought Bianca wanted nanites. Wasn't that her goal? My brow wrinkled as I mulled it over. Doctor Graham had said the healing power of nanites could keep drones from dying off. He believed Bianca was trying to acquire them, but she just called them poison. I had a hunch that somehow, nanites had freed those workers. The infection must have been underway before Keenan and I ever got here. Inside, I kicked myself. We should never have come to the pyramid! If I'd only known. Me and Keenan could've just hid in the bar while the plague spread.

Blonde Bianca waved her hand again. The giant eyeball-screens flickered in response, and a new image of the Border collie appeared, down on his side on a steel surgical table. He lay still except for a few slight mouth movements that told me he was alive. The camera zoomed in as a robotic arm swiveled, bringing a long needle down to stab the dog's eye. With a strangled cry, I turned away, wiping away tears of pity and revulsion.

That horrible woman! I hate her. I hate her so much. I won't cry in front of her. I won't! I refuse to give her the satisfaction.

"We were so careful," Bianca whispered with the black girl's lips. "Only one of my children ever touched you, a specially prepared son, difficult to infect. A significant effort went into that one." She twitched her chin at the gray drone, and then turned back toward me with a resentful pout. "Combining species isn't easy, you know."

My attention was still on the gray man. Was it my imagination, or had a flash of pain crossed his face?

"Combining species?" I repeated mechanically, my voice a dull monotone. "I wouldn't know, I've never tried."

"Well, I've never tried to separate a girl from her nanites before. But I'm willing to perform the dissection," Asian Bianca snapped.

It took a moment for that to sink in. *Dissection.* Bianca wanted to cut me apart, like a frog in biology lab. I stumbled backward, panic rising. I spun, reflexively looking for an escape route. All around the walls, giant eyeballs swiveled in their sockets, watching me. The immense gray drone still blocked the only door.

Bianca pointed the Asian girl's small, delicate finger at me. "Take her."

The drone strode toward me, hands out to grab. I faked left, dodged right, and made a desperate break for the door. The horrid forked feelers of the insect eye by the door reached out and stroked the back of my neck as I passed. I fucking hated bugs, and Bianca's giant, bio-engineered ones made me want to squeal. I flinched from the repulsive touch of the black, fuzzy antennae, right into the drone's arms. He twisted my right arm, pinned my wrist behind my back and lifted me painfully to my toes. As he marched me out of the command center, I thought my elbow was going to explode.

Despite the pain, I screamed and kicked and fought all the way down the ivory stairs and back down the hall, the same way we came. No other people were in the passageway. The feeding room was deserted except for a small cleaning crew. My heart sank. Maybe the rebellion had already been crushed. I gasped in pain as my skin slipped against the drone's toothed palm. That time I had no gloves to protect me, and the gray man's grip burned like fire.

I struggled anyway, thoughts of needles and scalpels filling my mind. Whatever dignity I had fled, and I sobbed like a little girl. "They're going to dissect me! Please don't let them, please, please."

The real, human man that drone had once been was gone, locked into a corner of his mind. He'd become a machine, and it wasn't programmed to care. The gray drone pushed me ahead of him, occasionally losing control of one of my blood-slicked hands. Screaming and cussing, I grabbed door frames and dug my nails into the leathery wall, trying to stop our forward progress. We left a trail of bloody handprints on the walls, bright scarlet on pale, living skin. The gray man recaptured both my wrists and pinned them behind my back, shoving me in front of him as he walked.

He stopped outside the door of the laboratory and held me there. I stood on tiptoe, arching my back to relieve the pain in my wrenched shoulders. My thighs trembled with fear and exhaustion.

Two middle-aged female nurses met us with the blank, unsurprised gazes of the infected. "Jaaacqueline," the first one crooned.

"Jaaacqueline," the second woman echoed, drawing out the sound in a way that grated on my ears.

I shivered. I'd never get used to the fact that every drone on the planet knew my name, though they'd forgotten their own. Behind the infected women, faint ammonia fumes bubbled from an enormous tank. A clean, stainless steel table lay empty, awaiting me.

"Come in, dear. Let us take care of you. We always take care of you," the first one said in a sing-song, maternal tone, like she was talking to a baby.

Those were about the most words I'd ever heard a drone string together, but I didn't give a shit what she had to say. I tried to back up, farther from the stainless steel surgical table, but the gray man had me in his iron grip. Biting and spitting, I flailed in his grasp. My heart pounded so fast that it filled my chest with a dull ache. I forgot about that when the drone deliberately twisted his razor hand against mine, tearing my flesh to the bone. White-hot pain exploded up my arm, and I screamed. He switched his grip to my left hand and dragged me through the door of the lab.

Chapter 15

Infected white-clad women got in my face, murmuring in concerned voices. "Jacqueline . . . Jacqueline. You are injured."

"No shit. Get away from me!" I flailed at them with my torn right hand, punching and clawing, droplets of my blood spattering their emotionless faces. The nurse-drones didn't react at all. One of them braved my flailing arm to spray cooling medicine on my mangled fingers. I had no idea why. Were they programmed as caregivers, unable to do anything else?

The tall drone reached over my shoulder, snatched up my free arm and wrapped both my wrists into one big hand. He lifted me off my feet and cradled me on my back like a baby, my knees pinned in the crook of his right elbow. I strained against him, grunting with effort. With wrists and ankles trapped, I couldn't punch or kick at all. I dimly wondered why he hadn't grabbed me like that in the first place. Would've made life easier for him. Nurse drones hovered around me with aerosol cans, spraying bitter, oily ointment on my hands and face. I squeezed my eyes shut tight. My split lip stung, and my stomach rolled as all the cuts and bruises healed at once. I was starting to loathe my nanites. They picked the worst times to kick in, and they left me exhausted. My head lolled, hanging backward off the gray man's forearm. I could hardly move. The drone's rough-skinned finger stroked gently across the cut on my lower lip. Pivoting, he dipped his bloody finger in the bubbling tank. Inside, something splashed.

I barely noticed. Dread weighed me down. I rolled my head against his thick arm, eyeing the stainless steel table. There were no straps on it. No restraints at all. That chilled me. Apparently, drones were compliant about being dissected. Anything for America.

Motherly nurse-drones stroked my sweaty hair. "Jacqueline . . . Jacqueline. Relax. It's all right, dear. Don't worry. We'll take care of you." I cringed from their touch. The women recited their compassionate lines perfectly, but their lined faces were empty, devoid of any real emotion.

The gray man inexplicably turned and carried me toward the laboratory door. Starvation and exhaustion had pushed me to my limits, and I could barely writhe in his arms. He turned sideways to bring my legs through first. A small splash came from the bubbling tank opposite the door. I glanced over my shoulder and gasped. My own face peered over the rim of the tank, hazel eyes bright with curiosity. My eyes. In my eight-year-old face. Wet, auburn hair, exactly the color of mine, lay smooth against the girl's small head. I'd lost all photos of myself as a child, but she was definitely me, except for one thing. Flat, webbed hands clung to the edge of the pool. With another splash, the Jackie-clone dove under the surface. Twisted, asymmetrical flipper-feet arced through the air as she disappeared. I went limp.

She was crippled.

That girl was no fantastic, bio-engineered mermaid. She was Bianca's failed attempt to re-make me. Those flipper feet were accidents, malformations. The poor child lived in a tank because she couldn't walk. They made her…from me. I was stunned. In a way, she was my daughter, or maybe my sister, stolen as if by magic. I felt violated. Robbed. Furious, in a slow, calm way I'd never experienced before.

It took me a few seconds to realize I'd been drugged. Sleep rose up and took me by force. That was more than nanite-induced exhaustion. The spray-on ointment was laced with sedatives. Rapid thoughts flitted through my brain as it shut down. *Bauer was wrong. Bianca wasn't looking for my cells. She got them a long time ago. She cloned me, only the kid didn't come out right.* I ached to help that little girl, take her with me. But they kept her in a pool for a reason. On those twisted feet, she couldn't run, let alone walk. *How could she get away? How could I help her?*

Yeah, like I was going anywhere.

I fought the drug, clinging to a dim awareness of my surroundings. I was being carried . . . through the dome-roofed atrium . . . down a ramp. I blinked my bleary eyes when the drone shifted my weight to cradle me in one muscular arm. A sealed hide door separated under his silver thumbnail. Maybe that was another lab, the lab where I'd be cut open, where Bianca would somehow separate the submicroscopic nanites from the rest of my body. The drug killed my pain, made my anxiety vanish. Everything would be all right. I only needed to sleep. The gray drone knelt and set me down on a warm, cushioned surface. Tiny, infinitely beautiful lights twinkled up through the tissue beneath me, bright silver stars tangled with new, unfamiliar strands of gold. The last things I heard before passing out were running footsteps and a boy's voice, calling my name.

I woke wrapped in Keenan's arms, my head pillowed on his folded brown Carhartt jacket. My palm lay on the bare skin of his chest. I traced my fingers down a patch of fine, light brown chest hair and glanced up at his sleeping face. Nanites had healed every scratch and bruise, leaving his skin smooth and perfect. His eyes were closed, his breathing even. Beads of moisture clung to his long, golden lashes as he dozed. Keenan was the bravest guy I knew. I'd never seen him cry, not since the day I met him, the day his family died. Had he given in and wept in secret while I slept? Cuddled close against his side, I slid an arm across his flat stomach, stretched to bring my face closer to his, and resisted the urge to kiss his parted lips. Instead, I sat up cross-legged, blinked blearily, and coughed.

Keenan cracked an eye, rolled over and passed me a big metal water bottle. "About time. You had me worried. You slept for hours, and I couldn't rouse you."

I sipped the cool water gratefully, the new, pink skin on my hands sensitive to every tiny scratch on the bottle. I wiggled my toes inside my socks. Keenan must have pulled my combat boots off for me and set them aside. That little gesture touched me. He'd never been the nurturing type, but now he hovered anxiously nearby, like any second I'd pass out again.

"What happened, Jack?"

"They drugged me. Some kind of spray," I said in a raspy voice. I inhaled sharply, looking down at the blue metal water bottle in my hands. "This is mine, from my black pack! Do we have the--" I began, but my excited voice trailed off when Keenan shook his head.

"Shark Man brought it, with these." He dropped three protein bars on the blanket, tore open a fourth, and handed it to me. "But not the EMP device."

"Aw." Not that I expected Bianca to deliver the weapon that could kill her. Food and water were surprise enough. Why did she want to keep us alive? Then something Keenan said registered in my drug-hazed mind. "Shark Man?" I repeated around a mouthful of protein bar. "Y'mean the gray drone?"

Keenan curled a lip in a disgusted grimace. "Yep. Bianca changed him. Covered him in shark skin. Flat little shark teeth are embedded in his skin, just like a real shark."

I shuddered. "Sharks have teeth in their skins? Seriously?"

"Yep. It's normal for them."

I tilted my head dubiously. "How do you know?"

Keenan shrugged. "Some kids liked dinosaurs. I liked sharks. My mom bought me all kinds of stuff on 'em, y'know, toys and books."

"Books. Um, nice." I couldn't help my raised eyebrow. Back at the diner, Keenan never read much more than comic books. I was always the one scrounging old paperbacks on foraging runs, not him. Not that I was gonna say that out loud.

Then something occurred to me. "Up in the control room, Bianca said something about combining species. That gray drone was made to be resistant to nanites. Maybe nanites can't infect sharks."

Keenan only shrugged.

I imagined the gray drone as a free man, before he'd been taken by the pox. He was a survivor. A dude with that much muscle obviously hadn't been scrounging and starving like the rest of us. He'd been doing all right, at least until Bianca got him. That kinda shook me up. If a guy like him could lose, what hope was there for the rest of us?

Keenan's gentle hand on my back snapped me out of my thoughts. His tawny head bent protectively over mine. "What happened in there, Jackie? I heard you screaming, it was awful."

I had a sudden impulse to cry, or maybe throw myself into his arms. I wasn't sure. It had been a fucked up day, and it might not even be over yet. From inside Bianca's flesh-crafted fortress, we couldn't see the sun.

I took a deep breath and my words came out in a rush, picking up speed as they spilled out. I told him about rebel drones tearing out their feeding tubes, and the three beautiful girls in the command center with giant eyeball-computers and how Joe's nanite-infested dog got taken by hunters and had his eye stabbed with a needle so they could build a spy camera out of him. Gulping, I even included Bianca's plan to dissect me in the creepy lab where they kept flipper-Jackie in a clone tank. It sounded like I'd lost my mind. I wondered if Keenan even believed me. His brow furrowed, but he didn't say much. Maybe he just thought I was high.

At the edge of our blanket, twinkling silver nanobots rose from deep within the living floor. I leaned forward, hands splayed, and stared into the pyramid's partially transparent flesh. The sensation was vaguely disturbing, like I might pitch forward and sink. I wanted to turn away, but something in there caught my attention. Deep in Bianca's warm, soft tissue, faint gold dots glittered where only silver had been before. As I watched, specks of gold joined together to form a chain that tangled around one tiny, silver star. The star's faint, white light flared brighter, then faded as it died. I wasn't sure what I'd just seen. Not individual nanobots--they were microscopic. Maybe every speck of light was an army, made of billions of the miniscule machines. If that was true, our team had just scored a point.

"Take that, bitches," I muttered.

Keenan's lips split in a wolfish grin. "It's been going on for hours. Nanites against nanobots. Bianca's infected, all right. And you infected her."

"Shh! Joe's dog infected her, I didn't." I glanced around, afraid the living walls would overhear. For all I knew, they already had. "Bianca's furious," I hissed out of the corner of my mouth. "She won't take either one of us because of our nanites, and she thinks I infected her on purpose. But what I don't get is--"

Keenan's sudden laughter cut me off. "Bianca's pissed because *you* infected *her*? That's priceless."

I had to smile, just seeing his grin. We were together again, a team. Relief and gratitude surged through me in a palpable wave, leaving me feeling strangely light around the heart.

"How can nanites hurt anyone?" I asked. "They heal me. And, uh, you too, now." I should have thanked him then, but the sudden lump in my throat stopped me. I was almost glad we didn't have the EMP device anymore. Now I wouldn't have to set it off. I wouldn't have to watch Keenan succumb to old age, his handsome, young face sagging. I wouldn't have to watch him die.

Keenan stared into space and spoke slowly, without looking at me. "Nanites heal everyone. They have to heal drones too. What if they repair the damage that Bianca does?"

I twisted to look into his amber eyes. "You think Bianca causes damage when she infects someone? Like . . . like brain damage?"

Keenan nodded. "She has to short-circuit something to take over, right?"

"I guess. That explains the drone rebellion, except for one thing." I bit off another chunk of protein bar and chewed thoughtfully. "The gray man got our blood all over him when he dragged us inside. He had plenty of time to get infected, and he's not."

"Maybe he is. He could be thinking for himself by now," Keenan breathed. "Do you think it was his idea to bring the food?"

"I doubt it," I snorted. "He wasn't exactly the soul of compassion when he hauled me off to the command center. But one thing was weird. He totally could've pinned me, but he let my hands slip away sometimes, so blood got all over the walls. Plus he went out of his way to drip some inside the clone tank, where my . . . my . . ." I hesitated, not sure what to call the flipper girl. Daughter? Sister? Clone? Either way, the kid was mine. And they kept her locked in that creepy lab, with no one for company except mindless nurse-drones. Tears stung my eyes, and I fell silent.

At first Keenan didn't notice. "Blood on the walls? See, I was right, he's infecting the pyramid. Sharkey's on our side!" His smile died when he caught my dark expression. "What?"

I hated to say it. Hated to ruin what little happiness we had left. I spoke slowly, my voice small. "Um, Keenan? Imagine, back when we lived with our crew at the bar and grill . . . if we found out the diner was infested with nanobots, what would we have done?"

"Left, of course. And torched the place on our way out."

"And if--" My voice broke. "If a couple of hunters ran out?"

Keenan's blond eyebrows drew together. "Burned them too."

I took Keenan's hand and sat in front of him, head bowed. "Yeah. That's why I'm thinking we . . . uh, we probably won't be locked in here much longer. They'll come for us. And when they do, it'll be over."

"I tried to break out, Jackie! I tried to go after you!"

I dropped his hand and recoiled. "It's okay. It's not your fault."

"It's not okay," Keenan snapped. "What did you think I did when they took you away? Just sat there? Look. Look at that." Keenan seized his white thermal shirt off the floor and shook it. Dark, fresh blood soaked the front.

I'd seen his knife stab through the living skin of the door. The drum-tight seal bled before it healed. But I hadn't faced the implications. "Bianca's blood. You . . . you got it all over, and you're not infected."

Keenan looked away. "Maybe I am. Maybe there's a nanobot war inside me right now."

"No, if that was true you'd be sick, and you're not," I said, trying to convince myself as much as him. "Your nanites are protecting you."

Maybe I was right. Maybe we couldn't be infected. If that was true, Bianca was gonna lose her shit. She handled frustration like a spoiled child. No doubt she'd kill us just for spite. I suppressed a groan. We were trapped, and time was running out. I didn't know what to do. So I said nothing, and just ran my fingertips up and down the bare skin of Keenan's back. There was no fat on him, and only flat, wiry muscles, but his shoulders were broad. I think he would've been a big guy, if I'd been able to feed him right. Damn. More regrets.

As if he sensed that, Keenan turned and folded me into his arms, one hand wrapping the back of my head. I melted against his chest, trying to forget everything except the warm scent of his skin.

"I never thanked you for leaving the space station," I whispered. "That was the bravest, most incredible thing anyone has ever done for me."

"You don't have to thank me, Jack. I did it because I love you."

A wave of emotion filled me. Keenan had left our crew, the safety of the orbiting base, and the first regular meals he'd had in years, all to follow me. Even when we got captured, he never regretted it. Never threw it in my face. In that moment, all I wanted was to be worthy of his sacrifice. But I still couldn't tell him I loved him. That felt like a betrayal of Dakota.

I glanced up at Keenan's brooding profile and felt warmth tingle my cheeks. I wanted him. Needed him. And for a lot more than cuddling. Pity I'd slapped him down every time he hit on me. Now what was I gonna do? I turned away and took a gulp of water to hide the longing in my expression.

When I handed the bottle back to Keenan, his fingers brushed mine. I glanced up, captured by his amber eyes. It felt like they looked right through me, saw all my secrets. Saw how bad I wanted him. The room suddenly felt too warm. I fidgeted on the blanket, shifting to my knees on the cushioned floor. Looking down, I traced my fingertips down the flushed skin of my neck and tugged my jumpsuit zipper open an inch or two. Keenan instantly noticed. Eyes lit, he sat up to face me, one of his long thighs stretched out, pressing against the outside of mine. I tensed when he put a hand on my leg, but I didn't pull away. I couldn't raise my eyes. As amazing as Keenan was, he wasn't Dakota. Dakota had always been safe and familiar. Keenan was anything but. He even smelled different, smoky and wild, with a savage edge that set my heart racing. With Keenan, everything was always a little bit out of control. He didn't follow orders, and if I got him started, he might not stop. That part was okay. I was pretty sure I wouldn't want him to.

His fingertips brushed my cheeks and ran through my hair, and his lips traced kisses along my left temple. My gaze strayed from Keenan's tight abs to the long bulge in his jeans. Part of me wanted to reach out and stroke it, but shyness stopped me, so I ran my hands ran down the broad muscles of his back instead. For a second I caught a whiff of orchids and musk, an intoxicating blend that belonged in a mountain meadow, or some faraway jungle. Not here.

Keenan pressed closer, his breath coming faster. "Mmm. I love your perfume. So sexy."

I parted my lips to tell him I wasn't wearing any, but he stopped my words with a kiss. Strands of Keenan's long blond hair lay across my black-armored shoulder, and his strong arm wrapped my narrow waist.

"Jackie," he murmured. Then more sharply, "Jack! Look at me."

I glanced up in reflexive obedience, startled by his stern voice. In that moment, Keenan seemed older, the clean, boyish lines of his face morphing to rugged manhood. Those golden cat eyes held me as he reached out a hand and tipped my chin up.

"Look at me," Keenan said again, lower. Pain edged his voice. "I am not Dakota."

"I know that." I fought down an irrational burst of irritation. Was this a huge mistake? Would Keenan and I grate on each other's nerves forever? Then a dark thought intruded. Forever might only be an hour, before Bianca's guards marched us to the pyre. We couldn't waste it.

"I know, Keenan," I said again. My voice came out softer that time, sweeter, more yielding.

"Do you?" he murmured, sliding his fingers up the nape of my neck and closing them slowly on my hair. That drove me wild. For once in my life, I wasn't in control, and I loved it. Keenan kissed me, his tongue plunging deep, making me want him. His hands roamed across my body.

"Oh my God, Keenan. Keenan." I whispered his name, intuitively feeling the sound of it settle his wild heart.

He kissed me again, hard and demanding, his tongue flicking enticingly across mine. My nipples tightened, and sweet tingles warmed that secret spot between my legs. Back arched and mouth open, I melted against him, but he suddenly broke contact, leaving me yearning for more.

Somehow I expected Keenan to take me hard, tearing my clothes off and slamming me savagely down on my back. He'd always been a wild man. But his touch was gentle, almost reverent, as he unzipped my jumpsuit to the bottom and peeled it off my arms, exposing my lacy white bra. He leaned forward and kissed my neck, refusing to hurry, even though Bianca's hunters could already be on their way.

One of Keenan's hands slid behind my back as the other caressed my breast, sliding under my bra to tickle my nipple. In a moment he unsnapped my bra, tossed it aside, and cupped my small breasts in his palms. His tangled butterscotch locks spilled around my face as I leaned back on our blanket, pulling him down on top of me. He smelled like smoke and blood and pure, feral male, and the scent drove me crazy. We kissed, deeper this time, and then Keenan rolled over on his back and stripped off his jeans. I wiggled out of my jumpsuit and let the heavy armor thud to the floor. The warm, moist air felt delicious on my naked skin. And so did Keenan's hands.

We collapsed and lay side by side, lost in each other's eyes. Keenan's fingers slid up my inner thigh, brushed aside my lacy, white panties, and touched the wetness inside. I gasped and parted my legs for him. In a moment I raised my hips and helped him tug my panties down. His fingers were gentle as he stroked me, on and on, sliding a finger inside me and then slicking it across my clit. Pleasure built, and I moaned, arching into his hand. My thighs tightened around his hand as I felt an orgasm coming. Reaching down, I wrapped my fingers around his thick cock and stroked it. My leg wrapped Keenan's hip, pulling him closer. He rolled on top of me, taking most of his weight on his arms. The tip of his cock touched my entrance, enticing me to push against him. Finally, unable to wait any longer, I reached down and guided him inside.

Keenan thrust hard and buried himself inside me, moaning in pleasure. His left hand slid under my neck, cradling it as he rocked my body with one powerful stroke after another. He whispered, deep and low. "I love you, Jackie."

Not ten strokes later, Keenan's cock pulsed inside me as he started to come. That set me off too, and we both cried out, clutching each other, limbs tangled and skin damp with each other's sweat. Afterward I realized I was crying, tears flowing across my temples and into my hair.

Keenan's warm lips kissed them away. "What's wrong, babe? Regrets?"

I held him close, arms and legs wrapped around his long, lean body. "Oh, no. No regrets. Not anymore."

"Good." Keenan's body went loose in relief. His weight settled onto me, warm and comforting. "Baby, I really do love you."

I opened my mouth. Tasted the words on my tongue. Formed my lips around them. And couldn't say it. I don't know why I couldn't tell him I loved him. I swear I felt that love in my heart, love and boundless admiration too. Keenan was fearless and free, a born hero. I know, we'd gotten ourselves captured and lost our only weapon, but none of that was his fault. I could have been in that pyramid alone. Instead, we were together, in bliss, at least for the moment. I buried my fingers deep in that beautiful hair, reveling in the feel of it between my fingers. His cock stirred inside me, getting hard again. "Keenan," I whispered, overwhelmed with love and stress and fear. "I--"

A soft, wet, tearing sound came from across the room, so faint I could have ignored it. Keenan's head snapped around. The hide curtain had parted when we weren't paying attention, and Shark Man stood in the doorway, his expressionless gray eyes locked on us. My whole spine jerked in shock. How long had he been standing there?

"Hey!" Stark naked, Keenan sprang to his feet between me and the intruder, fists clenched.

The drone didn't react. He stayed where he was, watching us, either oblivious to what he'd interrupted or completely unembarrassed by it. His razor thumbnail ran absently up and down the pale hide of the door, shredding the shuddering skin into two ragged sections, and then three, as blood spattered his calloused, gray feet. With a faint, liquid squelch, a scrap of white skin fell to the floor and lay there, curling and twitching. My stomach did a sick flip.

I scrambled for my clothes. Being dragged down corridors by that monster was bad enough--I had no intention of doing it naked. I stood, zipped up my black jumpsuit, and bent to toss Keenan his jeans. He caught them in one hand but made no move to put them on. I knew why. If a fight broke out, he didn't want to get caught with one leg in his pants.

Keenan was all set to do something stupid. His muscles were tense, weight on the balls of his feet, ready to spring. Attacking Shark Man naked--that could put a guy in a world of hurt. I cringed just thinking about it. Maybe Keenan wasn't that stupid, or that hormone-driven. Just in case, I stepped forward, made a gentle *stand down* gesture with one hand and gave a brief shake of the head. Keenan got the message, thank God, and wiggled into his jeans, commando style.

The huge drone strode slowly toward us, his long, gnarled toenails sinking into the soft floor with every step. For a heart-stopping moment I froze, wide eyed, gazing up at that stony face. Then, without a word, the shark man turned his back and walked ponderously out the door. Weird as it was, we'd clearly been summoned, either for another audience with Bianca or for our own execution.

Keenan shot me a wary look. "We have to go with him, Jack. If we don't, he'll just come back and drag us out of here."

I put my hands on Keenan's bare shoulders and stood on tiptoe to whisper in his ear. "We're not lettin' 'em burn us. If we die, we die fighting."

His only answer was a grim nod.

I peered at the dimly lit doorway, where shreds of skin still hung, writhing. The sight made me feel weak and shaky, and all I wanted to do was hide. Instead, I kicked Keenan's tennis shoes in his general direction and knelt to tie my boots. My fingers felt clumsy, and I fumbled with my laces, shooting sidelong glances at the door. The gray drone must be waiting for us outside. That was an odd bit of behavior, almost courteous, but I didn't have time to wonder about it. This would all be over soon.

Keenan lifted his bloodstained white thermal shirt between two fingers, grimaced, and dropped it on the hairy floor. He slung his brown canvas coat over his shoulder and stood, bare chested. I fingered our blanket, reluctant to leave it behind. A five-second fantasy flashed through my head, of escaping and huddling under that blanket with Keenan, somewhere out in the ruins, as we made our way back to the safety of Joe's tunnels. But in the end, I walked out empty handed.

Keenan wrapped an arm around me as we trudged from our prison. My stomach churned. All I could think about was fire.

Chapter 16

At the cell door, Keenan used his knife blade to hold back a strip of twitching, curling skin. I steeled my nerves and ducked under it, into the dimly lit corridor. The gray drone was gone, the corridor deserted. I don't know why that shook me up, but it did. He just disappeared, like . . . like something had swallowed him. I glanced nervously at the creepy, dark gaps where the walls met the floor, wondering if they could yawn wide and—I forced the thought out of my mind. A sour, body-odor breeze sighed from those gaps, cooling the sweat at the nape of my neck. I stood still, holding my breath, listening. The only sound was the ever-present electronic hum of the pyramid. Even that seemed hushed, as if waiting for something. My skin prickled.

Strange, overlapping flaps of skin festooned the walls, flickering with tiny, moving hairs. Air flowed through the space, but some of the hairs seemed to bend under their own power, resisting the current and then tiring and blowing in the wind. I pulled my gaze away. That way lay insanity.

Viktor's folding knife made a metallic click as Keenan snapped it closed. I jumped at the sound. "He's gone. What now?"

Keenan grabbed my hand. "We get the fuck out of here."

Hand in hand, we raced down the dark corridor. The milky-white light from the walls was dying, and once I tripped on a shadowed ridge of bone and almost went down. Faint vibrations came through the thick soles of my boots, growing stronger. We reached the bone bridge, with its narrow passageway through the bat-wing wall, and had to go single file. Keenan went first, springing lightly up the ramp and disappearing down the other side. I took the bridge at a run. As my boot struck the steepest section, a deep, rumbling groan came from the pyramid itself. The floor lurched. On either side of me, bone cracked and ivory arches ripped free of their skin coverings. Blood and fatty chunks of marrow slicked the bridge. I skidded, squealed, and instinctively grabbed the nearest rib. My right palm came away smeared with Bianca's blood. Or maybe it was my own. I had to face the truth.

The winter-pale color of the skin floor in our prison, glimmers of auburn from its nasty little hairs, even the sour, unwashed stench, all felt disturbingly familiar. I was pretty sure that Bianca had taken my cells and grown something monstrous. Keenan might have known it already. I couldn't bring myself to ask.

Gripping warm, seeping bone on both sides, I halted under the archway at the top of the bridge. The floor beneath me suddenly rocked, and the pair of slick, upright ribs I held separated, jerking themselves from my grip. I screamed as the circular, dome roofed chamber ahead stretched, elongating to twice its former width. Keenan staggered and fell. I picked my moment and jumped, but the floor moved backward beneath me, spilling me into a roll. My armored suit took the brunt of it and I came up on my feet.

"Which way?" Keenan shouted. Blood ran into his eyes. He wiped it away, wincing as the cut on his forehead healed.

Until that moment, I swear I was headed for the front door. But all I could think about was that little girl, alone and terrified. We couldn't just leave her. The lab. First archway to the left of the bone ramp, I thought. Or was it the second? They all looked alike, and the room had changed shape. I took a few hesitant strides that way, trying to decide. And then the whole room contracted around us. The walls rushed in, and the ceiling dropped down with a *floom* of escaping air. I screamed and dove through the nearest archway. Keenan stumbled through behind me, literally stepping on my heels.

I stumbled down the white bone ramp. The brightly lit hallway ahead of us stood empty and quiet. Our tentative footfalls sounded loud in the sudden stillness.

The laboratory was ahead on the left. "Maybe another forty feet," I whispered.

We paced on. Only there were no doors, not for the first hundred feet, or the second. No feeding station, no bloody handprints on the walls. No ivory staircase at the end of the hall leading up to the command center.

I whirled. "Keenan, we've gone the wrong way! The lab's in another corridor, we have to go back."

"The lab?" Keenan repeated. Understanding dawned on his face, followed by fury. "Jackie, you said yourself she can't even walk."

"Then we fucking carry her," I shrieked, and began to sob. "She's . . . Keenan, I can't help it, she's mine."

"She is not," Keenan shouted. And then, all around us, the walls let out an agonized moan.

We both froze. The leathery skin on the walls liquefied, running off or absorbing into the red, raw tissue below. Sparkling nanobots warred deep inside, silver against gold, sending tiny bolts of lightning crackling through the inflamed tissue of the pyramid. The fight intensified, brightening the interior until we gazed into it as if through murky water. For a second,

Keenan and I stood rooted, staring in horrified fascination as a submerged web of gristle shifted, tugging on the softening wall. Then we ran.

With Keenan in the lead, we turned and jogged back the way we came, our strides lengthening with nerves. On the right, I made out the filmy outline of a vessel as wide as our hallway, clear liquid sweeping along a soup of grainy specks and yellowish, mucus chunks.

"Come on!" Keenan sidestepped and shoved me ahead of him. Then I saw why. The corridor had narrowed.

With a deep creaking noise, stark white ligaments tore through the skin ceiling, spanning the hall from one side to the other. They began to contract, pulling opposite walls together. I let out a panicked squeal and sprinted, with Keenan hard on my heels. A few rootlike strands poked through the walls and wormed their way across the walkway, threatening to trip me. I jumped them and ran on, heart pounding and lungs ready to burst. Clumsy in my heavy combat boots, I got tangled and bulled through, ripping one tendon clean from the wall. It whipped up and struck the wall with a crack. The corridor groaned, its passageway thinning until my elbows brushed the walls on both sides. And then my ribs touched, and I could hardly breathe.

I shuffled sideways, fighting the suffocating press of flesh on both sides. Small, frightened cries escaped me as the living ceiling inched lower. Keenan grunted and gouged his way along behind me, slashing at the constricting tissue with Viktor's knife.

Inside the huge vessel on my right, something big moved, pacing us. Dread overcame me, and I lost control. Sobbing and thrashing, I gained another yard, and then two. We reached the door.

And it was blocked.

Twisted ligaments had grown across it, squeezing the springy ribs of the portal closed. The pyramid grunted and closed on us. My chest ached, and I fought for each breath. Unable to move or even fall, I let my face get pressed against sticky, skinless flesh. My lungs burned, and every breath was shallower than the last. Red spots floated across my vision. I barely reacted when the tissue under my lips thrummed. Something on the other side struck me again, hard enough to hurt a little. I blinked, opened my eyes, and saw my own face looking back. I'd never thought so before, but I really was . . . pretty. Blackness took the edges of my field of view, but I still saw myself in the middle, frantically pulling some underwater vine. In the dream, my long hair flowed back in a strong current and my webbed feet churned water, fighting to keep me from being swept away. Darkness overtook me.

A second later, the walls retracted and cool, fresh air rushed in. I collapsed to my knees, took a deep breath, and cried out when my bruised ribs suddenly healed. Keenan writhed on the floor behind me. He must have fallen when the walls gave way. Something bumped my head. I blinked and tried to focus through thick, gelatinous tissue. There really was a girl on the other side.

"The clone," Keenan croaked from the floor.

The little girl kicked the wall in front of my face again, waving one webbed hand to get my attention. With the other, she gripped a long, white root. Behind her, the torn, filmy wall of the vessel fluttered, spewing some disgusting, high pressure liquid. Kicking hard against the current with her flippers, the clone-child leaned back, pulling hard. Grimacing with effort, she jerked her chin to my left. Tiny air bubbles escaped her pursed lips. Low down, near the floor, a hole had appeared in the tangled vines that blocked the door.

I grabbed Keenan by the arm and tugged. "Look, she opened the door a little. Go, go!" He crawled past my legs, dropped to his belly, and slid through the gap. I followed so close on his heels I got myself kicked in the face, but I didn't care. We were back in the atrium, and we could breathe. I collapsed on the skin floor and gasped, too exhausted to shrink from the vile little hairs tickling my lips.

As soon as I could move, I elbow-crawled back toward the gap we'd come through.

Keenan made a limp grab at my ankle. His breath gurgled in his chest, wet and labored. "What . . . the hell . . . are you doing?" He asked between coughs. "Going back in there?"

I flailed my foot, shaking off his grip. "I just gotta make sure she's okay. She doesn't have gills, you know. What if she's drowning?"

Keenan crawled a few feet, seized the front of my jumpsuit, and collapsed to a shoulder, dragging me down with him. "What if she is? What can you do about it?"

"I don't know! I just need to try."

Keenan abruptly released me. "Fine, go. Just remember, if that door closes on you, it'll pinch you in two."

"Oh. Shit." That made an impression. "Good point. I'll stay on this side, and only peek, then."

I wormed forward on my belly, clutched a bent rib, and peered through the gap. Through a dirty amber haze, I could make out the snakelike shapes of ligaments, like submerged tree roots after a flood. The broken vessel still spewed yellowish liquid, chunks of snot, and bigger pieces of God-knows-what. But the clone-girl was gone.

I struggled to my feet, aching all over. The circular atrium was in shambles. Overhead, the domed ceiling sagged, and at least half the hide-covered ribs around the doors were cracked and seeping. The coppery smell of blood filled the air, along with a new, sickly sweet odor that reminded me of the time a mouse died in the wall of Joe's diner, right behind my bed. We couldn't find it, and it stank for weeks. *Oh my God.* Was the pyramid dying? Would we be trapped inside its great, bloated corpse, like mice in its fleshy walls?

That thought got me moving, circling the room. Keenan dogged my heels, refusing to shut up. "We need to get out of here. You're gonna have to forget about the clone. We don't even know her, it's not our problem."

I said nothing until he cornered me between some broken ribs and a torn flap of hide wall. "The front door, Jackie! Which one is it?"

I honestly didn't know. The atrium had been round, but now it was a misshapen oval, swollen on one side and crushed flat on the other. Only a few doors even looked passable.

Keenan loomed over me, his lips twisted into a snarl. He gripped my jacket, bellowing inches from my face. "Which fucking door?"

I slapped his hand off. "Back off, asshole! I don't know anymore, okay? You came in here the same time I did. Why am I supposed to know the way out, when all you have to do is follow me around?"

Keenan spun away from me, red faced and glowering.

I'd hurt his pride, obviously. But I didn't appreciate being manhandled either. If our crew saw him grab me like that, they'd beat him bloody. That reminded me of Dakota, and pain stabbed my heart. He was gone. There was nobody left in our crew who could beat up Keenan, except maybe Ash, and he'd never even try.

I paced the atrium, so mad at Keenan I couldn't even look at him. How did we go from making love to sniping like bratty kids?

"What are you looking for?" Keenan asked bitterly. "For a way out? Or for your *daughter*?"

"Whichever we find first," I lied. Turning my back on him, I chose a half-collapsed door, turned sideways, and squeezed through.

Angry as he was, Keenan's loyalty never wavered. He stomped through the portal after me, elbowing aside cracked and broken ribs. I immediately knew we had the right corridor. My bloody handprints still marked the pale skin walls.

"This isn't the way out," Keenan said.

"Nope." I kept walking.

"You did this on purpose, didn't you?"

I ignored him.

Keenan grabbed my arm and yanked me to a halt. "Listen to me. This place smells like, ugh. Like it's dying."

I wrinkled my nose. He was right, the pyramid was dying. Even the air felt moist and feverish. Around us, the corridor shuddered, and the faint rotten-meat stench was getting harder to ignore.

"It's okay. Leave if you want, I'll catch up. I just have one thing to do first." I turned away, knowing I'd never catch up. Not with a crippled child on my back. But I had to try. She hadn't let me suffocate. How could I leave her now?

Keenan coughed, gagged, swore, and bitched as he followed me down the hall. "Fuck. Fuck. Fuck. What the hell are you thinking? That's not your kid, Bianca made it. It's some kind of monster. Forget her. We need to get out of here! These ridiculous maternal instincts of yours are gonna get us both killed."

From inside Bianca's laboratory came the high, thin cry of an injured child. I burst through the door at a run, forgetting the nurse drones, their drugged spray, and the shiny, stainless-steel dissection table that awaited me.

Chapter 17

We skidded to a stop inside the laboratory. I looked around, confused. The scream had come from inside that room, I was certain of it, but the place seemed deserted. Shelves of glassware and scientific equipment lined the walls. The rubbery clone tank and stainless steel surgical table almost filled the middle of the lab, with three narrow, parallel walkways between them and along the walls. I moved cautiously to the tank, stood on tiptoe, and peered in.

Ammonia fumes bubbled from the gray water, stinging my eyes and making my nose run, but I held my ground. A dark tunnel, barely wide enough for a child's narrow shoulders, gaped from the floor of the little pool. So she wasn't trapped in there after all. Maybe she could explore the entire pyramid, swimming through tubes and popping up for air in different rooms. I swore under my breath. If that was true, I'd never find her. Then a whimper and a soft, wet slap came from the back of the lab.

Movement there caught my eye. A black stone bench ran along the far wall of the chamber. Silvery statues crowded its surface, each about two feet tall, with jointed legs and long, curving antennae. They reminded me of giant shrimp, except that their shiny, steel jaws opened sideways, like the mouthparts of a centipede.

"That's some seriously weird art," I muttered.

Then one of the statues twitched. Keenan sucked in a startled breath. "Holy shit, they're alive. Look at 'em. Those things could strip the meat off our bones."

I gestured for silence, but he had already alerted them. Sharp jaws clicked, scissoring open and closed, while iridescent metallic forelegs waved back and forth, tasting our scent on the air. Tiny, metal-sheathed claws tapped out a frenetic rhythm on the black stone table top. Meat or machine, those things sure looked like they could jump. I watched them warily.

"Cyborgs," Keenan breathed. "Flesh and machine, combined."

I always thought cyborgs were more like humanoid robots, but that wasn't the time to argue. Besides, Keenan might be right. He read a lot more comic books than I did.

Somewhere, a child whimpered.

"Aw, shit, she's under the bench." Without taking my eyes off the mechanical spiders, I edged closer, sliding each boot forward as smoothly as I could. The room seemed to be getting warmer. Itchy beads of sweat slicked my armpits and trickled down between my shoulder blades. *She's under the table. Maybe they bit her already.* Fighting down my fear, I forced myself closer.

On the table stood a rectangular, chrome box which I would have ignored, except that the pale blue eyeball mounted on the front suddenly blinked open and rolled to watch us. Unlike the oversized view screens in the command center, this eye was only about four inches long, but recognizably humanoid, like it came from a giant. Somehow that was worse.

Keenan sucked in a startled breath. "It sees us. She sees us. She knows we're here."

"Only if she's looking through that eye right this second," I said evenly, like I was some kind of expert on artificial intelligence. Truth was, I had no clue. All I wanted to do was grab the kid and get out of there.

Dumping his jacket on the floor, Keenan squeezed by me, slipped past the stainless steel dissection table, and bent to look under the black stone bench. Above his head, the multi-legged cyborgs seethed, their tiny, clawed feet tapping on stone. One of them crouched to spring. Before I could shout a warning, a mess of white tentacles sprang from the gooey lid of the eyeball gadget and arced toward the spiders, making the same damp, squelching sounds I heard in my nightmares. Waves rippled through them, like cracking whips. Hissing and clicking, the cyborgs retreated to the back of the bench, folded their jointed legs, and obediently lowered their bellies to the bench top.

Keenan snapped upright to check the benchtop. "What just happened there?"

I let out a shaky breath. "Never mind. It's okay, I think. I don't know."

The cyborgs lay still except for the constant, rhythmic ticking of those restless steel jaws. Arched antennae waved over their heads, each tipped with a bright splotch of a different color, so every individual was unique.

Keenan watched them for a few seconds, then crawled under the bench after the little girl. Tentacles cascaded off the edge of the bench and curled to follow him under.

"Look out!"

He turned his head, saw them, and kept on going.

I swore. "Keenan! Don't let those things touch you."

With typical, infuriating arrogance, he ignored me. I wanted to scream. Anxiety propelled me a few steps closer. The tentacles were on him.

Pale, slimy fingers caressed the bare skin of Keenan's back. If it was me under there, I would have come unglued. Keenen just brushed a curling, yellowish tendril off his ear and crawled farther in. The silver-sided box hummed a faint, electronic purr, and I caught a whiff of ozone. The blue iris on front rolled up in its socket, showing only white. Rows of green-lit numbers rolled across its oval screen.

I peered under the bench. Keenan's denim-clad butt blocked my view. "Is she in there?"

"Yeah." His voice turned soft and soothing. "Hey, it's okay. I'm not going to hurt you. Is it all right if I pull you out from under here?"

A child whispered. In a moment, Keenan wriggled backward with my clone-daughter in his arms. Up close, she was smaller than I'd thought, only as big as an average five year old, but her heart-shaped face seemed older, the hazel eyes wise and sad. If I had to guess, I would've said she was an adolescent, twelve or thirteen years old, despite that tiny, twisted mermaid body. Had Bianca stolen my cells that long ago, or was the clone really just a little girl? I couldn't tell for sure, but I knew one thing. She was my twin, a younger sister or a daughter. She was mine.

Keenan's shaggy blond head bent to look down into her face. "What's your name? Mine's Keenan."

"I know," the girl said. "I'm Jacqueline."

"I know." They shared a smile. "Do you want me to put you back in your tank, Jacqueline?"

Her tiny, pale arms squeezed his neck. "No. I want to stay with you."

Still holding the deformed child, Keenan eased himself to the floor, tenderness softening the angular lines of his face.

"We need to go," I hissed, pacing the lab, looking for something to wrap her in.

It would be freezing outside, and she wore only a pair of black, tight fitting shorts and a wrinkled beige top. I knew I should've brought the damned blankets. We didn't dare go back for them now.

A grungy white lab coat hung on a hook by the door. I took it and knelt beside them. As I reached out to cover the little girl, she turned toward me and whimpered. What I'd taken for a wrinkled shirt was her skin, dying and peeling off, exposing red, raw flesh beneath.

She had the same disease the pyramid did. *Oh my God. I caused this.*

I lurched to my feet. "You need medicine. What should I do? Where are your nurses?"

The child shook her head. "They're gone. Sick, I think. Maybe dead." She wheezed, coughed weakly, and worked to suck in another breath.

"You were sick like this when you saved our lives?"

She nodded weakly. The effort seemed to take a lot out of her.

"That's incredible. We can't thank you enough," I said.

Keenan gave her a brotherly squeeze, which she seemed to like better than anything I said.

Behind me, a tentacle, white as a blind cave fish, reached for the child. I slapped it away, crouched over her defensively as the whole mess of them erupted in agitated motion, like a nest of pissed-off snakes. "Keenan, move!"

"Wait, Jackie. Just wait."

I tugged on Keenan's arm. "Move her, move her, come on, we gotta get out of here."

Keenan didn't even try to stand. He shook his head, some awful, wordless message in his eyes. When a pale tentacle wormed over his naked shoulder, he let it. The clone-child extended a fragile, long-fingered hand, and it slithered onto her webbed palm like a big slug. She raised the fat tube to her lips.

"Don't," I cried, but she didn't listen.

The tentacle swelled, like a long, saggy teat overfilled with milk. With an airy, hissing sound, some kind of nasty, pressurized gas leaked from the tip. The girl inhaled, and her wheezing eased.

"Oh my God." My hands shook as I covered her with the stained white lab coat. "That's it, we're taking you with us."

"I wish I could, but . . . I can't," the little girl whispered.

"It's okay. We'll help," I said shortly.

Keenan leaned his head back on the wall and closed his eyes. Had he given up? Had I killed him by making this decision? Had he known it would happen, and followed me anyway?

"Come on, Keenan," I snapped. "We're taking her out of here."

His amber eyes flew open. "Don't you think she has the right to decide that? She's *you*, Jack. When has ordering you around done any good?"

What was he thinking? She wasn't *me*. Frustration built until I wanted to scream.

"Okay, okay. Fine." I knelt and looked into my own face, made tiny and vulnerable. "Look, honey, we need to get out of here, and we want to take you with us. You belong with me. With us. We . . . we're the same. We're family." Tears filmed my vision.

"Family." The child smiled, and her dry lip cracked. A trickle of watery blood ran down her chin. Keenan wiped it away with a thumb. Her thin arms tightened around his neck, and she gazed up at him adoringly. He had to be the first free boy she'd ever seen, the only one who wasn't a hunter or a drone. I'd never seen the gentle, paternal side of him before.

Even with Tito, Keenan was like a rotten older brother, teaching him to do bad things just for fun.

Distant footsteps came from down the corridor. Someone was out there, coming after us or only walking past, I couldn't tell. "Hurry up. You need to decide. Are you coming with us or not?"

The child's wide, hazel eyes were on me, but behind her, Keenan shook his head. I knew what he was telling me. There was no point. The kid was dying.

"It's okay," my clone-daughter whispered, a faint, teasing smile on her lips. "Leave if you want, I'll catch up. I just have one thing to do first."

My exact words to Keenan, not five minutes before. She'd overheard us. *She'll catch up? Not a prayer.* I put my face in my hands.

"What do you need to do?" Keenan asked her softly.

"I need to talk to them. They do things for me, sometimes." Before I could ask who, the girl pointed at the eyeball that blinked at us from the brushed chrome box.

The clone stretched, reaching both arms high. Like her feet, her hands were mismatched, both webbed, but one of them much longer, lumpy and painfully twisted. Long, red rope burns marked her palms, relics of her desperate effort to save our lives in that suffocating corridor.

"Oh, no. No," I muttered, eyes wide with dread, but Keenan boosted her higher. Little Jacqueline murmured, calling sweetly. A tentacle raised its faceless head, seeming to sniff the air. Then a thick, writhing mass of them squeezed from the rectangular, chrome-sided box. When they brushed her peeling fingers, I cringed. Their yeasty, rotting-dough odor triggered memories of the enormous false-flesh tentacles that attacked us during the battle at the array, killing kindly old Doc Stuart the day after he adopted me. No kid should be allowed to play with something like that, no matter how gentle these little ones seemed. I'd seen what they could do.

"Stop," I begged. "Keenan, make her stop."

He shook his head without sparing me a glance. "The kid lives here, Jack. She knows what she's doing."

The eyeball screen blinked its brown-fringed eyelid and read out a stream of numbers, green print mixed with alarming lines of red. Nurse drones could've interpreted that better, but even I could tell the news was bad. White, slimy tentacles slid from the box, more than it could possibly have held, but somehow they kept on coming. Soon the child's thin, pale arms were completely hidden under the writhing, wormlike mass. They wrapped her neck and draped her raw, red shoulders, while she smiled like a little girl with a pet kitten. I had to look away.

"They say yes," little Jacqueline announced. With faint squelching sounds, the tentacles retracted back into their container.

"Who?" I didn't understand, and my patience was wearing thin. "Yes to what? Does that mean we can go now?"

She shook her damp, auburn head. "Not yet. I have something for you, but you have to wait. Let me go now." The child struggled in Keenan's arms, and he released her.

"Keenan? Seriously, what the fuck? How much time do you think we have here?"

"What do you want me to do, hog tie her and throw her over my shoulder?"

"Yeah, good idea," I spat.

Little Jacqueline crawled off Keenan's lap and inchwormed painfully along the rough, bone floor of the lab. Her fragile arms couldn't hold much of her weight, so she wiggled along on her belly, bumping her chin on the floor. Wincing, I hurried over to help, but she disappeared under the black bench. A smear of blood and torn, dead skin marked her trail. That bothered me more than I wanted to admit. I needed to wrap her and hold her, put medicine on her scrapes--not let her freeze on the dirty floor, hiding under furniture.

I let out a huff of air that almost turned into a sob. "Keenan, please. Just grab her and we'll get out of here."

"We're not kidnappers, Jackie. Wanna leave without her? Fine. Let's go." He stood, chin up, eyeing me stubbornly, like he knew what I'd say.

"No." I paced toward the door anyway, quivering with impatience, and came right back. No matter how bad I wanted to run, I couldn't leave that kid behind.

Little Jacqueline's whisper came out from under the lab bench. "She's coming. She's coming! Hide."

I swore. A cold, familiar weight filled my chest, and my pulse fluttered in my throat. My gaze jerked from side to side, searching frantically for a place to hide. Too late. Bianca strode into the lab, wearing the black girl's tall, athletic body and dragging the teeny Asian chick by one arm. The clicking cyborgs instantly went silent.

"That's her, that's her," I hissed, grabbing Keenan's arm.

"Which one?"

"Both of 'em!"

The blonde teenager was missing. Dead or escaped, I didn't know, but it didn't seem like Bianca to let her playthings wander off. I swallowed the impulse to ask. The Asian girl had been crying, but her sobs abruptly stilled when she saw me. Recognition flashed in her lovely, slanted eyes, and something else—hope.

Keenan backed me into the narrow walkway between the clone tank and the steel dissection table. The harsh chemical scent of its disinfectant filled my nostrils, making me queasy.

Bianca shoved her captive hard, sending the girl stumbling toward the gray drone. "Take her. That sniveling is getting on my nerves."

Shark Man seized the girl's delicate wrist. She froze the second he touched her, and I knew this had happened before. Despite her careful stillness, trickles of blood ran down the back of her small, golden hand.

Bianca stalked toward us, and my spine went stiff. Then she veered away to lean over the clone tank. "Jaaacqueline! Where's my little darling?"

Bianca's high, fake tone set my teeth on edge. Keenan's lip twisted, and we exchanged a horrified glance. The Asian girl started sobbing all over again, and I wondered if she knew what was going to happen.

"Coming, Mommy." The clone's small, quavering voice came from beneath the shelves on my left. While I wasn't paying attention, she'd wormed halfway around the room.

"Mommy?" I echoed under my breath. I was her mother, if anyone was.

Bianca paced down the walkway in front of the shelves, the heels of her white leather pumps tapping impatiently on bone. "Jacqueline! Get out here this instant, or I'll teach you a lesson."

Tiny whimpers and grunts told me the kid was moving as fast as she could, injuring herself in her haste. Bianca squatted, reached under the shelf, and yanked the little girl out. The child squealed as her skin tore on the rough floor.

"Stop it," I screamed. "Can't you see she's sick? Stop hurting her!" I lunged toward them, but Keenan threw an arm around my chest and hauled me back. I struggled against him, grunting with the effort.

His sweat smelled rank with fear. Hot breath hissed in my ear. "Jack, no. Don't piss her off."

Ignoring my outburst, Bianca stood up, holding the crippled child. All of a sudden, she looked like any other mom. My muscles went loose. I knew Bianca was nothing but a computer-generated mind in a stolen body, a machine imprinted with some dead woman's personality. She wasn't human, and she wasn't gonna be, no matter how many human bodies she took. Could an AI be a mother? Could she really love her child? Maybe that was why she hadn't taken over the clone. And she hadn't, I was sure. Besides me and Keenan, that kid had the only free mind in this place. But why? Love couldn't be the answer.

Still carrying the child, Bianca strolled around the clone tank to the narrow walkway that passed between it and the dissection table. She faced us from the end of the aisle. Even from twenty feet away, I felt the prickle of her artificial, electronic presence, kind of like static from a television screen, but strong enough to stop hearts. A wave of weakness passed through me, leaving my legs tingling like they might fold. I clung to Keenan's shoulder. He drew me backward, away from Bianca and the sad little copy she'd made of me.

Bianca looked the little girl over critically and sighed. "You didn't turn out near as well as I'd hoped."

The child hung her head and did not answer.

"Pay attention, now." With her long, broken nails, Bianca pinched the delicate webbing between the clone's fingers. Little Jacqueline winced. Her face had gone stark white, and she was biting her lower lip to keep from crying, but she never even tried to pull her hand away. Those round, hazel eyes had gone vacant, like the person inside had fled.

"You are a disappointment, it's true. But all that's going to change, because I brought you a present," Bianca said cheerily, poking the girl in the ribs. "A brand-new body, just like yours, only better. Yours was never right in the first place, and now it's sick. This new one is healthy. It can walk, even run. Plus, it goes everywhere with him." She pointed at Keenan. "Bonus. Isn't he cute?"

My brain went numb with shock. *She just offered my body to the clone. Can she really do that? I thought only Bianca could possess people.*

The clone's eyes brightened, and she sat a little straighter in her mother's arms. From her smitten expression, she was an adolescent, all right, even if her body was stunted. She looked me up and down, envy written all over her face. "She's more grown up than me. I want to be pretty and curvy like that."

"You won't be *like* that. You'll be that. You'll be her," Bianca explained, casual as a mom taking her daughter shopping. Only they were shopping for a new body. Mine.

From the other end of the walkway, the Jackie-clone blinked dreamily at Keenan, who stood bare chested, his long, tawny hair cascading over his shoulders. She flushed red when she met my angry stare, but her gaze slid back to linger over him again. "Oh no, I couldn't. It wouldn't be right," she finally said.

But I saw the temptation in her eyes. My hands clenched into fists at my sides. Maybe she wasn't my daughter after all. Maybe she was a monster, like Keenan said. A monster who stole my face. I'd be damned if she got my body too.

Keenan and I backed away from them until we bumped the black stone lab bench. The spidery cyborgs on it had hardly moved. They were huddled together, as flat as they could get, bug-eyed faces hidden and metallic flanks pressed hard against one another. Jewel-tipped antennae arced over their heads, gleaming in a rainbow of colors. Every now and then, one of the small bodies quivered. I felt an unexpected pang of sympathy. They obviously felt fear, even if they were half machine, and Bianca terrified them. I felt sorry for them, for the clone-child, for all the possessed people. Fury burned in my chest. And I had no weapon, no way to stop her. I shuddered.

Keenan put an arm around me and bent to whisper. "It's gonna be okay, baby. I love you."

I tipped my chin up to look into his eyes. "Keenan I . . . I don't deserve you."

"Sure you do." He kissed my forehead, and I leaned on him gratefully. I should have said I loved him. What the hell was wrong with me? Would it have cost me that much?

Bianca's whisper poisoned the moment. "See how he loves her? Once you take over her body, he'll love you too, just the same."

I whirled on my clone. "He will not! That's not how people are. You don't know anything, because she keeps you locked in here." Keenan squeezed me around the middle, keeping me from rushing them. Panic took me, and I gasped for air, suffocating under the pressure of his arm. I pried at his wrist. "Keenan, dammit!"

"Quit! You'll just get yourself killed," he grunted.

"See how she treats him? After all he's done for her," Bianca purred. "I know you'd be nicer."

Flipper-Jackie nodded solemnly. "I would."

The Asian girl twisted her hand slowly in the drone's grip. Scarlet blood spattered his bare feet. I barely noticed.

Tick. Tick. Tick. Tick. Bianca's heels clicked on bone as she carried the clone down the middle aisle toward the back of the room. Toward us. Her gauzy, white gown swished softly around her tan legs. Keenan and I rounded the surgical table and fled up a parallel aisle in the opposite direction, to a patch of open floor near the door. There, we skidded to a stop, panting. The gray drone guarded the only exit.

When Bianca and the clone reached the black stone bench, the spidery cyborgs erupted into anxious clicking. Bianca sat the kid on the edge of the table and stood over her. "Just like we practiced. Pick one, hop inside, and from there, into the girl. Now, go, and be quick about it."

The child squirmed. "I . . . I can't."

"Did you hear that?" I hissed, digging my nails into Keenan's arm. "The kid can possess people! She's human. Keenan, she's not . . . she's not mine. I should've listened to you, we'd be gone already."

Keenan shook his head. "Fuck. I knew it."

Bianca leaned on the black stone lab bench, arms folded, staring coldly into the clone's small, cute face. "This is a present, a healthy new body just for you. Mommy will be upset if you don't take your gift. You don't want to upset Mommy, now, do you?"

The child looked down at her lap. Her reply was barely audible. "No."

That twisted my gut. "Oh, God. Don't do it."

The clone turned to regard the herd of frightened cyborgs. She raised a webbed hand and slapped it down hard. Cyborgs scattered, springing off the table and scuttling along the floor. Keenan and I split up and danced out of their way. One animal was left behind, squirming in Jacqueline's long-fingered grip. She held on for mere seconds before her head lolled and her body went limp. Bianca let the child fall, and the kid's skull hit the floor with a sickening crack. I groaned.

Bianca lifted the cyborg to her face, its eight jointed legs kicking or clinging nauseatingly to her bare hand. "Are you in? You have control?"

Violet-tipped antennae waved.

"Good. Go."

Bianca tossed the creature onto the dissection table and it landed skidding, legs scrambling, picking up speed as it headed for me. I screamed. Pivoting, I tracked the thing as it leaped the aisle to the clone tank, shot along the rim, and sprang onto a high shelf. A tall, glass flask shattered on the floor and the whole pack of cyborgs exploded into motion. Spiders orbited the room faster than the eye could follow, a living tornado, leaping from floor to wall to floor again, razor jaws snapping. Keenan snatched his heavy canvas coat off the floor and whipped it around his head, taking out any that got too close. Their chattering, clicking, and hissing almost drowned out our panicked shouts.

"Which one's the clone?' I yelled, spinning in place. "Where'd she go?"

She leaped for my face, metallic jaws gaping wide.

Squealing, I ducked, and Keenan slapped her out of the air. He followed up with a stomp, and her metal-sheathed carapace cracked on the floor, leaking greenish blood topped with a silvery sheet of floating nanobots. The 'bots formed up into the sluglike formation they used for travel and began a slow migration to the wall. The cyborg's broken body got left behind, her antennae twitching feebly as she died.

Then I noticed. Those antennae were tipped with tiny spots of brilliant yellow, not violet.

"Wrong one, wrong one," I shouted as another spider pounced. Had I seen a flash of violet, or only imagined it? I ducked and spun away, stomping an injured bug with half its legs already broken. The Asian girl's screams blended with my own. Somehow she'd gotten loose, and the path to the door was clear. She bolted that way, white dress flying, but a cluster of hissing, knee-high cyborgs drove her back. Panicked spiders darted about the lab, dodging twenty-foot tentacles that whipped from the blue-eyed box.

"Jacqueline, end this. Take her now," Bianca shrieked from a corner in the back of the lab. My head snapped around, but she was talking to the clone, not to me.

The gray drone lay sprawled on the floor by the door, and I never even saw what took him down. The big man rolled slowly upright and sat cross-legged, holding his huge head in his hands. A pack of clicking cyborgs took his place at the door. Three more milled around him, jumping onto his lap and scuttling along his leg to perch on his knee.

"Be still," he said, so softly I wondered if I imagined it.

Every one of the survivors instantly obeyed, sitting on their butts like dogs, their faceted eyes bugged out and jewel-tipped antennae pointed attentively. Like that, they were almost cute, but I still would've smashed them.

Using both hands, the huge drone pushed off the floor and stood. He stepped carefully between cyborgs and shambled toward his post at the door, arms out to the sides for balance. I watched him intently, hoping he was sick too. Maybe he'd drop, and we could get away.

At the portal, the gray man fixated on me in that eerie way he had, without making eye contact. "Jacqueline, primary host. Peace through cooperation."

"Fuck off. I'm not cooperating," I snapped.

I followed his pointed gaze to the spot where he'd fallen. A cyborg body lay there, legs shattered, her violet-tipped antennae limp and still. *He killed her. He killed the clone.* I forced my gaze away, trying desperately not to care. She was just another demon, like Bianca, her real mother. Rogue tears still filled my eyes.

Behind the drone's head, the living wall flexed. I looked up, already cringing, expecting the ceiling to drop down on us. High on the wall above the door, a large, teardrop-shaped tumor appeared. Maybe it had been there all along, and I only noticed it when it began to move. The thing seemed to be squeezing through a tube just under the skin of the living wall, sliding gradually lower. Maybe the pyramid had cancer now, thanks to me. Maybe it was only taking a dump.

Bianca didn't seem to notice. She paced the laboratory, scattering living cyborgs and kicking their dead sisters savagely out of the way. "Jacqueline? Where are you? Did you get yourself crushed, you little fool?" She locked her blazing eyes on me. "This is all your fault. I swear, it's got to be genetic. This bloodline is ridiculously headstrong. We need to start the training when you're younger and more compliant."

"Well, it's too late now." I tossed my head defiantly.

Bianca curled a lip at me. "Actually, it's not."

Something tickled the tiny hairs on the nape of my neck. I whirled, my heart clenched in a powerful electric field. Bianca stood right behind me, now in the body of the Asian girl. I'd almost forgotten that the petite beauty was a threat. She stood an inch or two shorter than me, but when possessed, she was formidable. Energy crackled off her slender body, and a mad gleam lit her dark, slanted eyes. I stood my ground, determined not to show my fear.

Off to our left, the freed spokesmodel shuddered as she retook control of her own body. Watching us intently, she crept along the wall toward the door. Asian Bianca had her full attention on me. Rising to her tiptoes in her tiny, embroidered slippers, she sniffed me audibly, one side of my head and then the other, like a curious dog. That weirded me out, and I backed away. So much for looking brave.

Asian Bianca flashed me a wicked smile. "Congratulations, it's a girl. Just what I always wanted."

I gaped, open mouthed. "What?"

"You're pregnant, dear. Teenagers are so susceptible to pheromones." Bianca smirked. "A few carefully selected chemicals in the air, and you might as well be puppets."

Keenan came to my side, his yellow eyes lit. He slid an arm around my waist and laid his other hand protectively over my flat belly. His voice was low, intimate, despite Bianca's presence. "Jackie, is it true? Can you tell?"

I didn't bother to whisper. "Not this early. So don't believe everything that bitch says. She lies."

"Only when it suits me." Bianca giggled. "Here, I'll prove it to you. Tell me, does this scent bring back memories?" She reached out one small hand, and a pale tentacle oozed across the dissection table, lifted its front end like a cobra, and slid its eyeless head onto her palm. She raised the vile, slimy thing, pointed it at us, and squeezed. The room filled with the familiar, intoxicating odor of orchids and musk. Without really meaning to, I pressed closer to Keenan's side.

He stepped in front of me, chest out and muscles tensed, the testosterone surging almost visibly through his body. "You had nothing to do with that, Bianca. What happened was private, between me and Jackie."

The scent of orchids lingered, and I knew he was wrong.

Bianca rolled her stolen eyes. "Of course it was private, dear. You're in love, and all that. So predictable. So boring. But useful."

"Useful how?" I blurted. "Why do you want me pregnant?"

Asian Bianca tilted her pretty head and looked at me hard before she spoke. "You are the primary host," she finally said. "The only one who won't sicken and die once infected. I require your bloodline. But there's a genetic issue, a problem with the wiring in your brain. It makes you hard to possess. You probably don't remember, but I've tried to take you before. I've literally been in your cells, and failed."

"No way," I breathed.

"That's why I created the clone," Bianca said. "But I ran into the same problem with her."

"She's lying, Jack," Keenan growled. "You were never infected."

As much as I wanted to agree with him, I didn't. There had been too many close calls, too many incidents of spattered hunter blood or questionable meat.

Bianca raised the back of a hand to her forehead and let out a long-suffering sigh. "You have no idea what I've been through. Can you believe that stupid clone resisted me? People would fight for the honor of being my host."

Keenan quirked a lip and shot me a dubious glance. I rolled my eyes.

Bianca just kept on ranting. "And then the little fool went and got herself killed. Luckily, I have a replacement. And this time, I'll go in early, take control as the brain is developing. During infancy, or better yet, in the womb." Asian Bianca flashed me a self-satisfied smile, her teeth a row of tiny, perfect pearls.

I backed away, both hands over my stomach. "No. Not my baby. No."

Keenan stepped forward, glowering. "Get away from her."

Bianca jumped back into the body of the athletic black girl and strode up behind us. We spun to face her.

"America, celebrate! We're about to acquire a brand-new primary host," Bianca announced, in the girl's clear, spokesmodel voice. "The embryo will be weak and compliant. She won't resist me, and I'll acquire the healing ability I've always wanted. In her, I could live forever. It'll be glorious." She laughed, high and wild. "Global America. One mind, one planet, one--"

"Shut the fuck up, Bianca," Keenan interrupted. "You destroyed the real America."

"You don't know anything, boy," Bianca spat. "I *am* America."

"What you are is nuts."

I was hardly listening anymore. *I'm pregnant. I'm really pregnant. We have to get out of here, save our baby.*

But the gray drone blocked the open doorway, hands outstretched, gripping the ribs of the portal. Where his nails dug in, the wall bled sullenly. Over his head, the tumor bulged in its tube, and a long slit appeared in the skin beneath it. The mass inside slid lower, like the living pyramid was laying an egg. I shivered. I didn't want to see the horror that would hatch from that.

Bianca raised both hands like a sorceress casting a spell, and tentacles shot from the blue eyed box. Curving and twisting, they wove themselves into a cage. I forgot all about the tumor and everything else.

She marched toward me, dark eyes glittering. "This will be your home for the next nine months. We'll surgically implant an umbilical port, so I can feed you the way I feed my hunters. Once I get your baby, I won't need you anymore. You'll burn, like you burned my hunters."

I swallowed hard. Didn't even try to lie. "You . . . know about that."

"My children transmit until the moment of their death," Bianca said quietly. "I saw it all. I saw you burn them. I felt their pain." She bowed her head, hand over her face, like a grieving mother.

That struck me in the heart. My crew had burned more than a few hunters, before we knew that the people they'd been were still in there, helpless passengers in their stolen bodies. But I was the only one who really cared. Bianca didn't. She pretended well, but the grieving mother thing was just an act. I shook my head and turned away. The gray drone watched me, his silver-gray eyebrows drawn together in a scowl. His heavy jaw swung back and forth, pointing at me, then Bianca, then me again.

Bianca pointed at me. "Imprison her now."

The drone took an unsteady step toward me, like a toddler learning to walk. That was weird. He'd never had trouble moving before. Behind him, the slit on the wall stretched, and, like a great silver egg, the EMP device rolled onto the floor. He pivoted toward it awkwardly, hands out.

"Get it," I howled. Me and Keenan lunged for the device, the soles of our shoes skidding on bone. The gray man was closer, but we were quicker.

The tentacles struck like snakes, knocking me off my feet. I hit the floor hard. False-flesh tendrils wrapped my body, pinning me like a fly in a spider web. I cried out as they whipped around my neck and slammed my head against the floor. Straining, I raised my chin a fraction of an inch and glimpsed Keenan in a slimy cocoon at my feet. A damp tendril slid over my lips, filling my nose with the sour, yeasty scent of rotten bread dough. The Asian girl saw her chance, leaped my trapped body, and dashed out the door.

The drone let her go. He stood over us for a moment, holding the EMP device, and then trudged slowly toward his mistress. When he shoved the heavy silver sphere into Bianca's arms, I sobbed and Keenan swore.

Bianca took the device uncertainly, her full, red lip curled in distaste. "What's this?"

"Look, Mommy, I brought you a present," the drone rumbled in his deep, manly voice.

"Jacqueline?" Bianca gasped. "You wretched clone, is that you in there? What are you doing? That's the wrong body, you fool. The female was for you, not the hybrid."

"I know." Grinning like a little girl, he reached out and pressed the button. The first green bar lit as the EMP device hummed to life. The gray drone's deep, booming laughter filled the room. Under it, I could almost hear the giggles of the little disabled girl who possessed him.

Bianca stared down at the green bars spreading slowly around the equator of the device. Her face went slack with horror. "Jacqueline, what have you done?" The sphere slipped from her hands.

The gray man caught it and her in a crushing bear hug, trapping the device between them. Her tender skin tore under his toothed grip, and blood stained her lacy white dress. Bianca screamed, took a breath, and screamed again.

Twisting and panting, I fought the web of tentacles that held me down. When the chain of little green bars encircled the sphere, the device would detonate. Keenan and I would age instantly. I'd become a wrinkled old crone, and the baby in my womb would die.

"Jacqueline," I cried. "Jacqueline, help me!"

The gray drone still clutched Bianca let out a guttural shout, and the tentacles abruptly released us. "Go," he rasped. "Run!"

Keenan seized my hand and jerked me to my feet. We bolted out the door and raced down the corridor toward the exit. A line of blank-faced workers came our way, trudging along in step. I elbowed past them, vaulted up the ramp, and practically fell into the crushed remains of the dome-roofed atrium. Freed slaves packed the small space, milling around in confusion. A portal yawned open, dead ahead. Cold, smoky air hit me in the face.

"Go, go," Keenan bellowed, pushing me through the door ahead of him.

We sprinted down the passageway, trailed by a line of ragged men. A blast of neon-blue light bathed us, and then were outside, on the red clay wasteland that surrounded the pyramid. Freezing air bit my bare fingers and whipped my hair around my face. Only gray, diffuse sunshine penetrated the layer of oily smoke in the air, but it was still the prettiest thing I'd ever seen. Keenan swung his coat around his head and let loose a triumphant whoop. We were free. We'd done it. We won!

Joe's black and white stray bounded from the crowd. Tail wagging, the dog jumped up on me and licked my face. Somehow, miraculously, he still had both his eyes. I laughed, dancing in circles with him, and then we dashed away across the plain.

A tickle of static electricity touched the back of my neck. My elation fled.

Keenan loped impatiently beside me. "Come *on*, Jackie!" His skin glowed gold, so he looked like a demigod, running shirtless with his long, tawny hair blowing in the cold wind. He gripped his brown canvas coat in one hand, and his jaw was clenched in desperation.

I caught a glimpse of my fingers, and I was glowing too. The tingle on my neck turned to a buzz that itched and stung. My legs ached, and the electric sting on my skin turned to a prickling burn, like the bites of a thousand fire ants. The Border collie yelped in pain, tucked his tail between his legs, and took off like a shot. I dug deep for the last of my strength and ran after him. The ground began to slope uphill, and loose dirt underfoot made the going harder.

Keenan grabbed my hand and hauled me up a little ridge. Behind us, a deep, electronic thrum rocked the pyramid. A mechanical scream split the air, long and high. The sound reverberated, as if the pyramid itself was shrieking in pain. Freed slaves dropped as the spreading ring of force caught them. Keenan and I dove over the far side of the ridge and tumbled down the other side. As I lost consciousness, I thought I heard a baby crying.

I woke to the faint, heartbreaking sound of a man sobbing. I'd passed out face down, and grit coated my lips. Arching my back, I pushed myself up with my hands, scrubbed my mouth with the back of a hand, and spat. Bare, red earth surrounded me, gleaming with a thin layer of frost. The sun was either rising or setting, I couldn't tell. I'd lost all sense of direction. The pyramid was invisible on the other side of the low ridge, and fog had swallowed the distant ruins. Keenan was gone. I sat up to look for him, and then, with a surge of horror, I remembered that I was old. Tracing my face, I felt rough, scaly skin under my fingertips. A small cut stung my knuckle. Unhealed. So my nanites were dead, too. With a sob, I collapsed back to the frozen ground.

It was worth it. My crew can come back to Earth now. They'll be safe.

I closed my eyes, but unconsciousness and death both eluded me. My body shook with cold, and I had to move. On hands and knees, I crawled to the top of the low ridge and looked down. Bodies littered the red plain. Some writhed. Most lay still.

"Keenan, where are you?" I shouted, but it came out hoarse, the voice of an old woman.

I stumbled down the hill, back toward the pyramid. That was okay. Bianca was dead, and I had nothing left to lose. I moved slowly and stiffly, my knees and hips aching. The pyramid looked vacant. Its neon blue light had gone out, and the walls were ashen and still. The seething, silver layer of nanobots that had covered them were gone.

Shark Man sat sobbing in the dirt outside the tall, narrow door. "Look what she did. Look what she did to me. No one will ever touch me again. No one can."

The Asian girl knelt beside him. "That's not true," she said firmly. "See? This direction works just fine." She reached out and stroked his face, smoothing the inlaid fangs in his skin down flat.

The gray man met her eyes, and something beautiful passed between them. I looked away, embarrassed that I'd accidentally witnessed something private. As I hobbled off, a sweet sadness welled up in my heart. Keenan and I had paid with our lives, but we brought love back into the world.

Chapter 18

"**K**eenan," I shouted. "Keenan!"

No answer.

I started back toward the ridge where I'd last seen him. He must have aged, the same as me. Maybe he had a heart attack, or got dementia and wandered off. Either way, I had to find him. Had to know.

A horse-drawn cart rolled down the red dirt road toward me, followed by that same, familiar black and white collie. I stepped off the trail to make room. As the wagon got closer, I saw that it was really a blue Ford pickup with the doors and the top of the cab torn off. Four mares pulled it, two bays, a gray, and one painfully thin paint with a wide, hairless scar on her side. The horses wore no bits or bridles, only harnesses, but they didn't walk or breathe in step.

Are they still slaves, even now?

The wagon rolled up beside me and stopped. When the driver got out, I recognized him with a start. He was the lean, thirty-something drone I'd seen with the team of injured horses, the night I crashed my shuttle. It felt like a long time ago. The freed man acknowledged me with a nod.

"Thank y' kindly, ladies. Take a rest," he called to his team. The horses lowered their heads with contented sighs.

"They aren't infected anymore," I murmured. "But they still pull the wagon?"

The driver gazed fondly at the mares. "Strictly on a volunteer basis. Me an' them, we're still kinda . . . connected."

A burly, graying man clambered from the passenger side of the old Ford and came around the rear of the vehicle, moving with a familiar uneven stride.

"Joe!" I hobbled toward him as fast as my aching body would let me.

Joe had abandoned his business suit and canary yellow gangster tie, and he looked like he ought to, in denim and worn flannel. He wrapped me in a warm, fatherly hug. "Aw, honey. I thought we lost you."

"I, um, I have to tell you, you kind of did. I won't be around much longer." I took a deep breath and spit it out, the EMP device, sudden aging and all. "So . . . that's why I look like this now. You must've recognized me by my clothes."

Joe laughed. I didn't. He took me by the arm and led me over to the truck's cracked, dusty side mirror. "Take a look."

My own face looked back, covered with mud and sweat and blood, but still mine. And still sixteen. Relief made my knees weak. Determined not to cry, I pressed my lips hard together and wiped at a crusty patch of dirt on my cheek.

Joe grinned. "Got any other crazy ideas?"

"Um, yeah. Bianca's dead. Keenan's missing. And I'm pregnant."

"You're pregnant, really?" Joe almost danced. "Congratulations, honey! About time. We've been hopin' fer long enough. And Keenan ain't missing. He's in back o' the truck there, all wrapped up. We found him passed out in the snow with no coat on, not even a shirt. He damn near froze to death last night, but he'll be fine."

"Oh, thank God." I stood on tiptoe, trying to see into the bed of the truck. "He's not . . . he's not, um, old?"

"Cold, Jack. That's all. Go on, get up in there." He patted the side of the dented blue wagon. "We'll take you back to the Tech Center, or what's left of it. Headquarters is there. The Air Force boys keep on radioing us, askin' about you. They'll be wantin' you back up there right away." Joe pointed a thick finger at the sky.

"Right." I should have expected that, but I was still shocked that we won at all. I never figured on surviving my confrontation with Bianca, so I had no plans for the future at all. I needed to get back to my crew, eventually get them all settled on the ground, now that the planet was ours again. The idea made me smile.

Joe boosted me over the tailgate, and the collie jumped lightly in after me. Someone had thrown an old mattress in there, and Keenan was stretched out on it, wrapped in blankets. The collie turned around and laid down beside him, tongue lolling happily. I slid under the blankets on his other side, crept into Keenan's arms, and fell asleep. He never even stirred.

The sun was sinking low in the gray sky when the wagon rolled to a halt, waking me. We were at the airfield. Joe and our driver got out and went to talk to some people standing on the edge of the runway. I blinked, sat up, and looked around, feeling disoriented. Deer wandered among the humans, close enough for them to touch. A flock of tiny, black-capped chickadees swept over my head and landed on the men, perching on their heads, hands, and shoulders. Every guy had become a living perch, except for Joe. Not a single bird landed on him.

The landing strip was mostly clear. My wrecked shuttle had been dragged to one side, and Keenan's shiny one sat at one end of the runway. The jarring sound of metal scraping on concrete startled me, and I twisted to look over my shoulder. Two spotted milk cows and a huge, black buffalo slowly went by, horns lowered, working together to push a wrecked car from the runway.

The noise scared Keenan awake, and he sat up gasping, kicking the blankets frantically off his legs.

"Hey, it's okay," I soothed, squeezing his shoulder. "They're volunteers. Not infected. There's some kind of connection between the formerly infected. Even wild animals aren't afraid of us. We're all on the same team now."

Keenan watched them suspiciously, gripping his blanket in sweaty fists. "I don't like it. That's a bad sign."

I smiled at the ragged men, standing in a circle with wild birds on their shoulders. "Those guys seem happy enough. The world's a different place now."

Joe appeared beside our wagon. "It sure is. I'm guessing hamburgers are a thing o' the past, now that all the freedmen and animals are linked. But we don't have time to talk about it. They're sending you two back up to the space station straight away."

"That's because Jackie's pregnant," Keenan said. "We can't risk her, in case Bianca's not dead."

I shot him a sidelong look. "Don't say that. She's dead, all right?"

"She'll be dead when the fucking cows stop helping us and wander off to eat grass, like actual cows," Keenan shot back.

"Enough, you two," Joe rumbled. "Into the shuttle."

One last hug, and I found myself in a padded black seat in the shuttle's cockpit, listening to the reincarnation of the feminine autopilot I killed when I wrecked my own shuttle. I was pretty sure the bitch still hated me. I could hear it in her clipped, mechanical tone. "Destination, International Space Station, confirmed. Secure for launch."

"Yes, ma'am." I rolled my eyes and clipped in. Our sleek little ship took off like an airplane, and the ruins of the Tech Center dropped away below us.

I took a deep breath and let my muscles relax. "We did it, Keenan. We're safe."

He squeezed my hand. "I love you, babe."

"I love you too." I smiled. That wasn't so hard to say, after all. "We're gonna see the crew! I missed them so much. I want to cuddle Tito again. And the boys are gonna go nuts when they hear about the baby."

"I can't wait to see the admiral. In your face, Bauer. We saved the planet. Is that good enough to buy our oxygen?" Keenan chuckled and entwined his fingers with mine.

Off the left wing, Bianca's pyramid caught the last rays of the setting sun. From the safety of our ship, it was absolutely beautiful.

"Computer. Hey, autopilot," Keenan snapped. "Circle the pyramid before you take us into orbit."

"Acknowledged."

I sat up straight, instantly alert again. "What? Why?" As the shuttle banked for a sweeping left turn, I leaned on Keenan's shoulder and stared out the window on his side.

"Look at that, Jack. Am I wrong, or is that thing a hell of a lot shinier than it was this morning?"

He was right. The tiny, faraway pyramid glinted, rippling as if water was flowing down its walls. As we circled it, the whole building shuddered, and then an enormous, silvery sheet of nanobots rolled off one corner, leaving the pyramid dull and lifeless again. We groaned as the 'bots formed into their sluglike travelling formation and began inch-worming across the red plain. Only this time, the worm had to be a hundred yards long. The last golden light of the day hit it, and thin tendrils of black smoke curled into the air. The inchworm humped along faster.

I gripped Keenan's arm. "Excellent. It's gonna burn!"

He shook his shaggy, blond head. "Only a little. Not enough to kill 'em all." The giant worm reached some ruins, where it split into ten thousand quicksilver streams and sank out of sight.

We sat in shocked silence as our ship gained altitude, and the blue sky began to turn black. The Earth hung below, grayer than before, but with new gaps in the clouds where blue water and patches of land showed through. A few, faint stars appeared above us.

"This isn't over," Keenan finally said. "We'll have to come back and finish her off. Or I will. You won't be doing any fighting until after the baby is born. Maybe not even then."

"You can't tell me what to do," I blurted, and then let out a frustrated sigh. "Seriously, are we going to argue like this forever?"

Keenan leaned over and kissed me softly on the lips. "Oh, yes. Forever."

The End . . . until Book 3

About the Author

Courtney Farrell lives on an orbiting space station, where she pens novels while evading pox-infected animals. She tweets messages from behind enemy lines as @CAFarrell.

Where to connect with the author

Blog
http://www.courtneyfarrell.com

Facebook
https://www.facebook.com/pages/Courtney-Farrell/405475149467821

Twitter
https://twitter.com/CAFarrell

Goodreads
http://www.goodreads.com/user/show/7894049-courtney-farrell

Amazon
http://www.amazon.com/-/e/B001JPBU6S

Other books by the author

The Nanobot Wars
Bait
Stolen Eyes

The Enhanced Series
Enhanced
Sacrificed

The Mexican Drug War
Gulf of Mexico Oil Spill
Terror at the Munich Olympics
The Abortion Debate
Methane Energy
World Population
Mental Disorders
Green Jobs
Mongol Dawn
Children's Rights
Human Trafficking
Save the Planet: Using Alternative Energies
Plants Out of Place
Build it Green
Save the Planet: Keeping Water Clean